To Ellen Picotte

I hope you enjoy
the book.

**In loving memory of my nephew,
Isiah Andrew Edwards**

It has been a pleasure
getting to know the
most landlady I've
ever known. !!

Take Care,
Gerald

After the Games Are Played

After the Games Are Played

GERALD K. MALCOM

A novel by the author of

THE NAKED SOUL OF A MAN

Published by **MUDDY BOSOM PUBLISHING**

http://www.muddybosom.com
Albany, NY 12202

ISBN # 0-97909709622-2-3

Printed in the United States of America

DEDICATION

This book is dedicated to four very strong women that have endured a lot over the past few years. The strength that I think I have, is nothing compared to the strength they've got. If we all knew how to battle adversity and come out on top like they do, we would all be better off.

This book is dedicated to my mother, Peggy. My sister, Rochelle. My niece, Jasmine. And my good friend, Evelyn. I love you all very much and I'm behind you 100 %.

ACKNOWLEDGEMENT

First, I would like to thank God for watching over my family and me this past year. Without you, where would we be? I want to thank my family for all the support that you have given... again. Words can't express the love that I have for you guys. Mercedes, Warren, Davion and Denzel, let's take this amazing ride as far as it will take us. Denzel gets the front seat on the way back. Mercedes, where would I be without you? (Don't answer that.) I would like to thank my brother and sisters; EB Jammin', Rochelle, Aqueelah and Bendelia. To my family in Newburgh, thanks for letting me crack jokes on you all of my life. To my family in Philly, I promise to be down more often. My other brother, Cortland...way to keep me positive. Mantic meets Muddy... Extra special shout out to my brother again. We should've argued years ago. It's good to have a real ear to shout in and a true shoulder to lean on. I love you, Little Buddy.

I want to send luv to my two moms; Peggy and Joyce!!!

I want to thank my editor, Shelly Rafferty, for helping me through this rough period. You definitely came through. You have showed me a whole lot over the past few months. Way to keep it real! (Wrifraff@aol.com) Big shouts to Jayson for showing me how to do it on the computer.(Mr.Pagemaker) Thanks to all that contributed to the "revised" edition. It's well worth the wait!!! Super shout to Kate at Boyd Printing.

I would like to thank ALBANY for backing a brother. I love the support. Shout outs to the End Zone, Tru Images, 3 Star Soul Food, Claytons and JAMZ 96.3. Special pounds and half-hugs to some of my Negros: Karl, Kay-Dog, K-Will, Keith, Derek, Nuke, John F., Lionel H., Dave Brown, Magic, Corey(ATL), Jimmy, Rob(DJ Nameless), Slick, C-Nice, and Mr. Music (Mark Ford) I would like to especially thank Goat-T (Terry) for all the talks during lunch about life and making our kids sit through it *and* like it. Thanks to Angell for giving me a chance to be Mr. Mom and Charla for taking care of the kids. To all, thanks for the conversations!

Super shouts to a few people putting Albany on the map, all over: Boxing champ- Tony Marshall; Navy point guard- Demond Sheppard; Xavier point guard- Lionel Chalmers; NFL runningback- Chad Dukes; Winston-Salem point guard- Devonaire Deas; Le Moyne point guard- Jason Coleman; Loyola 2guard- Lucious Jordan; Houston Astro- Glen Barker; Grammy nominated jazz musician- Stephon Harris; movie producer- John Horne; actor- Todd(Dog) Foster; writers Mars Hill and Ronnie Tanksley, just to name a few. Keep representing so no one can ask, "Where is Albany?"

A heartfelt good-bye to classroom 100, Sal, Brenda, and Room 245, where you can always smell collard green juice. Triszan, I told you I would put you in here. Marcy, keep doing your thing and walk across the stage, even if it's in the summer.

Shout outs to Yolanda and Denise. You guys keep coming back here! Lena, thanks for showing me the power of words. You can make washing your hands, sound exotic. Erika, thanks for giving Traci all of her attitude. Jade, love the vibe you got going on in the city. Spread the love. Glinessa, thanks for the slamming website. (www.epreciousthings.com) Tyneka and Fashia, thanks for taking care of my woman!(smile)

Thanks to Cyndi for everything. Dawhan, thanks for making it ghettofide. Eno, thanks for all the PR. I hope I don't have to pay you. Dina, thanks for letting me have, I mean, use your laptop. Tanya. (What, what...) Thank you for all the help you've given me. You are definitely God sent. (Eye boogers. LOL) Shout out to Kenny from Urban Voices. You've been very instrumental in getting me off and running, I appreciate it all. To the computer whiz for all the help; Bae Seang (Peter). To my cuz in DC; Shannelle. I luv the way you took me in without knowing me. That's family, and family = love. It is by far, the best PR firm in the business. (www.laurencommunications.com

Shouts to my grandma Alma for giving me the slamming Corn Bread Stuffing recipe that helped feed me throughout this whole rewrite.

Shouts to my little bro's: Morgan, Jordan, Aaron and Jamal.

Shout outs to Soul Kitchen... thanx for the start and the name that no one would ever understand-(Muddy Bosom) An extra shout out to the fathers and others that are making it happen. It's nice to see you out there doing the Little Leagues, After School Programs, Educating and Mentoring: Clem Harris, Mel Hood, Dancin' Danzy, Jermerle, Trison, David Gamble, Dave Graham, Alan G, Lionel Chalmers Sr., Toby, Aaron B, GoGo, Pookie, Terry Marbale, Ralph Tucker, Vince, Life, Tracy Ford, Troy Kennedy, Frank (at Lasalle) and all the women that are filling that role of fatherhood. Dave Bullow, I want to thank you for stepping in when I was looking for some-one to guide me. Your work never goes unnoticed. Nelce G, thanks for guiding the kids with your STERN hand at Hackett.

Much love to BlackPlanet and all those that have showed support

See ya at the book signings. If there's any questions or comments, hit me on the website; www.muddybosom.com

After the
Games
Are
Played

Chapter 1

"Excuse me, Miss, I'm looking for Room 315," I said.

The woman at the desk was about sixty years old and tired. She had the thinnest lips I had ever seen. Her lips were so thin that if she put on lipstick, she would only be covering her teeth. I got this thing with lips. For some reason I've always loved big hips and big lips, and this chick definitely didn't have either. Not that she was attractive, but being a man, I looked anyway.

"Right around the corner. Take your first left then a right, then another right, and it's the door to your immediate right," she said. She never took a breath. I guess she didn't have to. She had no lips.

"Thank you. I'm sure I'll find it," I said.

It was like a maze. I wondered if there was gonna be cheese at the end. I really didn't want to be here today. It was four o'clock on an otherwise pleasant Friday afternoon, and look where I was. Part of me hoped she didn't show up. But just in case she did, I was looking smooth. Who in the hell said that image was nothing, and thirst was everything? She's gonna wish that when she sees me, she could guzzle my black ass up. I didn't want to seem like I was trying too hard to impress her, so I decided to put on this smooth casual number: black jeans, black shoes and a ribbed black sweater that showed off the pecs.

Finally, my man Tony has been getting me into the gym. Tony is a gym rat. All he does is work out. He's the type of brother always trying to show off his arms. He would be the type to wear a sleeveless vest to a black tie affair. He always said, "Yo', I can't help it if women always want to feel on these pipes." Well, I can remember times when it was more than women that wanted to feel those pipes. He gets mad when I remind him of the time he had to go get his woman out of the gay bar. Gay guys of all colors and creeds were jumping up. I have never seen that brother run so fast.

When I turned the corner, I looked up at the ceiling and noticed that it resembled a large, vacant building that had been around since Jesus.

While walking around the corridor, all I could smell was stale air. It reminded me of those old buildings that were always being worked on but were never going to be totally fixed. *There it is, Room 315.* My palms were sweating and I really didn't know why, because *I* really didn't want to see her. I did want her to see what *she* lost. I wanted her to want me. I wanted her to sweat me. I wanted her to beg me to come back. Then I would look into her eyes, grab her hands and say, "Hell no!" I wanted her to feel the hurt that I felt. No! My mother always told me that two wrongs don't make a right. But hell, two wrongs didn't make it right. *How could she make that mistake?* I'll never forget walking into…

"Mr. Styles? I'm so glad you could make it," a man said as he opened the door. "You can have a seat right there." I was doomed before I even started. The man sat down at the head of the table, leaned back and eyed me curiously. I felt like I was gonna be interrogated. He reminded me of one of my old math teachers. *Damn midget!*

"Thank you," I said, sitting down. This sure was a cheap looking room. It was about as big as four cubicles. The room even smelled of undone construction. There was one picture on the wall and one long table with six beat up chairs.

"My name is Timothy Shoemacher, but feel free to call me Tim. I will be, what you would call the mediator today," he said, pausing to take a sip from his cup. "I'm terribly sorry, but it seems like Mrs. Styles will be a little late. She left a message with the receptionist. Would you like a cup of coffee? There's some over in the corner that was brewed about an hour ago," he said, pointing to the table. The coffee maker was circa 1920. "It's not much, but it will help you stay awake," he chuckled.

Who was this guy? And why is it that when someone is late, they offer you a cup of coffee that they wouldn't drink? I don't want that nasty ass cup of coffee! Would you drink it, Mr. Cheap-Ass Suit?

"No thanks. I'm fine. I think I'll go to the drink machine and get a soda." I went toward the door, but just as I got there, I heard a knock. I quickly sat back down in my chair and awaited death.

Tim got up and answered the door. "Hello."

Damn she looks good. She was wearing the black skirt set I had bought her for Valentine's Day. I got it 'cuz it showed off her ass-sets.

"Hello," she said, giving her hand to Tim. "I'm, Serene Styles and I apologize for being late. Somebody rear-ended me at my job as I was leaving, but luckily, everything worked out. The man got out, gave me his card and waited with me until the police came. It's nice to know that chivalry isn't dead," she remarked, eyeing me.

Tim was apparently stunned. He didn't know whether to

take her hand, or one of those breasts that was calling him like a fly to shit. "I'm so sorry to hear that ma'am, it's not a problem. As a matter of fact, me and…um…um…"

"Styles. Mr. Styles!" I butted in.

"I'm sorry. Mr. Styles and I were just talking," he replied. *Just what I thought. I was doomed before I even started.*

"Hello, Jordan. How are you doing?" Serene said, sitting down across from me.

I'm doing about as well as I can be since I'm not with your conniving behind. How am I doing? How am I doing? I don't give a shit how good you look. You still ain't…

"I'm doing fine, Serene," I replied, hoping my voice wasn't shaking. *Come on, Styles, get a grip of yourself. This is Semean-ass we're talking about. You know, the same one that cut your clothes up. Even your favorite black Armani suit. She was also the same one that put holes in all four tires, and a brick through your windshield.* Boy, I snapped out of that funk quickly.

Tim cleared his throat. "Ugh umm. Let's get this show on the road. Well, you both know why you're here. We are getting started a little late, but better late than never." *Shut up and cut to the chase.*

"I'm here to mediate, and as you know, I don't know either party. Hopefully we can work together to come up with an agreeable solution that is conducive to everyone."

He then pulled two notebooks and two pens out of his bag. "Here. These notebooks are for you to either take notes, or when it comes time, to write what you desire." I glanced at Serene. She still looked finer than ever, but for some reason she made my stomach turn.

Tim asked, "Who would like to begin? From what I understand, you two were, excuse me, *are* married. That is all I know, besides the fact that Family Court wants you to iron out some problems you're having with who gets what." No one said a word.

Serene finally spoke up. "I'll speak first, Mr....?"

Embarrassed by his blunder, Tim quickly responded, "I'm so sorry, Mrs. Styles. Forgive me. I don't know where my mind was." *In her shirt, Polyester Man.* If he paid more attention to his job and not other things, he wouldn't have forgotten his own damn name.

"Timothy Shoemacher," he said as he gave his hand again, slightly brushing hers. *Maybe it was habit. I hope it was just habit.* "But please, call me Tim."

"Well, I was saying Mr. Sch..." She abruptly stopped her sentence short. "Tim. I would not mind expressing myself first. Should I write it down or say it?" Serene asked. She was trying to get her voice on. You know the voice that people use when they're at work or on the phone. He was definitely going for the bait.

Tim replied, "Well for starters, you can just tell me why you are here. And remember, we are all professional adults."

I see professional adults get their ass kicked every day.

Serene blurted, "Well, I prefer to get things out in the open. We might as well cut through all the shit. I really don't have time to be wasting." She was looking directly at me. I felt like walking out but I wanted to get this thing over with as much as she did. "I don't think that this marriage is going to work out. He repeatedly verbally and mentally abused me. I'm not even going to mention what's-her-name," Serene screamed, rising above Tim. *She was definitely working on my nerves.*

Tim stood up and quickly stopped her. "We need not get *too* personal, Mrs. Styles. We want to keep things in control. You can continue, but please, relax." I was happy to get some points in there. I was starting to think that I was in a no-win situation.

"Well, like I was saying, Tim," Serene sighed, sitting back down. "I know that this will not work out. All I want is alimony, the car, our son, the house and he can keep the dog. I never liked the dog anyway. His hair was always all over the house. And Jordan never cleaned up. I was doing it all."

Did she ever stop? I couldn't take it anymore. I got up and shouted, "Would you just shut the hell up! It's been like this for the longest, Tim. You don't understand." I turned to Serene to finish my tirade. "And where do you get the gall to come here late as hell and then start yelling about my dog? He ain't never done nothing to you! He should've bit off your little ass pinky toe."

Tim slid to the edge of his seat. "You two have to understand that we will never get anywhere like this. Now I want to know what the problem is. You have ten minutes to mull it over. If you two could refrain from all the talk, maybe we can get something done."

We both sat there like kids who were being scolded for fighting. I started writing what I thought the problems were.

It only took me a few minutes to write my problems down. I slid my paper over to Tim and just as he received it, she threw hers. He forgot about mine and took hers, accidentally brushing up against her hand, again. She gave me that crazy looking smirk that she always does when she thinks she's getting over. He took my paper and placed it underneath hers.

"Well," Tim began, sifting through her list. "It seems like Mrs. Styles has a problem with alleged mental and physical abuse."

Serene jumped up. "There is *no* alleged on that paper! My doctor says that I am suffering from back pain caused by Jordan pushing me into a wall. He also shouted profanities at me almost daily. I can't take it anymore. I watch the talk shows and they say that we women shouldn't take it anymore. We have rights and I'm taking a stand. Every woman should be persistent because what happens when he pushes once? He'll push harder and harder until a push becomes a tug, which becomes a shove, which becomes a grab, which becomes a snatch then a slap followed by a hit then a punch and the next thing you know they're finding me in a plastic bag outside. I need some coffee," she screamed, getting up to get herself a cup.

She was really working herself up. I knew this was coming. I started tapping my foot as I felt my temperature rise and I couldn't take it anymore.

"Serene, I never put my hands on you! I grabbed you, but you were *never* physically or mentally assaulted. And if you were, why is there no account of any violence? You're always crying wolf. What's gonna happen if you ever really get assaulted?"

"See! There you go threatening me. I'm not going to take this threat lying down," Serene cautioned, strutting back to the table with a cup of stale coffee.

"Who's threatening you? You always make something out of nothing. That's the problem with this whole relationship. Truthfully, Tim, you don't even have to read mine. I'll tell you what it says. I caught little Ms. Styles with another woman!" Tim's jaw dropped. "That's right. I snuck home and she and her good friend Mona were on the couch. Maybe they didn't think that I would be home so early. I fooled them though, 'cuz when I walked in, Serene was lying on the couch with her…"

"That's enough, Mr. Styles. I don't think we need to go into any details. I think we have heard enough on both parts to know that we cannot do anything today." Tim was sweating like a pig wearing corduroys. "Thank you, and someone will be in touch with you both regarding your court date. I'm very sorry that things could not be worked out. You both can see yourselves to the door. I have paper work to do."

He didn't even look at us. It was as though we were a waste of his time. I was rather embarrassed about the outburst, but I was not going to be made a fool of. Not this time. As a matter of fact, I wasn't going to be made a fool of any time.

We both got up and left. It was a long, quiet walk down the hallway. She walked in front of me, but I didn't look at her. Her ass would not get her out of this one. It had happened too many times before. We would argue and the next thing you knew, her hand would find my zipper. As soon as I got hard, she would stop and say, "I'll see you about ten o'clock tonight." And like a dummy I would come. For some reason, people say that the ex makes the sex spectacular. I don't know whether it's because I felt so comfortable with her, or because it was that good. Regardless, she would call, and like a dummy, I would go.

We went down the elevator in silence. I was hoping that Monica would be downstairs waiting for me. This was one of those times when I hoped she was wearing that little black dress I bought her for her birthday. It showed every inch of hip. Women, for some reason, always seem to judge their ex's new girl. We haven't been together for a long time. It never fails though, every time I break up with a woman, they always call the new female a 'fat bitch.' They could be 5'5 and a hundred and twenty pounds and they would still call them an ugly, fat bitch. Maybe it was a competition thing. I never referred to any of their men as ugly or fat. Go figure.

As soon as we walked out of the lobby, I saw my baby leaning on her car, looking fine as hell. She was thick and beautiful.

God definitely gave her more than her fair share of ass and hips. She walked my way with a big smile on her face. "Hey, Baby. Sorry I'm late. I was seasoning the chicken."

"Don't worry. I just finished," I said, giving her a kiss on the lips.

Serene saw her and damn near flipped. She yelled in my direction, "Jordan, can I talk to you? It's about Kendal."

Here we go with this shit. It never fails. Every time a woman is near, Serene finds something to talk about. "Um…hold up for a second, Monica. I'll just be a minute."

I went over to Serene. She was sitting on the hood of her car. "The teacher said that Kendal was acting out in school and maybe you should stop by and talk to him before you go home. Not unless you have something more important to do?"

I motioned toward Monica to give me a little more time. Serene quickly jumped in. "Oh, no, it's nothing secretive. All I want to know is if you can stop by and check on *our* son. It's a simple yes or no answer."

I had to get away from Serene. As soon as I stepped away, Monica came over, grabbed my hand and whispered, "Go check on Kendal, Jordan. I have to grab something to drink at the grocery store anyway. Just hurry up 'cuz you're food will be done soon, and I am marinating under this skirt." She kissed me on my cheek, got in the car and drove off. This woman was cool. Not only was she beautiful, but she was understanding. It wouldn't have helped any if she was on my back as well as Serene.

I turned to Serene. "Okay. I'll follow you down to the house." She gave me that smirk again.

Chapter 2

As I pulled up to the house, my stomach was turning. Serene always seemed to pull a trick out of her hat to get me over to her house, but because I loved my son, I had to go. Monica always told me to go because I never knew when something was really wrong. I'm just upset that Monica has to go through all of this. She's definitely one of the sweetest women I have ever known. My homeboys, Tony and Dallas, always told me that I was one of the luckiest niggas they knew, minus the bad luck that I had with Serene. Between the both of them, they had no luck at all.

Kendal opened the door, looking just like me. He's thirteen years old and tall. All of my female friends told him that when he got older, they would be waiting for him.

"Hi, Dad. Mom went upstairs to change," he said, slapping me five.

I walked into the house and plopped down on the couch. "Kendal, what's going on in school? Your mom just told me that there was a problem today."

His eyes got real big. "No," he said quickly. "There wasn't a problem in school today. Some girl was trying to pinch me and I got mad and threw a piece of paper at her. Next thing you know, the teacher said that I was throwing things in the classroom."

I had heard all of this before. It was nothing new; just Serene's way of getting me over there. "Kendal, when people do things to you that you don't like, just ignore them and if it persists, go tell the teacher. You're getting a little old to be throwing paper in the classroom." I knew that it was going in one ear and out of the other, but I had to say it. Just as I finished my sentence, Serene walked downstairs in a black silk robe. She sat on the love seat a few feet away.

Kendal got up and ran upstairs. "Bye, Dad. I got some homework to do."

"Remember what I said!"

Just like old times, it was just Serene and I, alone.

"I hope you told him that that's not a way to handle himself in school."

"What did you think I told him?"

"I didn't call you over to argue."

"Yeah, yeah."

The house looked the same every time I went there. She didn't move anything, except for the picture that we all took at Disneyland.

"Well, Jordan, I hope I didn't inconvenience you," she said, eyeing me up and down like I was a smothered pork chop. "You know I don't like to come in between new love."

Here we go with the bullshit. "Serene, first of all, you know that my son comes first. Second of all, there is no new love between anybody. Monica is just a friend of mine," I said, becoming more agitated with each passing minute.

She gave me her little smirk. "You don't have to explain anything to me. I don't have any papers on you." She thought about it. "Actually I do, until we get this divorce done."

"Can we cut the shit, Serene? I got things to do. Is there anything else you want to discuss before I bounce?" There was nothing like coming into your own house and wanting to leave.

I was thinking about Monica marinating. She never put any pressure on me. The good thing was, she knew my situation and helped me through it. Since I've met her, about six months ago, we've spent some good times together.

"You're not saying anything so I'm gonna leave." As I slid off the couch, Serene got up and stood in front of me.

"Jordan, can you do something for me before you leave?" She definitely had an ulterior motive.

"What?"

"I need you to help me hang a mirror in my bedroom. That son of yours can't lift a piece of paper."

I was caught between a rock and a hard place. *You mean, her rock with your hard place.* The hell with it. "How big is the mirror?" On the way upstairs, I kept telling myself to keep my pants on and just hang it. It'll all be over, I kept repeating.

Just get it over with and get the hell out!

Chapter 3

The phone was ringing off the hook.

I'm not answering it.

It stopped. I put the covers back over my head, a pillow in between my legs and I was about to go into a coma when it started again. *Who in the hell!* I threw the pillow at the phone and knocked everything over.

"Hello!" I yelled into the phone.

The voice on the other line was stern. "Hello, Mr. Styles, I'm Officer Franklin, and there was a report that your 1997 Volvo was found broken into."

I woke up real quick.

"Excuse me! Who are you?"

"Officer Frances, and I just..."

Relieved, I yelled, "Shut the hell up, Tone! You can't even lie straight. First you were Officer Franklin, then Frances. You don't know your ass from your elbow."

He laughed. "What's up, Styles? I had to find a way to wake your ass up. You probably still got green shit in your eyes, and if I'm not mistaken, I can smell your breath over the phone.

"Fuck you!"

"We got fifteen minutes to get there, and you're always late."

"Where's Dallas?"

"I'm on my way to get him now. I hope he's ready. Knowing him, his girl is probably fixing him breakfast." He paused. "You better get up!"

"Get off my nuts, Tone. You know I get there before the first game starts anyway. If I'm a little late, hold a spot for me."

"Alright. Fifteen minutes or I'll be there, ringing that beat up bell of yours. Peace."

I got up, remembering that I had no intentions of playing shit today. It was a ritual that we all went and played ball. We got together with about ten other guys and rented this old gym out. We would usually play for about two hours and then head to the End Zone to have a couple cold ones. I loved Saturday. It was the only chance we could get together without any women. Dallas' chick always had to be with him. Nothing wrong with that, but damn, can't a brotha breathe? If he was walking and stopped suddenly, she would need tissue to wipe up the mess. Tone didn't have that problem, usually. He did have a crazy chick that used to watch who he worked out with. She used to try to hide behind the weight machines. Serene didn't follow me, but she used to give me hell. She would always say, "You ain't making the pros, so why don't you give it up?" Every Saturday, we had the same old argument. It seemed as if it was basketball or the family. Can't a brotha get one day to shoot the shit?

After playing ball, we made it to the End Zone and Tony started playing the lawyer role.

"I see you got home a little late, Styles. What's up with that?" He turned to Dallas. "I got ten dollars that Styles goes back to the hill."

The hill is what everyone called the condo complex that I *used* to live in with Serene.

Dallas laughed, "That's a sucker's bet. I got ten on the same thing." Dallas then looked at me and said, "You looking kinda whipped. I ain't never seen a five-foot two woman make a brotha squirm."

I had enough. "Shut the fuck up, Dallas. I ain't ever seen a midget white lady make a *real* brotha squirm. As a matter of fact, why don't you try pulling some of your shit on a sista? She'd probably have you doing the dishes. Hell, your timid ass wouldn't even approach a black chick." Dallas was getting heated. I turned to Tony, "I got fifty that Dallas couldn't even get a sista to let him smell it."

Dallas turned to the waitress, "I'll take another beer."

"Shit, give him a glass of Kool-Aid and I bet he'd throw up!" I yelled toward the waitress.

Tony said, "Chill, Styles, you know he's sensitive. Let's go half on a How to Date Black Chicks book." We both burst out laughing.

It was dark in the club. That's the way I like it. The club was kind of small, with brick walls. It was nice and cool in the summer. There was a small stage where you could dance and a huge dance floor in the back. It was empty now, but in about two hours, everyone and their momma would be arriving for the drink specials.

Tony moved closer. "Styles, what happened last night? Did you slip up and slip in?"

I knew he must've seen my car on his way home. He lives about a block away from Serene. "Nah. I had to talk to Kendal about school and then Serene asked me to do some fixing up."

Tony pushed his chair back, shaking his head. "Boy, you're good. Had I caught my old lady…"

I shot him an icy cold glare that seemed to hit him in the pit of his stomach because he caught on and stopped. I had never really told Dallas why Serene and I broke up. I told him that we were having some difficulties with her attitude. Dallas was the type of man that got in trouble, and his only way to get out of it was to bring up other people's shit. He told his girl everything. Not that you're not supposed to share things, but *damn*, can't some things be kept confidential?

"I didn't do anything but fix the mirror. Even if I wanted to, I couldn't have. I had to type up some reports for work. You know, with this new merger, I got to be on my toes. You never know when the axe is going to fall."

Tony replied, "Yeah, I know. It must be tough not knowing if you're here today and gone tomorrow."

Dallas' pager started blowing up. He said there must be something wrong at the house. He went by the bathroom to use the phone.

"Yo', Tone. There is no way there is an emergency every Saturday. She got homeboy on lock down. As a matter of fact, she probably has a chastity belt around his jock strap. I'm about to get out of here anyway. When Dallas gets through checking in, let him know that I'll catch up to him later. Peace." I gave Tony the pound and left.

It was still early and I wondered what Monica was doing. I opened the sun roof and took in some of the cool air. The air slid across my head and down my back. It felt good to have absolutely nothing to do. I decided to pick up my cell phone and call.

"Monica, what's up? This is Jordan and I was wondering if you were going to be free this evening. If you are, hit me on my cell. Bye." She wasn't home. *Damn!*

I decided to just drive around, taking in the sights. Whoever said that Maryland was boring definitely had to be out of their mind.

In the middle of my thoughts, the phone rang. I was so deep in thought that I almost ran right through a red light.

"Monica, what's up?"

"Jordan, I gotta talk to you!"

"About what?" I hated when women hit you with that statement.

"Don't ask what it is. I just want you to tell me that you'll make it." She sounded a bit off.

"I can meet you wherever. If now is a good time, then I'll meet you now." I wasn't feeling her vibe. She was giving a brother some nervous energy.

She hurriedly said, "Meet me at Haynes Park." I knew exactly where in the park she was talking about. We had met there when we were set up on a blind date by one of Tony's bodybuilder friends.

I arrived there a little early, sat on the bench in front where we would have a clear view of the Washington Monument and awaited death. When she arrived, it was obvious that there was something wrong. She had a look that I wasn't quite familiar with.

"Hi, Baby. How are you?" I waited for her to sit down. I hoped she wasn't mad about last night. I didn't call her back after I left Serene's house but she knows that with my son, anything can happen.

"I'm okay. What about you?" she asked, sitting down next to me.

"I'm fine. What's the big rush? Is everything okay?" I was a little nervous.

"I know that we don't have any commitment, but after I cooked dinner for you last night and waited, I got to thinking. I am too old to be going through any of this. Did you know that I ran into Serene at the store this morning? She made sure to let me know that it wasn't over with you two. She also said that she has been having an off and on relationship with you for the last year. I told her that you and I were really just friends, but she was persistent. Jordan, all I want to know is if you have anything to do with her outside of Kendal." Monica leered at me, confused and angry.

I looked deep into her eyes, "Listen, there is nothing like a woman scorned. She's been harassing me for the longest. I don't know what to do. She comes around and tries to disrupt my relationships, even if they are just friends. She feels threatened and uses our son as a pawn. Monica, I just don't know what to do right now. Do you really think that we have something personal going on?"

Monica picked her eyes up from the ground. "Honestly, I don't know what to think. If you were in my position, what would you think? Would you go through this? I have enough problems with my own life." She intertwined her fingers with mine. Her thumbs caressed mine. It was a soothing massage that comforted me.

"What do you want me to do? What would make you feel at ease?"

"Well, Jordan, it's funny you would ask me that." There was an awkward silence. "I was thinking that maybe…" She seemed to be stuck or she just didn't know how to say it.

"Maybe what?" I was sensing this conversation was going in a direction I hadn't anticipated. She untied her fingers from mine.

"Well, I was thinking that maybe we can take it to another level."

I almost choked to death.

"Another what?"

"You know, another level. Like being together."

"Don't you think that we need to wait a little while? I'm saying, I really like you and all, but you know that it's been hell the last few months and I really don't know if I need to be jumping into something right now."

Monica was tapping her foot on the ground. "Jordan, don't you think that I deserve more? I mean, why be idle? I'm not rushing to get married or anything, but c'mon. If I'm good enough to sleep with, then I should be good enough to be with. Or is it just a sexual thing? I want to know what's going on. You make the choice. We can be an item or we can just be friends."

I really didn't want to answer her at the moment. I really didn't *have* an answer at the moment. I was in a no-win situation. I pulled her next to me and pleaded with a softness in my voice, "Can I think about it?"

She pulled away. "No," she belted, staring at me hard. "I want you to answer me now! I don't care if it hurts me. I've been hurt before and I would like to know if this relationship is worth trying to salvage. Why waste another six months on something that may never materialize!"

Damn! Just when I thought that everything was cool, Bam! It's not that I didn't like her a lot, it's just…maybe, I'm not ready. I didn't want to hurt her feelings though. *Think, Styles, think.* "Monica, I really like you. As a matter of fact, I think that I have had more fun with you than with anyone else in a long time." It was difficult to actually say what I felt because I didn't have words for it. "Right now, I think that it would be better if we remained friends."

Tears welled in Monica's eyes. Mascara ran down her face like a mudslide. I turned my head because I hated to see women cry. It was like Kryptonite. I went to put my arms around her and she stood up and walked away. "Monica!" I screamed after her. "Monica!" I started jogging towards her, fully aware of the looks people were giving me as they sat in the grass reading their books.

"Just go away!" She didn't turn around. "Jordan, just leave! I need to be alone!"

I bowed my head dejectedly and murmured, "Alright." I didn't know what to say that would comfort her. I hated to leave on a bad note so I added, "Maybe I can stop by later and cook dinner."

She spun around. "What about after dinner? You want me to eat, have sex with you and make like everything is okay? No! I am not some puppy that you can pet on the head to make things all right. I need time to figure things out."

She was fuming and I didn't know how to ease her pain. Maybe I really didn't know her. At least I knew Serene. I knew when to tell a joke, when to hug her and when to console her. I was lost. As Monica put her key into the car door, I reached up from behind and wrapped my arms around her. Her butt was pressing up against my body. I wanted to hold her badly and tell her that it was going to be all right. I wanted to kiss away the pain. I wanted to rub her shoulders and back until she responded with moans of approval. I kissed her gently on the back of her neck.

"I'll wait for things to calm down and then maybe you'll call me. I won't call you. I'll give you time."

She got into her car and sped off.

I won't call you; you call me.' What a jackass. This was not the time to be playing Billy Hardass, Styles.

Chapter 4

"Mr. Simmons, you wanted to s-s-see me?" I stammered. I was nervous as hell. I was right in the middle of writing a proposal and Mr. Simmons wanted to see me. I never had to deal with him before so maybe that's why I was shaking.

"Good morning, Mr. Styles. Have a seat," he said, fumbling with his pen. "As you know, there is a merger proposal on the table and we've been waiting for the word from the CEO. If you haven't heard by now, I want to be the first one to tell you that we've accepted the proposal."

Fear was beginning to turn to anger. I wished he would just get this over with. I knew in the back of my mind that it was possible, but I just didn't think that it would ever happen. I had heard of others being laid off, but it never occurred to me that it would hit home. As coolly as possible, I said," Mr. Simmons, could you just give it to me straight."

"Well, Mr. Styles, we have decided to merge with Twin Tech and they have requested to bring their own tech support staff. That means that we have to keep half our managerial team and three support tech staff members. Now with you being the newest hired, we regret that we have to let you go."

"Fine," I hesitantly replied, trying to remain calm and under control. "I understand."

Mr. Simmons got up to offer me his hand. "Thank you, Mr. Styles. If there is anything we can do to help you, like giving you a recommendation, it would be our pleasure."

Just like that. I give them three years of my life and all I get is, "We will give you a recommendation." I went to my desk ready to go postal, but I realized that this was a message from above. Mom used to always say that everything happened for a reason. Maybe it was time to move on. I still had other avenues I wanted to travel.

I needed to find my niche in life. There were job openings for tech support staff in other companies, but after dealing with the merger, I wanted something different. It left a nasty taste in my mouth. I liked traveling, so I thought why not look into something that would interest me.

Wanted: Entry-level position working at BC Airport. Great opportunity for growth. Excellent benefits. Paid vacations and holidays. Please inquire within.

I decided to send my resume in the next day. I was so excited about the possible change that I wanted to treat myself to lunch. I wanted badly to call Monica, but I remembered I said I wasn't going to call her. She had to call me. She needed to see that she needed me. She just didn't know it yet. Next thing you know, I'm on the phone calling.

The other line quickly came on with an announcement. "The number you have reached, in area code 301-422-4136, has been changed, the new number ..." I reached for a pen to write the number down. "...at the customer's request, is unlisted." *Ain't that a bitch?* I was stunned and confused. It's probably another dude. It never fails. Every time things don't go a woman's way, they look for a replacement.

After watching the games on TV all day I looked at my clock and it read seven o'clock. I was getting edgy so I searched desperately through my phone book to find a number that would fulfill my needs. Right now, I needed someone to talk to. I needed someone to give me that killer massage, you know, the one that makes your toes curl.

Tanya…nah. She was crazy. Shameka…nah. She was one of those chicks that likes to get their tease on. Darlene…oh, hell no! I heard that honey is burning dudes. I was running out of names until I remembered Kym. She was cool as hell. I dialed her number hoping she wouldn't be upset that I hadn't called her since our last encounter.

"Kym, what's up?"

"Jordan." She sounded pleasantly surprised. "And what do I owe for this call?"

"I was wondering if you had time to go grab me to bite. I mean grab a bite to eat," I laughed.

She cracked up. "Actually I have about an hour to kill before I have to head to bed. Early day tomorrow."

"I remember the feeling," I said rather dryly.

"What did you say?"

Not wanting to kill the mood, I replied, "Never mind. I just want to know if you're going to bring that fine ass over to Clayton's?"

"Let me know the time."

"Eight o'clock. I'll see you there. And by the way, wear something comfortable. Peace." I hung up before she had a chance to change her mind.

I arrived at the restaurant at about ten after eight. I was

always fashionably late, even when I didn't try. She was sitting at a table in the front, looking good. She had on a short red skirt that exposed those thunda thighs that I loved.

"Give me a hug, woman!" I shouted as I approached her.

Kym stood up and greeted me appreciatively. "Mr. Jordan Styles, things definitely have not changed, except you are looking finer than ever," she said as she pressed her big round breasts up against my chest.

"Ms. Jackson, you are the one looking better than ever. I know you're still killing 'em dead, huh?"

We sat down and Kym informed me that she took the liberty of ordering for the both of us.

"Kym, you think you still know me? Maybe I've changed."

She must've taken her shoes off because next thing you know, I felt a foot in between my thighs. "You may have changed a little bit, but I still know that both of you can't turn me down," she said, brushing her foot up against my thighs.

She definitely knew me. I never could resist Kym. She had a man's mentality with a killer body. "What did you order?"

"C'mon, Jordan, we go through this every time. I got you the thighs and breast dinner, with red beans and rice. I bet you thought I forgot that you're strictly a breast and thigh man."

I smiled as I reminisced about her breasts and her thighs.

"So what have you been up to, Jordan?"

"Same old thing. I just got laid off and I'm trying to get that off my mind."

Kym put the straw in her mouth and began seductively licking it. "Is there anything I can do to help you do that?"

"Now that you mentioned it..."

She perked up. "Yes?"

"Can I be honest with you?"

"That's the best way."

"I don't really want to eat...food. Let's get this to go and bounce to your crib. I want to make love to you right now."

"Jordan, as well as you know me, I know you too. Why wait? Let's go to my house, open the refrigerator and pour any sauce we see on each other."

I raised my hand to the waiter. "Check, please."

Chapter 5

It was after ten o'clock and the lawyer was late. Hopefully this would be the last court date, but having been in the system this long, there was no telling. It seemed like they put us in this cramped waiting room to sweat to death. I looked around and there were some pitiful people here. Some of the people that piled into the waiting room were nothing but trash. Hell, I don't know how half of these people ended up with kids anyway. I guess there's somebody for everybody.

I looked around and inhaled slowly, only to have my lungs filled with the smell of pampers and milk. There was a fat black lady in the corner, breast-feeding, while another child clung to her leg. The child she was breast-feeding looked too old to be sloppily slurping from her dangling breast. I found myself staring at her. For a second, I thought I was looking at a woman out of a National Geographic magazine. I believe that when a child's legs start touching the floor, it's time to get him off the tits and into some grits.

"Mr. Styles, sorry I'm late. Parking around here is for the birds."

I'm paying you one hundred and seventy five dollars an hour and you're late? Let somebody pay me that much, I'll be early as hell. Shit, I'll beat the janitors to the courthouse.

He looked around the corner to see who showed up. "Did they call you in yet?"

"No. Actually I got here a few minutes ago and I haven't seen Serene. I hope she shows up, because this thing has been dragging on for too long." I wanted to get this over with, bad.

"Well, let me go in and find out what's going on. Hold tight, I'll be right back." He disappeared into the back room where all the other lawyers were. I had a newspaper I was getting bored with. I finished most of the word jumbles and got stuck on one, so I made a word up, turned the page and was now reading Dear Abby. She definitely didn't give answers from a male perspective. Not that she would, but can the fellas get some love?

I heard her mouth from all the way around the corner. Why did she always come to court with an entourage? I just came with the Maryland Gazette and myself. But here she comes with her lawyer, two of her best friends and an aunt. It was ridiculous. All they did was stare at me and laugh. I just wanted to go over and pull off their tired looking weaves. They sat in the corner and talked about everyone. They looked me up and down and turned up their noses, but I wasn't the one with herpes and a drug problem. That's the only thing wrong with telling your husband everything. If you happen to break up, he always knows a lot of personal shit about your friends and family.

My lawyer came back in and spotted Serene and her entourage. "I see they made it," he smirked. He handed me a pile of papers. "All you have to do is fill out these financial statement papers."

"Bill, I'm tired of filling out these papers. All they want to know is how much I make so they can bleed me dry. Does it even matter? They're gonna take out what they want anyway. I have to pay for everything. Half of the day care, I can deal with. Half of the medical expenses, I can deal with. Half of the living expenses, I can deal with, but half of her hairdos and nails? Man, she can kiss my black…"

"Whoa, Jordan. Relax. It's just a formality."

"Fuck a formality! She wants money for everything. When I come down here, the courts want W2's, tax returns, finger-prints and mug shots. All I want is a fair shake."

"We're up," Bill whispered. "Calm down, everything will work out. Just think of the best." That's easy for him to say. He probably sees a whole check. I get so many garnishments I should be decorating platters.

When we walked into the courtroom, I knew that it was over. My lawyer went up to meet her lawyer in front of the judge. I had just sat in the waiting room for what seemed like five hours and when we finally got in to see the judge, she adjourned the court date another two weeks. It was going to be another two weeks of being nice to her.

The elevator rides out of the courtroom are awkward times. My lawyer and her lawyer talk as if they didn't just try to tear each other's throat out. I couldn't understand it. I hated the woman.

As we walked outside, everyone walked away leaving Serene and I alone. She looked over at me. "Do you want to talk about this? Maybe we don't have to go through any of this."

"Why don't you just have your lawyer speak to mine."

"I'm tired of the damn lawyers Jordan."

"What do you have in mind? I'm open to talk, just let me know when and where," I said, trying to avoid eye contact.

"Maybe we could meet on Friday. Say about eight-thirty." Serene was trying to get her voice on but today I had my earmuffs on. Nothing she said was going to get to me.

I turned and looked at her. "Okay. I'll see you then." I made sure that she knew I was all about business. At this point, I was willing to do anything to get her to sign, and the sad thing was, she knew it.

Chapter 6

I still heard no word from anyone regarding a job. I wasn't at the point of desperation. I was supposed to meet the fellas at Friday's in Greenbelt to eat, and there was no telling if Dallas was really going to show up. I knew Tone was like money in the bank. Dallas, well, you can never tell. We were cool, but he wasn't the one that I would call if some shit went down. Mostly he came around when he and his girl were arguing.

Dallas was into white women. When we were in black clubs, he would feel awkward, but put his ass in a white club and he was like Karl Malone. The white chicks were all over him. He said it was because he had a white aura. I told him that if the cops caught his white aura in their neighborhood, he would have to call me up and have my black aura bail his ass out.

I found them at the table located near the window. "What's up, fellas?" I gave them the pound and sat down. "Did you order something to drink yet?"

"No. Not yet," Dallas said. "We were waiting on your slow behind. Did you get caught up in some business last night?"

Dallas was always trying to fish for dirt. He would probably get in trouble for hanging out for more than one day this week, so he needed some ammo to bring back. You know, "Sweetheart, Jordan got caught up in some shit and he needed me."

That's why these women always hated me. I was the excuse for their man to leave the house.

"I didn't get into any shit. Why? You concerned about a brotha, or are you going to bring back the drama for your little white mama?"

"Fuck you!" Dallas yelled.

What I did was none of his damn business. I spoon-fed him information that I wanted him to know about me. I didn't tell him anything that I didn't want his woman to know.

I decided to be nice. "The first round is on me." That was all it took to get them smiling. Dallas could clinch his butt cheeks and squeeze silver out of a quarter. Cheap ass!

A dark skinned sista wearing a Friday's uniform passed by. She looked like she didn't want to be working today.

"Waitress. Excuse me. Can I get a drink for my peoples?" I beckoned.

The waitress came back, snapping her gum. "Huh?"

"Six Molson's and two shots of tequila," I said.

As she walked away, I turned to Dallas. "Now what do you think about her? Is she bangin' or what?"

Dallas turned his nose up. "It's definitely 'or what.' She's okay. And why are you asking me anyway? You know I don't like those ghetto booties. You and Tone are the ones that like those booties that look like watermelons," he laughed.

Tony turned to Dallas and said, "What's wrong with that fool? How can a brotha not like a fat ass? I mean, who wants a skinny ass Barbie doll?"

"I know," I joined in. "My mom would definitely whip my ass."

"I just wouldn't do it," Tony said. "Not because of family pressure, but because they still haven't given me my forty acres and a mule."

I burst out laughing. "You mean to tell me that if a white woman came to you with forty acres and a mule, you would hit her off?"

"Now you know that ain't what I meant," Tony said. "I just can't overstep those boundaries."

Dallas was quiet as hell. When our drinks came, he took his beer and began guzzling.

I took a shot of tequila. In between coughs, I pulled my chair next to Dallas'. "So, D, why do you only date white girls?"

He put his beer down and circled the rim of the bottle with his fingers. "I date *all* women. I don't narrow it down to one race like you guys do. I am beyond that forty acres shit," he said. "It just so happens that I am *currently* involved with a white one. Love has no color."

"Love has no color? Didn't you watch *Jungle Fever?* I know I did," Tony asked.

Dallas jumped out of his chair. "Well you can't say anything, with all those bodybuilding hoes you go home with!" If Dallas were white, he would've been red. "Every time we get together, it's gang up on Dallas day. I got news for you guys; I've had it with this shit!" Dallas reached into his pocket and pulled out a twenty. "That's for my round!" He reached into his pocket and pulled out another twenty. "As a matter of fact, I got the next round after that! Have a couple of White Russians on me!" he screamed as he bolted toward the door.

"Yo', D, relax. Chill," I said, trying to stop him. By then, he was half way out the door. He left and it was just me and Tony, sitting there looking stupid.

"Damn, Tony. Was that called for?"

"I was just joking," Tony said with a guilty look. "Man,

when a brotha got problems at home, it's hard to joke around. You know I got to defend my sistas, but when have you known me to discriminate?"

"You're right," I said. "I've seen you with some ugly black chicks. As a matter of fact, I've seen you with some ugly white ones too," I laughed. "That's just not my cup of tea."

"C'mon, Styles. You can't sit up here and say that you never dated an ugly black chick. As a matter of fact, I know you have dated a white chick before."

"Dated?" I questioned, with one eyebrow cocked.

"Dated, slept with, it's all the same shit."

"Not in my book it ain't. The answer to your question is, no. I have never actually dated or slept with a white chick. I came close though. She was Spanish, but she looked white. I couldn't take the look from the sistas when I went out in public. They looked at me like I was the plague. If I looked like Shabba, would it matter who I dated?"

"It always matters. They're even saying now that the ugly guys are getting attitudes."

I slapped Tony on his back. "Well, that must explain your negative persona as of late."

"Fuck you!"

"When I decide to hang out with the apes, I'll tell them that you gave them an open invite. But seriously though, the problem with me dating white women is, I don't want to teach anybody shit. You know how back in the days, we always wanted a virgin? The hell with that, I don't want to teach a woman shit. And with white women, you got to start with the basics."

"I feel you," Tony said. "When I dated this white chick one time, she cooked dinner for me. She didn't use any seasonings, and you know that the sistas throw all kinds of seasoning in their food."

"I know what you mean. I was talking to a bunch of women at the job, and they were buggin' out. The white ladies were trading their candied yam recipes. Who in the hell bakes a sweet potato and then puts butter and sugar on top? Not me. Besides that, I'm talking about basic things like music, life experiences and family matters. I'm a firm believer that white women can't understand the black man."

"Don't tell that to Dallas," Tony said. "He says that there are a lot of white women that could cook me under the table."

"That ain't hard brotha. I know a couple of Japanese guys that could fry chicken better than you," I laughed. "It's not just about the cooking though. It's everything. I remember one white broad coming up to me shouting, 'What's up, my nigga.' That chick almost got my big black boot in her ass. She said that she heard my friends calling me that, and she didn't see anything wrong with her doing it. She just didn't understand."

"Not all of them are like that though."

"Don't get me wrong. I'm not saying that all of them think that way, but I just don't want to put up with any slipups. I have friends who date white women, but when things went bad, the first thing to come out of their mouth was, 'You dumb ass nigger!' I know I couldn't deal with that."

Tony finished his drink and started to order another. "You want another drink, Styles?"

"Nope. I'm cool." I pushed away my empty bottle. "I don't want to get too toasted."

"Check it, not to jump off the subject, but what's up with you and the chick in Baltimore?"

"Who are you talking about, Monica?"

"Yeah. She's the fine little brown-skinned honey with the

cherry red Blazer, right?"

"That be the one. She's doing okay, I guess."

"You guess?"

"She bugged out on me. All of a sudden, she had a problem with me and Serene. She must've thought that I was still sleeping with her. I tried to tell her that I wasn't, but I guess she wasn't trying to hear that. Then get this," I said, pausing to finish the little drop I had in my bottle. "She wanted me to take it to the next level."

"What! Get the hell out of here! She wanted *you* to take it to the next level? What did you say?"

"Well, you know," I started. I had this image to uphold. Tony and Dallas had the impression that I was always in control. "I told her, if that's what she wanted, she would have to wait. I told her that I wasn't ready to be on that level yet and I would call her when I was ready."

"She just took it?"

"She cried a little bit, but what am I supposed to do?"

Tony was shaking his head. He didn't have the balls to say anything like that. Not that I did either, but it could've happened. "So are you going to call her?"

"Hell no! She needs to cool off a bit. And anyway, I'm not ready to jump into anything yet."

"I'm feeling you. Sometimes you just want to be with someone without all of that title shit."

"Word! Why can't we continue doing what we were doing? Women always want a title. Does a title really make or break things?"

Tony had this crazy look on his face. "Now you know they always want to be something. I always get that dreaded question." He mimicked a woman's voice. "Tony. What if someone asked you who I was, what would you tell them?"

He continued, "I always tell them I would say that they were my lady friend. Boy, they hate that shit."

"I know. But how else do you explain to them that you just got out of a relationship and you just want to take a deep breath? I want to avoid that rebound stuff too."

"You're stupid."

"It sounds that way. But seriously, how many times have you broken up with a woman and the next one you meet, you're with?"

"You're right."

"Damn right, I'm right. The next one that comes along is usually perfect, or so we think. She seems so understanding, so we jump right on her. I don't give a damn what no one says, it's hard to go from being with someone, to sleeping by yourself."

"Yeah, but going into another relationship isn't really worth it, is it?"

"Is what worth it?"

"Is it worth going through all these women to find the right one?"

"For me, it becomes easier to find the right one. Now check this out. When I first left Serene, I dated a few chicks."

Tony tilted his head. "A few?"

"Okay, maybe slightly more than a few. But what I found is, the more relationships I go through, the easier it is to see the signs."

"What signs?"

"You know how when you first meet a chick and she is a little concerned."

"About what?"

"Anything. Actually, a better word to use is, when she gets a little jealous."

"Yeah."

"I used to think that it showed that she cared about me. Well, after dealing with Serene, that shit definitely ain't cute. The problem is that I don't know what I want; I just know what I don't want. It's kinda like looking for an apartment. After seeing a bunch of shitty ones, you know the one you want as soon as you walk in."

"So you're saying that when you see a female, you check to see how many different outlets she has so you can plug in your appliance?"

"Kiss my ass!" We both cracked up.

"So what are you going to do with her?"

"I don't know. I guess I'm going to just wait it out and see where things go. One thing is for sure; I won't be forced into a relationship. I've learned a couple of things since I've gotten older."

Tony shook his head. "Boy, I don't know how you do it, Styles. You are definitely the man," he said, finishing his drink. "Are you ready to go?"

"Yeah." As we were leaving, I threw a twenty on the table.

As we got near the door, Tony put his hand over his mouth. "Oh shit! Ain't that Monica that we were just talking about?"

I peeked around him to see. She was walking toward us, and she wasn't alone. *Gather your thoughts, Styles. Breathe.* "Yeah, that's her. She must be with her cousin from out of town."

"Damn!" Tony said, pointing and laughing. "If that's her cousin, there must be some incest going on."

I didn't want to pass by her on these terms. Especially after I just lied to Tony about how we broke up. "Listen, she's a grown woman and she can do whatever she pleases. I didn't put a ring on her finger. I'm glad I dropped her ass anyway!"

Just like that, out with the old and in with the new. *Damn! Couldn't she wait until I at least forgot her name?* Women were getting just like us with each passing day. Next thing you know, they'll be sexing us and throwing us out of the back door.

Where is the love?

Chapter 7

My sister, Renee, asked me to pick up my niece from school today. Renee had an appointment at the doctors. This chick lived and breathed the doctors. If it wasn't one thing, it was another. One time she had a bean stuck in her ear. Another time, she was getting her stomach stapled. For four thousand dollars, I would've gone down her throat with my own stapler. She was crazy, but I guess it kind of ran in the family. People said that Renee and I had the same personality, while our brother, Darnell was nothing like us.

When I arrived at the day care, I prepared myself for the smell of shit. I could never work in a day care center. The constant smell of shit mixed with a hint of piss wasn't my cup of tea.

I walked up the stairs and saw an older lady writing something down while yapping on the phone. She must not see me standing in front of her face. *C'mon Aunt Jemima.*

"Excuse me, Miss. I'm looking for the toddler room."

She looked up at me with disgust. She seemed a little ticked off that someone would actually bother her while she having her "quiet time."

"It's the first room on your left, but before you go in, you have to check in at the office."

As I walked down the hall, another worker shouted, "The

office is right there!" She was big too, only she was pushing a cartful of snacks instead of talking on the phone.

"Thank you very much!" I shouted back. I hoped I wouldn't get any crap about picking up my niece. Renee better had called and let them know.

I opened the door and almost fell right back through it.

"E-e-excuse me. I'm looking for the office to sign my niece out." I was astonished. She has to be the sexiest sista I've seen in a while. She was fine as hell. I loved chocolate women, and just looking at her made my cavity hurt. Her lips were luscious, with thick hips to match. Her black business suit showed off just enough to wet the lips without quenching my thirst.

"You must be, Mr. Styles," she said, extending her hand. "I'm, Traci Johnson, the Director. Renee called and said that you were coming to pick up Janay."

"Can I just go in and get her?" I questioned nervously. I was nervous as hell and I didn't know why. *You know why, Styles. Look at all of that...*

"Yes, you can. She is right around the corner, to your left," she said, extending her hand again.

I shook her hand again and looked around her office, noticing the oil paintings of different flowers. "I see you like flowers," I said, pointing to a painting of a dozen red roses.

She smiled. "I like paintings because they never die. I have bad luck with flowers," she said, shaking her head.

"Gotta use aspirin," I replied quickly.

"I've tried it all."

Someone yelled into the loudspeaker, "Ms. Johnson, you're needed in room 203."

She reached for the phone. "It was very nice to meet you, Mr. Styles. Duty calls."

"You can call me Mr. Sty... I mean, Jordan." Embarrassed by my blunder, I made a quick exit.

What the hell is going on, Styles? You see women everyday and you don't act like that. It's not like she was giving you any vibes.

I tried to shake off the encounter. When I walked in the room, I saw about ten kids and two staff members. There were some big ass women working in this building. One of them had a head wrap on; looking like a big ass Erykah Bah-Don't. The other one was sporting some huge Bugle Men's jeans. There was a lot of ass in the house.

"Hello, Uncle Jordan. Wanna see my cubbies, I drew pictures and one is for mom and the other is for you, wanna see my cubbies?"

"What's up, Janay? How are you doing?" I picked her up and gave her a big hug. Either she was getting big, or I was getting weak. Janay looked just like Renee; big nose and all. She was a pretty little chocolate girl. "Uncle Jordan has to get going. Are you ready?"

"Yes, Uncle Jordan, I gotta go get my homework outta my cubbies. Can I get something to drink before I leave, I'm real thirsties?"

As we were leaving, all I could think about was that damn director. Damn! I didn't even check to see if honey was married; Renee would know something.

As I pulled up to Renee's house, I thought about Renee's situation and was relieved that I had gotten out of mine. Renee was still dealing with a lot of shit with her husband, Andre. I don't know how she did it. I didn't ask any questions; I just had her back.

As I got out of the car, Renee came toward us.

"What's up, Whore-don?" she laughed, directing Janay into the house.

I gave Renee a kiss on the cheek. "What the hell are you talking about?" I said, fanning hard particles of dirt and rock off of the porch so I could sit down.

"Watch yourself," she said, wiping her face off. "I don't know where your mouth has been."

"Need you talk?"

"Anyway, Janay's school just called and said that you left your pager there. Knowing you, you must've seen Traci and pulled your 'leave something behind' stunt."

"I left it by accident this time. I swear on your bunions. Seriously though, it was by mistake. As a matter of fact, it must have fell when Janay jumped on me." My sister was glaring at me. She was trying to get me to laugh, because she knew that when I laughed, I was lying.

"Well, she said that you could pick it up before five-thirty, or she would give it to me tomorrow."

"I might as well pick it up today because I'm waiting for an important call regarding a job," I said as I prepared to speed to the day care.

"How is your job hunting coming along? You know, I can still get you down there with me at the disabled home," Renee added, trying to sound sincere.

"Just being on the porch with your bean in the ear, stomach stapled ass, is enough to know that I don't want to work around you and your friends. Birds of a feather, flock together." She tried to slap me in the back of the head, but I jumped off of the stairs.

"I'll let you go. I don't want you getting a speeding ticket trying to see someone that doesn't want to see your tired ass."

Whenever I was feeling good about something, Renee had the ability to make me question my judgment.

"What did you tell her?"

"Nothing." I looked at her, waiting for her to crack. "Honest. I didn't say one word about you being married and that you get around. Did I forget to mention that I didn't tell her that you didn't have a job either?"

"I know you aren't talking. Doesn't your husband know that you were just reformed when he met you?"

I jumped in the car and pulled off before she had a chance to shout a comeback. I pulled onto the turnpike and all I could think of was Traci. I had this thing with chocolate. I've had some light skinned ones, but I have always had a thing for fudge.

I was right in the middle of a traffic jam, and no one was moving. It's five-twenty five and I was only five minutes away. This traffic was killing me. I had to get there.

I didn't know what the hell was going on with me. For some reason, I just had to see her again.

With each passing minute, I felt like opportunity was slipping away. I needed a damn time machine.

When I finally arrived, the building was closed.

"Damn!"

Chapter 8

I got home and checked my messages.

"Hello Jordan, this is Monica. If you didn't know, I got my number changed. If you get a chance, give me a call at 555-7985."

I debated whether to call her or not. Fuck it! I had nothing to lose. Even though I didn't want to deal with her shit, at the same time, it made a difference when I found out that she wasn't waiting for me.

"Monica, what's the deal with you?"

"Damn! Can't you say hello first? And what do you mean, what's the deal with me?"

"You know what I mean. What's up with you and that guy? Is that your new man?"

"No!"

"Did you have fun the other night?"

"It was alright."

"Have you two known each other for awhile?"

"Yes."

The terse answers were making me boil. "What, you can't talk? You got company?" I felt myself losing control. *Get a grip, Styles.*

"That's none of your business, Jordan. What is wrong with

you?"

I was starting to sweat. "Nothing is wrong with me. What's wrong with you? I mean, I just think that you're moving too fast. After we had that argument, did you go right to the next man? You ain't..."

"Watch your mouth! You were the one that said that we should spend some time apart."

"I did, but damn, did you have to get your number changed?"

"I needed to clear my head, Jordan, and I couldn't do that with everyone and their mothers calling me. Besides, no one has my new number but my parents and now you."

"Is that supposed to make me feel better?"

"Listen. I don't have time for this right now. I've got deadlines to meet," she paused. "I'm not trying to be rude but I have to go."

I needed to salvage something. *Speak up, Styles. Don't bitch up now brotha.* "After you get off of work, do you mind me coming over and cooking you a little dinner?"

"Didn't I just say..."

"C'mon, Traci!" I shouted. *Oh sweet Jesus! I know I didn't just say that.* There was silence on the other end. *Relax Styles. Think.* "C'mon lazy, what's the deal?" *Lazy sounded a lot like Traci.*

"Huh?"

"C'mon, Lazy, what's the..."

"Alright," she said, begrudgingly. "You can come over. Let's say about eight-thirty? And Jordan...?"

"Huh?"

"Never mind the cooking. Just bring your appetite."

"Okay." *Whew. I made it.* "I'll be there." I hung up the

phone before anything sank in. Why did I have Traci on my mind? I don't even know her. Regardless, Monica didn't seem to pick it up. *Good thinking, Styles.*

I showed up at eight-forty. Monica answered the door in a two-piece lingerie set. It was black satin and it exposed those perky tits that I had grown to love. By the size of her nipples, it was either cold in the house or *someone* was happy to see me.

"Hello, Mr. Styles."

She never called me Mr. Styles. Something seemed a little off but if it was, then why was I here? *It's just your imagination, Styles.*

"Hello, Monica," I smiled, stepping into the dimly lit apartment. It was dark, minus the light that flickered off two candles that were atop the mantelpiece. The room smelled just like vanilla.

Monica grabbed my hand and led me to the bedroom. As we approached the bedroom, I heard jazz music dancing off the walls. She pushed the door open and candles flooded the room. I followed her toward the bed.

She ordered me to sit down. Loving the directness, I sat on the bed and leaned backward, steadying myself with my hands.

Monica stood in front of me and let the top piece of her lingerie fall to the ground. The light hit her caramel skin and made it glisten in the dark. Her nipples were still erect. This time, I knew it was because of me. I tried to stand up to greet them properly.

"Sit down, Jordan. Let Mommyca take care of you. Didn't you say that I could have you?"

I couldn't speak. I only nodded my approval.

Damn! I loved when a woman wasn't afraid to take control.

"Take off your pants," Monica demanded, pulling my shirt over my head while I pulled my pants down.

When I finished taking off all of my clothes, she looked at me up and down, nodding her approval.

Monica pushed me onto the bed. "Lie down". She reached over and grabbed the baby oil. She rubbed her hands until they were dripping wet. "Get all the way up on the bed, Jordan." She was working the hell out of my name. I scooted up until I was all the way on the bed.

She climbed on top of me, positioning her clitoris on top of my dick. I was ready to explode, but it was going to have to wait. I was really going to enjoy this one. She began rubbing me with what seemed to be a thousand hands. All I could feel were the saxophones picking at my soul and her mouth tasting my nipples.

Instinctively I gave her *the nudge.*

She responded by kissing my stomach. I flinched every time she went back up and licked my neck. It felt good but it made me jump.

"Am I making you feel good?" She was making my pinky toe stand up all by itself.

"Ahhhhhhhhhhhhhhhhhh." I felt like a baby. I could neither speak nor move. Tongues were everywhere, or so it seemed.

Monica moved toward my belly button. She started playfully licking all around my stomach, while her hands found my balls. She bypassed everything and began licking my thighs. I wanted her badly to taste me. Between her tongue and the massaging my balls, I thought I would die.

I couldn't decipher anything. I opened my mouth and whispered, "Monica, please."

She looked up at me with a sly grin. "What?"

"You know what." I said, placing her hands around my dick.

She began stroking the shaft up and down while gently placing her mouth around the head. "Is this what you want?" she moaned in between licks.

"Hell, yeah!"

Monica came back up and kissed me on the lips. I wasn't in the habit of tasting myself but I would do anything to get her back down there. She went from my lips to my ear lobe. "If you want me to go back down, you have to ask me nicely."

"Please," I begged.

"Alright," she said, sliding back in between my legs.

She started licking me like I was an ice cream cone. I flung my head back and yelled, "Damn!"

"You like that, huh?"

"Yeah!"

She then stroked me with her hands and started licking my balls. The song went off and all I heard was Monica noisily slurping. I didn't want her to stop. Just when I thought it wouldn't get any better, she told me to lift up my legs and began licking underneath my balls. I thought I would lose my mind. It was feeling so good, that while she was still searching and licking, I began stroking myself. I was minutes away from sleeping for days.

She began kissing the head again. I started pumping inside of her mouth, like I was actually inside of her. I started to feel come boiling deep within, when all of a sudden she stopped.

What the hell is going on? She grabbed my dick tightly, stood up and said, "I would finish but I don't think that Traci would like you coming in someone else's bedroom. Lock the door behind you!"

Chapter 9

Still no word on a job and Serene was breathing down my neck. Everybody needed money: the lawyer, the landlord and Serene. Next thing you know, they'll be charging for air. The phone started ringing, but I ignored it. The last thing I wanted to do was get up. Finally it stopped, and started ringing again.

"Hello!" I yelled into the phone.

"Are we having a bad day?"

"What's up, Serene?" *Damn! When it rained, it poured.*

"Get your lazy ass up," she laughed.

"It's not a good time for your bullshit, Serene. I'm not feeling too well," I lied.

"Quit crying. I just called because the court date is coming up, and I wondered if you would stop by, so we can talk about Kendal's report card. I also made your favorite, and if you're good, you can have some."

"What?"

"Spaghetti. If you would let me finish."

"Whatever," I said, trying not to feed into her bullshit. "What time is good?"

"Whenever you can make it. Kendal went over to my sister's house for a bit. He should be back by the time you get here." Serene was up to no good, but I can control myself. I wouldn't do anything that I didn't want to do.

"Alright. I have to be downtown soon, so I'll stop over about seven o'clock."

"So, I'll expect you by seven-thirty?"

"Whatever," I said, slamming the phone down.

I showered and got dressed. I had to go take my money off the big screen that I was trying to buy. Money was getting kind of tight. I wasn't at hobo status, but I was starting to get the five o'clock shadow.

On my way downtown, something must've come over me because I came to a screeching halt at Tasha's Florist. Traci was on my mind. For some reason, I couldn't shake this lady that I only met once. She made an impression that gave me butterflies.

I walked to the back of the store. "Pardon me sir. How much is it for a dozen roses?" *Too much, Styles. You don't want to scare her.* "I mean, how much for a rose?"

The man behind the counter had a beard like Santa. He scratched his beard, searching for an answer. "One dozen is fifteen dollars, and single roses go for three dollars."

"I just want one."

"What color rose would you like, sir?"

"What color?" *What's up with this color shit?* "Any color will do. Does color really make a difference?"

"Yes sir-e-Bob. Is she a girlfriend, wife or friend?"

I thought about it for a second. "She isn't any of those."

"We don't have roses for enemies, sir," he said with a loud chuckle.

"I don't really know her that well. I just want something that says that I was thinking about her."

"If I were you, I would go for the yellow rose. It means

friendship."

I looked at my watch. *Hurry up, Santa.* "I'll take the yellow rose." I gave him three singles and grabbed the rose.

"Would you like babies breath?"

"That's okay. She can let one of the babies at the day care breathe on it for free."

As I drove near, I wondered how I would give it to her. Should I go inside of the building and give it to her? Nah. I decided to stick it on her windshield. Now the only problem was finding out if there was a director's spot with a car occupying it.

I arrived in front and it looked like the coast was clear. I was in luck because I saw a black 2001 Volvo with "1 Traci" on the license plate. It was the new top of the line model, and it was shiny as hell. We had similar taste, but different years. I found a little piece of paper in the glove compartment and decided to write a little note and wrap it around the stem. "Use two aspirins and cut the stem." I cautiously walked over, placed the rose and the note on her windshield and drove off.

On my way to Serene's house, I couldn't help but to think about Traci. My mother always said, "Watch what you wish for, because you might just get it." I wanted Serene and look what I got, a beautiful red Macintosh apple, with a big worm in it.

I finally made it over to Serene's house. I got to the door and thought about using my key, but that came with a lot of bullshit, so I knocked and awaited death.

"Hello, Jordan. How are you doing?" Serene said, opening the door.

"Fine. And you?" I said, walking into the house.

"I'm okay. Why don't you grab a seat?"

"I do believe that I bought this house. I know I can have a seat."

"Don't start, Jordan. We are going to have a decent evening, for once."

"Whatever," I barked, easing myself onto the couch.

"Do you want to do this or not?"

"Let's just get this over with."

"You act like this is torture. Nobody put a gun up to your head and made you come." She was starting to get agitated.

Serene got up and walked over to the stereo. A second later, I heard the slow jam tape that I made for her, blaring out of the speakers.

She came back and sat on the edge of the couch. "Jordan, do you think we can really work this out?"

"Where is Kendal's report?" I said, trying to change the subject.

"I don't know where he put it," she said, looking around.

"Well, can I have something to eat?"

Serene moved toward me with a big smile.

"Something to eat like food," I quickly interjected.

"I knew what you were talking about. I can't even joke with you anymore. You are so sensitive."

"Well, you would be sensitive too, if you went through some of the shit I've gone through. I just want something to eat!"

"Okay, Starvin' Marvin. But before we eat, could you fix my TV stand?"

"I'm hungry now. I'll do it after I eat."

"Jordan, the noodles aren't even done. That's going to take ten minutes and you'll be done by then."

"Alright." I followed her upstairs. She pointed to the TV stand that was half standing and half leaning. "How did it get like that anyway?"

"Don't ask me, ask your son." I put the TV on the floor and dragged the stand to the bed. While I sat on the bed, trying to fix the stand, Serene stood up on the bed to fix the light fixture. Next thing you know, she fell on me.

"You ain't slick. Could you please get off of me?" I said, trying to push her away. "You know that's not a good thing to do."

"C'mon, Jordan. I promise that if we can make love one more time, I will leave you alone," she said as she began rubbing my chest.

I didn't want this shit, but *he* was responding.

I stood up. "Stop, Serene. That's enough!"

"I just started," she said, pushing me back onto the bed. "Lay back, relax and let me handle the situation. I got you."

"Yeah, you got me... in trouble."

She unzipped my zipper and started massaging my dick. Within seconds, *Sambuca* was standing at attention. I called him that because two shots of Sambuca and you were definitely feeling nice.

"Do you mind if I have a shot of Sambuca? I've been thinking about him."

I said no, but he said yes.

I looked down and watched Serene devour me. She was licking, massaging and eating like she was starving. I wasn't at the point where I was going to stop her either.

My body and my balls were fighting and it seemed as though I wasn't invited. Needless to say, my balls whipped my ass.

Serene went to the bathroom to freshen up and I looked around. Why did I let her go down on me? All that coming made me sleepy and I would've killed for a bed. My own bed.

I called Tony and told him to start paging me in two minutes.

Serene came out the bathroom and sat next to me on the bed. "You said you were hungry, right? I'll go fix your plate."

My pager started beeping.

"Do you have to use the phone?"

"No, I'm straight. I'll use it when I get home. Dinner can't be that long."

"So now you're going to rush me. You get yours and you're ready to leave. You ain't shit and I'm glad I'm giving your ass a divorce!"

"Good!" That's why I couldn't mess with her; she changes like the wind. One minute she was kissing my ass and the next minute she was kicking my ass out. I walked downstairs, leaving her on the bed.

"And Jordan…?" Serene shouted.

"What?"

"I'll see your black ass in court and don't forget to bring the Band-Aids!"

"For what?"

"Because I'm going to bleed your ass to death!"

I slammed the door so hard that I'll bet her teeth were still rattling.

Chapter 10

I approached Clayton's and looked into the window and saw Dallas sitting at the bar. Clayton's served the best Caribbean food in the area. We go there at least once a month to eat jerk chicken and drink shots of Jamaican Rum. There was a bar on one side and the other side had tables set up for people to eat and relax.

We exchanged pleasantries and I nestled into a seat across from Dallas. I looked around for Tony because I knew he was usually the first one to arrive.

"Tone went to the bathroom about ten minutes ago. I thought he might've fallen in but his big ass wouldn't fit in the bowl." He turned his head toward the bathroom. "As a matter of fact, here comes his big ass now."

I reached out to give Tony the pound, but quickly pulled my hand back. "I hope you washed your hands. I don't want to see yesterday's meal under your nails."

"I know you ain't talking. Ain't you the one that took a shit in the graveyard and wiped your butt with poison ivy?"

"You know that was my cousin, Juan. You remembered that shit. That happened way back when your mother was sporting that wet curl." I looked at Dallas, almost forgetting that he was still one of Jheri's kids.

"My mother didn't have a curl," Tony said, defensively. "She's part Indian."

"You're right. She's part Navaho, Compton hoe and a bona fide DC hoe." Dallas and I cracked up.

"What the fuck are you laughing at, Dallas? You got to have the last curl on earth. As a matter of fact, aren't they becoming extinct? There's probably a doctor over in Africa injecting little babies with curl juice and dispersing them throughout the world."

Dallas stood up and yelled at Tony, "Your mom ain't got no gums. Just teeth and throat."

Tony and I looked at Dallas like he was crazy. He always jumped into the conversation with those dry jokes.

"Did you order?" I asked Tony.

"We just got here," Tony said. "I'm getting the usual anyway."

"I know. A fat chick with a side of cellulite."

"Funny. Where'd you get that joke from, your job? Oops, my fault."

"Kiss my black…"

"Are you ready to order?" the waiter interrupted.

Dallas looked up. "Give us three bottles of Molson Ice."

Tony looked at me and pulled on my shirt sleeve. "What's up with last night?"

Dallas quickly turned around. "Yeah, what did happen last night? You don't tell me anything."

"Because if I do, Becky always finds out," I said.

"It's Paulette," he corrected.

"Becky, Paulette, what's the difference? Anyway, last night I went over to Serene's to talk about court and Kendal and she started buggin'."

"Get out of here!" Dallas said. He enjoyed the juicy gossip.

No wonder he taped Jerry Springer before he went to work.

"You guys act like you've never dealt with an ex that wanted you and the feeling wasn't mutual."

Tony claimed, "If someone would try to bring me through that bullshit, I would be out."

We all looked at Dallas, awaiting his response. "For some reason, you act like I don't go through the same things that you guys go through. White girls give me the same headaches that black women give you." Dallas looked at me and whispered, "They even get caught cheating."

I quickly turned toward Tony. "You got a big ass mouth! You told him, didn't you?"

Dallas jumped in, "No he didn't. I was in the room when you were talking to him. What? You think I'm stupid? I catch onto things."

"It doesn't really matter. I just can't get over the fact that she cheated with another woman. I mean, what can a woman give her that I can't?"

"My woman and her friends talk about that stuff all the time," Dallas said. "She said that most of the time it's not even a physical thing. They just want to be close to another person and they feel that sometimes, a man can't provide them with that."

"Hold up," I said. "I want to be close to people sometimes and if a woman is not available, I'm just going to have to wait until one comes around. Can you imagine me saying, 'Tony, my girl ain't around, do you think you can stop by so we can snuggle?' That is some crazy shit!"

"You're right about that," Tony said, inching away from me. "I can't understand why women do that either."

"So, Styles," Dallas said, "you would never date a woman that was a lesbian?"

"Hell, no!"

"But would you sleep with two women?"

"Hell, yeah!"

"That's why you can't find a decent woman."

"What?"

"I'm just saying that maybe you should try sleeping with women that you could see yourself marrying. Maybe that would reduce the number of partners you have and I bet you wouldn't still be sleeping with Serene."

I understood where he was coming from. "You're right, Dallas, but before I do, I would love to be with two lesbians."

"Thank God I have," Tony said, jumping back into the conversation.

Dallas yelled, "Yeah, right."

"What reason do I have to lie to you guys?"

Dallas sat up in his chair. "When was this?"

"About a year ago," Tony said, taking a swig from his beer. "I was working out and two chicks came to me and asked if I could train them. I told them that I'd be able to work something out if they trained together. When I asked what they would be willing to pay, they told me if they could pay together, it would be worth my while."

"Were these some bodybuilding chicks?" Dallas asked enthusiastically.

"No. They were just a couple of Plain Janes just trying to get in shape. Anyway, we worked out a few times and then they invited me to their spot. Next thing you know, we were all in bed."

"How come you've never mentioned this before?" Dallas asked.

I slid back into my seat, looking around the restaurant. "I

heard that bullshit story before."

"You two are nuts," Dallas said. "Maybe I'm just old fashioned. I can't get into that ménage stuff."

"You're either old fashioned or scared," Tony said.

"I'd rather be old fashioned as opposed to being the freak of the week," Dallas snipped back.

I started licking my fingers. "I can't help it that I love eating everything from the toes to the elbows."

"If that's the case, don't be drinking from my cup," Dallas said, snatching his cup away.

"Whatever, O.J."

My pager starting ringing.

Dallas tried to look at the number. "Who's that paging you?"

"None of ya damn business."

Dallas said, "Seriously, who was that?"

"I don't know who it was. They left me a voice mail message. Tone, do you have your cell phone on you?"

"Where's yours?"

"Home."

"Damn! Make it quick."

I took the phone and went outside so I could hear and to get away from nosy ass Dallas.

I called my answering service and the message played. "Hello Mr. Styles. I want to thank you for the rose. It was very nice of you and if you get a chance, give me a call this evening. My number is 555-1469. Bye."

I listened to the message over again. I rushed back in and gave Tony that phone. "I gotta go."

Chapter 11

I contemplated whether or not to call her right away. I didn't want to seem too eager, but I didn't want to play myself either. I picked up the phone to dial, but quickly put it back on the hook.

It was nine-thirty five and I hoped she wasn't an early bird. I said the hell with it and dialed the number again. The phone rang six times and just as the answering machine came on, someone picked up. I hung up.

I decided to wait about twenty minutes before calling her back. Test number one: if she didn't have a lot of people calling her, she would know it was me. If she did have a lot of callers, she wouldn't know who it was and therefore, she wouldn't be calling me back.

Twenty minutes later and no call.

She won this round. I called back. This time she answered on the second ring.

"Hello." Her voice was sexy and soft.

"Hello, can I please speak with Traci?"

"This is she."

"Hi. This is Jordan." There was an uncomfortable silence on the phone. Dead air was a killer.

"I hope you didn't mind me paging you?"

"It was a surprise. How did you get my number anyway?"

"I did some investigating."

"Huh?"

"I'm just joking. I called Renee and told her I needed to call you. I really appreciate the rose you left."

"No problem," I said confidently.

"No problem? You act like you're the masked rose bandit or something," she chuckled.

"It's not like that. I'm just saying it wasn't a problem. You just seemed like a nice person."

"So, you're saying that you give roses to all the nice people you meet?"

"No. You're getting me-"

"I'm just joking," Traci jumped in. "I thought that was very nice."

"Thank you." I was relieved. "Well, are you ever free for a drink?"

"Yes."

"Okay."

"Jordan, I'm not going to bite you. Relax."

"It's just that I've been under a lot of stress with…" I stopped myself. Rule number two: men are not supposed to talk about drama. Women hate to walk into the middle of baby mama drama. "With umm…work."

"Me too. I had a rough day today and that rose sure brightened up my day."

"Are you willing to have a nightcap tonight? I promise I'll have you home by eleven."

Hook me up.

She paused for a second. "Okay. Where?"

"Where do you live?"

"I live two blocks from the day care center."

"I think that there's a bar around the corner from it. It's called The Shelf or something like that." I knew the name of the bar, but I didn't want to seem like I frequented bars often.

"I know where it's at," Traci said.

"I'll be there in about twenty minutes."

"Bye, Jordan."

Being a brother that's always late for everything, I was surprised when I checked the time and I had arrived at The Shelf right on time. I scanned the room and there was no sign of Traci. There were about fifteen people sitting around listening to music and drinking. Some were at the tables off to the side while others were at the bar noisily socializing. This place wasn't like the End Zone. The people that came here were a little younger and wilder. I sat in one of the empty booths next to the bar.

I hoped that she would be able to make it. I checked my pager and waited for a call that I didn't want to get. I was really looking forward to seeing her. For some reason, just thinking about her made me smile. *Styles, get a grip. She might not be your type. She might be crazy. Hell, she might be out there. She might have simple chronic halitosis. Anything.*

"Hello, Mr. Styles."

I almost jumped out of my skin. "Hello, Traci," I said turning around. "You scared the crap out of me."

She playfully waved her hand in front of her nose. "Well, that must explain the smell," she smiled.

"Funny. Have a seat." I pulled a chair out for her.

"Thank you very much. And who says that chivalry is dead?"

Damn, Styles, you just heard that recently. "Would you like something to drink? Oh, I forgot to ask, do you drink?"

"Yes. I don't drink the hard stuff. I like wine. What do you drink?"

"I drink liquor and beer. Not a lot though. I like to stay in control of my actions." I looked for the waitress. I spotted one and gestured for her to come over. As she was coming near, I got a chance to look at Traci and damn she looked good. My eyes caressed hers until I had to turn my head. I had a funny feeling in my stomach as we exchanged visual pleasantries.

"Can I please get a glass of white wine for the lady and I would like a Molson Ice."

"Sure. I'll be right back with your drinks."

"So," I sighed. "tell me something about yourself."

She smiled, while seductively brushing a few strands of loose hair behind her ear. "What would you like to know?"

"Anything. Hmmm, let's see. Why don't you start with…" *Why you're so fine? Start with why you look so good. Start with where is your man.* "Start with where you're from."

"That's simple, I guess," she said licking her lips. *Styles, pay attention.* "I'm from Chicago. I lived there until I was fourteen and then I moved. I've been living out here ever since. What about you? Where are you from?"

"I'm surprised Renee didn't open up her big ass mouth and offer any information about me. She's good for doing that kinda stuff."

"Well, to be honest, all I did was hand her your pager. We didn't get on the subject of you."

Damn, Styles, no inquiry? Maybe she's not feeling me. Minor thing.

The waitress returned with our drinks.

"I'm from Albany," I said, grabbing my beer and pushing the white wine in front of Traci. "The capital of New York."

"I know it's the capital," she giggled. Where exactly is it located?"

"It's about two hours north of the city."

Her eyes widened. "Is it like the city? You know, wild and everything?"

"Nah. Some people say it's country, but it's cool. I met a lot of people there that were down to earth. I always said that if ever blew up, I would put Albany on the map. Then people would know where it is."

"So, why did you move to the D.C. area?" she inquired, taking slow sips of wine.

Styles, save the drama for another time. You got her. Don't scare the poor woman. "For more opportunities. I wanted to broaden my horizons."

Traci had a sly look on her face. "You wanted to broaden *who's* horizon?"

"No ones. I felt it was time for a change. Why? You've never felt like you needed a change?"

"Yes. I guess that's why my family moved. So you're off the hook with that one." She gave me a wink.

"Thank you," I said, returning the wink. "You are so understanding to the black man's struggle."

Her forehead wrinkled. "What struggle?"

Yes, Styles, way to go. Way to change the subject. Rule number three: when it starts getting too personal, talk about current events. Chicks dig current events.

"The struggles that black men have to go through every day. We struggle at our jobs, with white people every day, hell, we even struggle with the black woman." *Ahhh shit! Styles, you just opened up a can of woman worms.*

She sat back in her seat and folded her arms. "What do you

mean you struggle with black women?"

"Well, you know, sometimes we get a hard time about things."

"What things do *we* give you hard times about?"

Damn. She was trying to represent all women. I needed Johnny Cochrane. I was squirming in my seat.

"You know, things like taking the garbage out. Nothing major."

She laughed. "You're crazy."

"Some people think I should be admitted to a psych ward anyway. So are you um…" I was about to ask if she was married, single or divorced.

"Huh?"

"Nothing. I was just gonna ask you if you were hungry." *Way to go. Rule number four is no matter what, never ask questions you don't want to be asked.*

"Not really. I have to get going anyway."

Damn, what's up with that? You losin' your touch, Styles?

"Well, if you're not busy, then maybe we can meet sometime at a decent hour," I said in between sips.

"Sure. I don't have a problem with that."

I got up and pulled her chair out. She stood up to leave, and all I saw was the light bouncing off of her mahogany silouette. She finished the last of her drink and I realized I hadn't finished mine.

I grabbed my bottle and downed the last of the beer when she turned and asked, "Are you married?"

Beer shot out of my mouth.

Chapter 12

BANG...BANG...BANG...BANG

"Open the door!"

I was still in bed, groggy. Someone was banging at the door and I felt like shooting whoever it was. Didn't people respect others who needed sleep?

I got out of bed and realized that it could only be one person. Tony was the only person with balls to come to my house this early in the morning.

"I'm coming," I yelled.

"Hurry up Rip Van Winkle," Tony shouted through the door.

"Shut up! Mess around and your monkey ass might not get in."

"If I don't, I'll just call the landlord and tell him that you ain't got a job."

"Whatever," I said, opening the door. He was wearing a bright red sweat suit. Big people should never wear red. "You got your outfit on. Shit, you could've climbed down my chimney."

"Ha ha. What's going on?" he asked, stepping into the house. "I was in the neighborhood and figured I'd stop by and check a brotha out. How did everything go last night?"

I sat on the edge of the couch, tired as hell.

"Believe me when I tell you, she is fine."

"Where did you end up going last night?"

"The Shelf."

"So what's the scoop? Did you make it back to her spot?"

"She's not like that. And even if she was, I didn't want to go at her like that. You gotta know when to hold 'em and when to fold 'em."

"So you're saying that if she had given it up, you wouldn't have taken it?"

"Even if I had sex with her, it wouldn't make me want her any less."

"What do you mean, less?"

"You know when women always say that if they sleep with a man too soon, he will lose respect for her? They come with that crap about how all of a sudden, we wouldn't want them like we used to."

"It's true."

"I don't think so," I disagreed. "It's true to an extent, but I think that if a man is going to respect you, he'll do it regardless. I'm going to like them regardless of how long it takes to sleep with them. That's one of the biggest myths they've got with us."

"What? That we want to get some on the first date?"

"No, that we'll respect them more the longer they make us wait. There have been times when I've waited and that only pissed me off. Shit, I ended up getting what I wanted anyway and then leaving. I've had women that I slept with after months of waiting that I didn't like and women that I slept with rather quickly. And to tell you the truth, some of the women that I slept with quickly were some of the ones I ended up caring about."

"So you're saying that if she offered, you would've turned

her down?"

I shook my head. "I don't think I would've slept with her."

"Yeah, right. When was the last time you turned down sex?"

"When your mother tried to take her dentures off and give me some head," I said, nearly falling off the couch. I was in the mood to talk shit.

"Fuck you. I have never known you to turn down anything."

"We're even then because I've never known you to get offered any."

"I've had more than you will ever smell," Tony boasted.

"It's not quantity, it's quality. When was the last time you wanted a female because of her and not sex?"

"When was the last time *you* did? As a matter of fact, when have you ever?"

"I do. Right now," I said, getting up to put some pants on. "If I knew that she wouldn't sleep with me right now, I would still talk to her. And that's saying a lot."

"Didn't you feel the same way about Serene? I remember you saying you got the one you wanted to get, and then what happened?"

"You know what happened. She showed her true colors. Forget what Forrest Gump said about life; women are like a box of chocolates. You never know what you're gonna get inside. She seemed like the sweetest person, but then all hell broke loose. There is no way to tell what a person's like. I wish I had that woman's intuition thing. They can dislike someone or something and not know why and the craziest shit is, usually they're right."

"You're right. One time a woman told me that something was telling her not to kick it to me, but she went against it and look at what happened to her; I dogged her out. And the sad thing is I couldn't control it."

I was hungry as hell. I went to the kitchen and fixed myself a bowl of cereal. I yelled from the kitchen, "See, Tone, your problem is, you're not in touch with your sensitive side!"

He followed me into the kitchen. "What do *you* know about a sensitive side?"

"I know a lot. A lot more than I let you know about."

Tony grabbed a chair and flipped it around and sat down. "Like what?"

"We as guys, have to be well rounded." I quickly scooped up a spoonful of Corn Flakes and shoved them in my mouth. "You know, like a renaissance man."

"So being that you aren't educated, I guess you would be considered a ghettosance man, huh?" Tony laughed.

"Women like different things besides lifting weights and eating healthy. Let me ask you a question. Do you ever think about just picking up a pen and writing?"

"Writing what?"

"Letters, journals, poems or anything that involves writing."

"No. I don't have time to sit and write because I got better things to do. And what do *you* write?"

"A lot. You'd be surprised."

"You write what?"

"Poems," I said, awaiting laughter.

"Punk ass. Look at Styles trying to be Mr. Love Jones."

"You can joke all you want, but you can learn a lot through writing. That's why I know exactly what I want from a woman. I write poems about bad experiences and when I forget about what exactly happened, I go back to the poems. It's like taking a picture; without it, your memory fades and you forget what you saw."

"I guess I see where you're coming from. My father used to always say things like that. He'd tell me that I shouldn't sleep with every woman. He would always tell me to save some for the next man."

"That's what I've been telling you guys for the longest. All these women you see me with, do you think that I'm sleeping with all of them?" I paused. "No! I wish I was, but it's cool just being friends. Just like last night, Traci and I were just having fun."

"So, how is this Traci chick?"

I finished up the last of the cereal and threw the bowl in the sink. "From what I see, she's cool. We talked a little bit about where she was from and you know what she asked me?"

"What?"

"Out of the blue, she asked me if I was married."

Tony doubled over. "Stop playin'. What did you tell her?"

"Well, after I cleaned the Molson off of her arm, I walked her to her car and explained that I was going through a divorce."

"Hold up. You said you cleaned Molson-"

I shook my head. "Don't ask."

"I guess you got shot down, huh?"

"I don't know. I explained a little about what I've been going through, without hitting her with too much. Besides, who knows how much drama she has with herself anyway? I just told her that I would like to take her out to eat one day."

"With what money? You got bills to pay."

"I got enough to get me by. I'm sure I'll find a job and if worse comes to worse, I'll be working with my sister."

"How's Renee doing anyway?"

"She's doing okay, I guess. You know she's like a damn hermit. I won't even start on that Andre character."

"That's her husband though."

"I don't give a damn!" I had to pause to regain my thoughts. Just talking about them made me mad. "Anyway, I told Traci if she was interested in going to dinner, to call me later. I put the ball in her court."

"She didn't even ask if you had a job?"

"No, but I'm sure that's coming."

"What are you going to tell her?"

"The truth. I got caught in this merger and they offered me a lower paying salary and I wouldn't accept it."

"Is that what really happened?"

"More or less. I gotta check on this gig at three o'clock."

"Ring me later," Tony said.

I called Renee at work and left a message for her to call me ASAP.

When Tony left, I started to clean up a bit. I looked around, and there were clothes and papers everywhere. I decided to start in the kitchen. As soon as I saw all the dirty dishes, I decided to sit down and rest a bit.

The phone jolted my thought process.

"What's up, Jordan?" Renee asked.

"I need you to do something for me," I begged, getting up and drying a plate that still had crumbs on it.

"What's the magic word?"

"Now!" I chuckled. "Seriously, I need you to get me an application."

"Oh, so now you wouldn't mind working with *us*?"

"I don't need the extra shit. I just need an application."

"Jordan, does Traci know that she's dealing with an unemployed Negro?"

"Kinda."

"It's either she does or she doesn't."

"We got on the subject but we didn't finish the conversation."

"Well, if it means anything, I won't say a word if you can baby-sit for me sometime."

"Whatever!"

"I'll drop the application off to you when I get off work. If you're not there, I'll slide it under the door."

"Thanks. I'll talk to you later."

"I'll try to pull some strings."

When I got off the phone, I decided to put the cleaning on hold because I needed to get some sleep.

I looked at the clock and realized that I was only asleep for two hours when someone started banging on the door.

"Open the door, Jordan!" Renee yelled.

She knocked like she had big ass gorilla knuckles.

"I'm coming, Grape Ape," I laughed aloud.

"Open the door!"

"Or what?" I yelled, easing off the couch.

"Or I'm going to make your black ass collect unemployment until your pension kicks in."

"Do you ever shut up, Knuckles?" I screamed.

"Just open the door!"

"Did you bring it?" I asked, flinging the door open.

She sucked her teeth, turning her head in disgust. "No. I came over to look at your crusty drawers."

"Whatever. Did you speak to your boss?"

"Not yet. I wanted to make sure you could still fill out an application."

"Just give me the application," I said, snatching the paper away. "And why are you wearing those stupid ass shades?"

"I got a sty and it's oozing."

"How's Andre doing?"

"I don't know."

"What do you mean, you don't know?"

"I don't know. We got into a little argument and he went to his mother's house last night."

"Is he still acting stupid?"

"Nah. Everything's okay. I'll call you later and make sure you fill it out and drop it off by Friday."

Chapter 13

Dallas called as soon as Renee left, asking me to meet him at his house around ten o'clock tonight. It must have been important because he said to make sure I stopped by. He must be going through something with his girl or something. Dallas' girl was a certified nut. She was even crazier than Serene. She would follow him to bars, nightclubs and anywhere else he went. Being a 911 operator like he was, didn't help matters none. He said that he heard a lot of crazy stuff on the phone. I'll never forget the time he told me about a lady being stuck to her dog.

The weather was perfect for running, so I decided to go for a little jog around the neighborhood. I usually ran to the stadium and around Landover Mall. I looked in the mirror and noticed a little bulge around the stomach. I sucked my stomach in and decided that running would be in my best interest.

I ran for about forty-five minutes and was tired. I got back to the house, ate an apple and jumped in the shower.

The phone rang just as I finished putting lotion on.

"Hello."

"Hello. Can I speak with Mr. Styles?"

"Who's calling?"

"Traci."

"What's up?" I asked with enthusiasm, which she could probably hear over the phone.

"I just called to see if you were doing anything this evening."

"No," I quickly responded. Then I thought about Dallas. "Oh wait. I promised a friend of mine that I would go check him out. I could always cancel."

"No." Her voice got softer. "We can go out another time."

"It's no problem. He didn't want to meet me until midnight anyway," I lied. *Don't let her think that your friends don't mean anything to you. You gotta be dedicated to something or someone.*

"If it's no problem, when is a good time to meet?"

"It depends," I said. "What did you have in mind?"

"I was going to leave that up to you. I love when a man takes charge."

"Is that right?"

"Yes."

"Why don't I pick you up in about forty-five minutes?"

"That's fine. I'm low maintenance. I'll see you at seven-fifteen."

"I'll be there."

Before she got off of the phone, she gave me the directions to her house.

I hung up the phone, dialed Dallas' pager and let him know that something came up and I was going to be detained until about midnight.

I tried to think of a good place to take her. It would be our first official date and I definitely wanted to make a good first impression. I also didn't want to take her anywhere I would see some of my stragglers.

I figured I would just go with the flow. Thank God I had

just exercised and taken a shower. I went to the closet and decided to put on some blue jeans with my cream colored Banana Republic sweater. I sprayed on some Acqua Di Gio and left.

The temperature was perfect. If this was any indication of how the date was going to go, I was happy. It was about eighty degrees, with no wind. I rolled the windows down, blasted my Silk CD and sped to her house.

I parked the car in front of her house and got out. She wasn't waiting by the door, so I figured I would go and ring the bell. I felt like I was going to the prom all over again.

As soon as I rang the doorbell, I saw the light in the front room go out. She stepped out of the door looking beautiful. She had on a tight black dress. The hell with dinner, *she* looked delicious. If I had a biscuit, I would've sopped her up.

"Hello," Traci grinned, giving me a hug.

"How are you doing? I wasn't late, was I?" I said, looking at my watch.

She looked at her watch and shook her head. "No. You are a punctual brother, aren't you?"

"I try to be," I said, allowing her to go down the stairs before me.

"Thank God, because nowadays, people cannot keep track of time. I'm a real stickler for punctuality."

Shit!

I opened her door.

"Thank you," she said, sliding into her seat.

"No problem." I looked at her and could do nothing but shake my head. She was breathtaking.

It was only seven-twenty, so we had enough time to relax. I looked through my CD's to find something smooth. I decided on John Coltrane's, *In a Sentimental Mood.*

As I pulled off, Traci turned to me. "This is nice. Are you a jazz aficionado?" She moved her head to the sultry sounds.

"No. I listen to everything except country. Are you one of those country girls?"

"I'm well rounded, but no country," she said, not missing a beat.

You ain't lying. You are definitely well rounded. Those lips are incredible. "No country? You didn't listen to groups like the Culture Club either?"

"No. Were they your favorite group when you were a kid?"

"No."

I changed the music to another slow melody. I changed to CD number six: Musiq Soulchild. I went right to track seven; *Love.* He started out, "Love, there's so many things I want to tell you." I wanted to keep the mood just right.

"Damn," Traci blurted. "Those are some powerful words that brother is singing."

"Yeah," I smiled.

We listened to the entire song, both snapping our fingers and singing along to the parts we knew.

When the song went off, Traci asked, "Where did you decide to take me?"

"It's a surprise. Don't you like surprises?"

"Yes. What about you?"

I remembered the surprise I got from Serene. "I don't like all surprises."

"Sounds like you had some bad ones," she said, patting me on the knee.

"I just had one and that was enough. So what do you like to eat?" I asked, changing the subject.

"Seafood. I love crab and lobster."

You won't be having crab and lobster tonight. This budget is killing a brother. "I can eat shrimps all day."

"Jordan, I don't mean to cut you off, but why do black people always put an 's' on the end of everything like shrimp and money. I'm not trying to be funny so I hope you're not offended."

"I don't offend easily. And I don't know why people say that, maybe because their parents teach them that way."

"Whatever it is, that's one of my pet peeves."

"Do you have any more pet peeves?"

"Yes. I don't like when guys yo' me and I don't like when guys wear suits with derby's. Do you wear those?"

"Wear what?"

"Those dumb looking derby hats."

"I couldn't do that anyway. I don't own any suits." Traci pursed her lips. "I'm just joking. Does it look like I don't own any suits?"

"Don't get me to lying. I just met you," she said, gazing at me conspicuously.

"Ha ha, very funny," I laughed, taking a left into a large lot.

"Where are we?" Traci asked, looking around.

"You said you like surprises, didn't you?"

She moved close to the door. "Yeah, but you could be a killer."

"Well, consider yourself dead because I have you for about three hours."

"Okay, Mr. Styles."

"Relax. You'll have fun. Trust me." I walked around to the passenger side and opened her door. It was getting dark, minus the few stars that lit the sky. "There's a lot of rock and gravel here, so if you don't want to fall, maybe you should hold onto something."

"Like what?"

"Like an arm," I replied, extending my arm.

She shook her head and smiled. "You are something else."

"I know." She wrapped her arm around mine as I led her into the building. When we got inside, we went down a long corridor filled with empty desks.

She took a few steps and stopped. "Jordan, where are we going?"

"I wanted to take you somewhere that you probably don't go too often."

"Where would that be?"

"Church," I joked.

"You better not be talking about God. He doesn't like it when people use him for jokes."

"Well, don't tell him that I was talking about him."

"Okay," she said, grabbing my arm tighter as I led her away.

When we got to the end of the corridor, I opened the door and let her go before me. We walked into a big room that was filled with about one hundred people. There was a dense cloud of smoke that filled the air. She waved her hand, trying to rid the smoke from in front of her.

"Jordan, where are we?" she coughed.

"You ain't never been bowling?"

"Not in a building without bowling lanes," she said, looking around for lanes.

"The lanes are in the back. Over there," I said, pointing to the older group of people, "is where they play bingo."

"Do you come here often?" Traci asked with uncertainty.

"Believe me, you'll have a lot of fun. Have you ever been bowling?"

"I've been to a bowling alley, but it was for a birthday party for one of the students at the center."

"Relax. You'll be glad I brought you here."

"If I'm not, I'm going to take you to court for having me do activities that are detrimental to my pleasure zone."

We walked through the haze of smoke and made it to the lanes.

"Excuse me sir," I said, attempting to get a little service.

The guy at the counter looked like one of the bowlers on TV. He was real thin, with thick glasses on.

"Can I help you?"

"I would like two pair of shoes, please."

"No problem. What sizes?"

"Fourteen for me and a…" I turned around and looked at her feet.

"Seven," she added.

"I know we have a fourteen for you sir, but that seven is going to be hard to find. It's a popular size this evening."

"I'll take a size eight if you have them."

"Let me check." He disappeared into the back.

When the man left, I turned to Traci and looked at her feet. "Damn! You got some big ass feet."

"That myth doesn't pertain to women." She then shot a similar glance at my feet.

"It does to me," I smiled, wiggling my toes.

The man reappeared with our shoes and sat them on the counter.

"Here you are. Lane 18 is open."

We found our lanes and sat down to put our shoes on. I watched Traci checking out her nails.

I leaned over, grabbed her hand and looked at her nails. "I hope you don't break a nail."

Traci put her hand in my face, showing her low cut nails. "I told you that I was low maintenance, didn't I?"

"I hope I don't break mines?" I joked, looking at mine.

"What?"

I put my arm around her shoulder. "I'm just playing around."

"You know what they say about black men."

"All the good ones…"

"Are either married or gay," we said in unison.

"I hope you aren't both," Traci spat back, arching her eyebrow.

"Well, after this divorce and sex change, hopefully I'll be neither," I said, winking at her. "We gotta get some balls."

She started looking around. "From where?"

I started to grab my pants and make a joke, but decided against it. "Damn rookie! There should be a ball to fit your hand on one of those racks," I said, pointing to the three racks in the back. "Just start putting your hands in the hole and if it feels good, grab it. I'll meet you back here in a few."

We both went looking for balls. Luckily, I found one right away. A minute later, she was back with a ball in tow.

"So, Jordan, I'll be nice and let you tell me something about yourself before I go inquiring. I don't want to dive into water that isn't ready to be plunged into."

I laughed and turned my head. I noticed that I do that when I don't want to answer a particular question. I hate it. "I am six-foot four, black-"

"It doesn't take a rocket scientist to figure that out," she butted in.

"Like I was saying, I am kinda shy and-"

She stood up. "Hold up! *You* are not shy."

"Yes I am. It may not seem like it, but I do get nervous

sometimes."

"I cannot believe that Mr. Jordan Styles is shy."

"I am. Especially when I meet someone for the first time. Like when I met you, I debated on whether or not to go up to your office to bring you the flower. And as you can tell, I chickened out."

"That's not being shy, that's being scary."

"I pointed to myself. "So, now I'm scary?"

"You can call it what you want."

"So, let's flip the script. Are you shy?"

"In the line of work that I'm in, I can't be. I have to hire and fire people and if I was shy, it would interfere with my performance." She paused. "Speaking of work, what type of work are you in?"

Relax, Styles. You knew it was coming. It was just a matter of time. "I'm in…"

Shit. To lie or not to lie. Fuck it, Styles. Tell her the truth. "I…I…I'm not in any type of work right now." I waited nervously for a reaction of any kind.

"Oh."

Say something before further damage sets in. "See, there was a merger and I was the odd man out." *It sounded like bullshit, but it was the truth.*

"I understand. It must be hard on you."

"Yeah, but I'm a survivor. I've been through worse."

"Me too."

My eyes widened. "You've been let go before?"

"Hell no!" She covered her mouth, gasping. "I mean, no I haven't been let go. I didn't mean it like that."

"It's okay. I deal with it." All of a sudden, I didn't want to be there. I was embarrassed about not having a job and also for having nothing else to say about getting a new one.

We began to bowl in silence. Traci threw two balls right into the gutter and sat down, vexed. I got up and rolled a strike, which didn't make her feel any better.

When she stood up to bowl again, I got up to instruct her. "You're doing something wrong. Try moving a little to your right." Traci moved to her left. "I mean, your other right."

She laughed, turned around and said, "I don't know my ass from my elbow sometimes."

I don't know about her, but I sure could tell that ass from those elbows. It wasn't that hard.

"Maybe you can come and help me."

"Alright. I think I know a few tricks," I said, getting closer. "See, you want to hold the ball like this." I demonstrated how to hold the ball correctly. I pulled her back to the starting point and walked behind her to show her the steps.

Out of nowhere, it started happening. *Relax, Styles. Think of Serene! For God's sake, think of anything to bring it down!* Sambuca was awakening and I couldn't control him.

"Did you say that you wanted something to drink?" I asked, stepping back from Traci. I hoped she didn't know how much I was enjoying teaching her the game.

"That would be nice."

"What would you like?"

Traci gave me a weird look. "I would like a glass of wine. Nothing too hard," she laughed, almost dropping her ball.

"Okay, I'll be right back," I yelled, putting my hands into my pockets. I jogged to the bar.

After a couple of drinks, she started to warm up. Time must've flown by because the next time I looked up at the clock, it read ten o'clock and I was starving.

"Let's get out of here and get something to eat," I suggested. "Are you hungry?"

Traci was sitting down, visibly fed up with all of the gutter balls. "I'm hungry too. Thank God I'm not a picky eater. I'll eat just about anything."

Get your mind out the gutter. We decided on Red Lobster. It wasn't in the budget, but what the hell.

As we were listening to music on the way there, Traci turned toward me and blurted, "Do you date white women?"

"What did you say?" I coughed, watching her and the road at the same time.

Not once taking her eye off of me, she repeated, "I said, do you date white women?"

"Why would you ask me that?"

"Why not? Is it something that you don't wish to speak about?"

"No. I was just wondering why you would ask that. Would it make a difference?"

"No." She turned to the window and gazed at nothing in particular. "I'm sorry if I'm getting a little too personal."

"I don't mind. Ask me anything you would like."

"Okay." She perked up and turned back to me. "Do you date white women?"

"No."

"Have you *ever* dated a white woman?"

"Not really," I said, pulling into the Red Lobster parking lot.

"What is not really?"

"I dated a mulatto chick one time."

"Oh."

"Why, do you date white chicks?"

"Very funny," she laughed. "I don't date white chicks or white men."

"Why not?"

"Because I can't forget everything we've been through and I grew up thinking that two people should have a lot in common. Nothing against the white guys, but I don't have too much in common with them."

"Damn, Angela Davis." I chuckled.

"No, it's not like that. I just love my brothers. There is nothing sexier than a black man." She must've reminisced about someone she knew because she turned her head, closed her eyes and bit her lip. "He is the strongest man alive and I hate to see them settle for anyone other than a sister."

The first person I thought of was Dallas. "So, do you think that a brotha that marries or dates a white chick is weak?"

"He might not be weak to others, but in my opinion, maybe he might not be able to handle a strong black woman."

"So, you're saying that a white woman couldn't compliment a black man?"

"She could compliment a black man. Just not a strong black man."

"A strong black man?"

"That's what I'm saying."

The cookout at Dallas' house was definitely out of the question. "Are you ready to eat?"

"Yes," she smiled. And with that, I decided that it was time to get off of that subject. I walked around and opened the door for her.

We walked in, and to my surprise, it wasn't too crowded. We walked to the host and he asked, "Smoking or non smoking?"

I looked at Traci and then at the man. "If she didn't bring the weed, then we'll sit in the non smoking section." Apparently by everyone's look, I was the only one that thought the joke was funny.

As the host led us to our booth, I let her walk in front of me, partly because I'm a gentleman and partly because I wanted to see her walk. She had a "my shit is good" walk. We sat down and a waitress came right over.

"How are you guys doing?" the waitress pleasantly asked. She was about twenty-five and thick as hell. I tried not to stare at her tits, but they were calling me. I was like a baby in a nursery ward. *Mama. Dada. Goo goo.*

Traci ran her finger up and down the menu. "I'll have a strawberry daiquiri,"

The waitress turned to me. "And you, sir?"

I must've been deep inside her shirt because Traci nudged me.

"Oh, I'm sorry," I said, trying to clear my thoughts. "I would like a Long Island Iced Tea."

As soon as the waitress left, Traci stared at me while her fingers aggresively danced on the table. "Is she attractive?"

"Huh?"

She nodded toward the waitress that had just left. "Is she an attractive woman?"

"She's okay, why?"

"Because you couldn't stop staring at her chest."

"I was just looking at her name tag because I like to call people by their name."

"Is that so?" she murmured, with a smug look.

"Yeah, that's so. And not to jump off the subject but I've

been thinking."

"About what?"

"About you."

"What about me?"

"What do you do outside of work? Do you have any friends or are you a loner? I want to find out what I can about Ms. Traci Johnson."

"Well, to answer your question, I do have friends. I was actually talking to one of them about you today."

"I hope you were being nice. You didn't dog, me did you?"

"Not really. I told the truth."

"Which is what?"

"She asked me how we met and I told her."

The waitress returned with our drinks and this time I kept my eyes directly on Traci.

"You told her what?"

"I told her that you came to the job to pick up your niece and you began stalking me."

I laughed. "Who was stalking you?"

"C'mon, Jordan, you know you were getting your stalk on."

"Yeah. And if I was, you were sitting there trying to be stalked. Calling me and telling me, 'I just love the flower you left,'" I said, imitating her voice to perfection. "What else did you say?"

"She asked me what you looked like."

My voice got heavier as I pulled my chair closer. "And what did you say?"

"I told her that you are a very handsome man."

"What did you really tell her?"

"It was nothing but women talk. You probably wouldn't understand it."

"I read Essence and Cosmopolitan."

"That's the problem right there. If you're reading Cosmopolitan, you definitely don't know what I'm talking about," she laughed. "I told her that you were very tall and chocolate with a very sexy build. I also said that you had dimples that I would love to stick my...fingers in."

"You're nuts," I blushed.

"You act like your friends didn't ask you about me," she sneered, waiting for confirmation.

"I didn't tell them anything." By the look on her face, she seemed a little deflated.

"That's okay, I like to be low key anyway." She grabbed her drink and sipped seductively from her straw.

"I'm just joking with you. I told my friends, Tony and Dallas, about you."

Her voice rose with excitement. "What did you tell them?"

"I told them that you were someone I met while picking up my niece."

"What else?"

"Nothing. I spoon feed them information most of the time." I thought about it for a second. "Actually, I tell Tony everything and Dallas is the one that I have to spoon feed information to."

"If you don't trust him, then why do you hang out with him?"

"I've known Dallas for ten years and I went to school with Tony. We were in the same gym class in the tenth grade. I met Dallas when I was working for the Boy's Club on Delaware Avenue and we've been hanging out every since."

"What do you guys do when you hang out?"

"Play ball."

"That's all?"

"No. Sometimes we go and get our drink on."

"Do you guys ever sit down and talk?"

"Hell no!" Traci threw her head back and squinted her eyes. I continued, "Not unless we're at the bar."

"Why does it have to be hell no? Men can't sit down and talk about life?"

"We can, but we just don't get into that stuff. We just don't get personal like women do."

She frowned. "What do you mean like women do?"

"Women go to the movies together and it doesn't look funny. But let two guys go to the movies and they look gay."

"Jordan, if two guys go to the movies together, it isn't a queer thing. It can be that they want to see the same movie."

"If we want to see the same movie, we double date."

The waitress returned. "Are you ready to order now?"

"Yes," Traci said, rubbing her stomach. "I'm starving."

Damn, Styles! Starving means more money. Please order something reasonable.

"Me too," I agreed. "I feel like I can eat a whole building."

"I'm going to order the shrimp combo. What are you going to get?"

Something cheap. Where the hell are the hot dogs?

"I'll take the Cajun Shrimp Pasta and another drink." Fuck it! If I'm going to be broke, I might as well be drunk. We both decided to get the house salad.

"Okay," the waitress replied. "I'll bring the biscuits and salad right out."

Traci looked beautiful under the lights. She had short hair that accentuated her face. Between the caramel skin and full lips I was already indulging. She reminded me of Nia Long. She had the same natural beauty with an attitude to match. Her dress was tough. It was cut into a v-neck in the front, exposing her full, caramel colored breasts.

"Uh um!" she said, clearing her throat.

"Huh?"

"Earth to planet Jordan."

"I'm sorry, I was just thinking."

"A penny for your thoughts," she inquired, placing her hands atop mine.

"I was just admiring your elegance."

"Thank you," she blushed. "It's nice to hear that every now and then."

"You sound as if you don't hear many compliments."

"I don't," she said, removing her hands and looking down at the table. "For some reason, I don't run into many gentlemen. I'm used to hearing, 'what's up baby,' and all that other stuff."

"Damn, where do you meet these guys at?"

"A little bit of everywhere. So after awhile, I started losing faith in men."

I looked at her with a funny expression. "So does that mean…"

She interrupted quickly, "No! I definitely don't go that way!"

"What way?" I laughed.

"Don't play with me."

"What are you talking about?"

"You can kill that noise," she snapped. She seemed rather agitated, like she was presented with that question before.

Our food came just in time. I must have touched a nerve because we had small talk throughout the rest of dinner.

The waitress came back and asked if we wanted dessert and

we both politely declined. She reached in her apron and pulled the bill out. It seemed as though she thought about where to put it before she so kindly slammed it in front of me, smiling, while looking down my shirt.

Asshole! This woman's lib shit was definitely fucking with me.

Pick up the bill, Styles. It can't be more than fifty bills. How much did you bring anyway? I hope Traci doesn't mess up her nails doing them dishes.

"Let me get the bill," Traci said, reaching for the bill. "You paid for bowling."

"No, it's on me," I persisted.

"*I* invited *you* to dinner, Jordan."

"It's okay." I reached for my wallet. "I can handle the damage."

"I know, but with your job and all…"

Fuck it, Styles! If she keeps begging for it, stick it right in her lap. 'I know with your job and all,' ain't that some bullshit!

"It's okay, maybe you can treat me to lunch one day."

I looked at the bill and it said forty-two dollars and thirty-five cents. I left the fifty inside the envelope and we left. She's lucky she's fine.

The ride home was just as silent as dinner. I decided to put on the radio and listen to the radio personalities talk.

I pulled up to her house and we sat in silence, both looking like her parents would start flicking the lights on and off, to let us know that it was time.

"Well, Sere…" *Oh shit! Think.*

I nervously coughed and started over. "Well, seems to me that I should get going. *Great thinking.*

"I guess you're right," she said, looking at me with those big lips puckered up.

"I had a good time tonight, Traci." I slid over in my seat and put my arm around her, playfully squeezing her shoulder. *Work it, Styles. Work it.* "So hopefully, I'll be able to see you soon."

"If you want to. I'm usually free after nine."

"Let me walk you to your door. I don't want anyone else stalking you. Two stalkers in one night are a bit much."

I opened the door for her. "You're right," she chuckled, stepping out of the car. "At least the stalker that's here is fine."

I looked over my back. "Oh, I thought the other one was in back of me." *Corny, Styles. That was pitiful.* "I guess I'll call you soon."

She approached her door and nervously fumbled through her bag to find her keys. This was my chance to make my move.

"Okay," she nodded, pulling her keys out of her bag. She leaned against her door, inviting me to her lips.

I moved closer to her.

Go for it, Styles. You've been in this position before. Mentally, I leaned over and kissed her, but in reality, I simply extended my hand. "Good night. It was a pleasure."

Good night. It was a pleasure. What an asshole!

Chapter 14

I woke up and looked at the clock. It was nine-forty and I had to be at the courthouse by ten-thirty.

I showered and decided to put on my blue suit because women told me that blue was a power color. This would be the end, I hoped. I didn't want her and she didn't want me.

I got to the courthouse at exactly ten-thirty and my lawyer was waiting.

"Jordan, they were just calling us. We can go right in." He sounded rather aggravated.

"Sorry, I was running a little late," I apologized.

"That's alright," he said, checking his watch. "Was there any progress that I should know about?"

Yeah, Mr. Take All My Money Man. There definitely was some progress. She took hold of my dick and progressively devoured all the evidence.

"No, we spoke briefly but nothing to talk about." I didn't want to get into all that with him.

"Well, I think we have reached a settlement with Mrs. Styles."

I wanted to do the running man all over the courthouse. I tried to remain calm.

"What happened?"

"Serene's lawyer told her that this could end up being a lengthy process. So she was advised to settle on getting the house, car and physical custody of your son. We agreed that we would split the insurance down the middle with you paying child support. I also stated that since you aren't working, alimony is out of the question. Do you agree with everything?"

"Yes!"

"Are you sure you want to go through with this?"

"Yes!"

"Well, all we have to do is go in there and agree to everything I have just stated and then wait for the papers to be drawn up and signed."

"What if she changes her mind after it's drawn up?"

"Well, that's another batch of eggs we'll have to deal with."

We walked into the courtroom and Serene and her pit bull lawyer were sitting down on the other side of the room. For some reason all the hatred I had felt for her left. I couldn't understand it. I didn't want to be with her, but at the same time, I didn't want to be without her.

We didn't exchange pleasantries or anything. How did I come to feel this way about someone that I had thought the world of?

Never mind that shit, Styles. She would spit in your face if you gave her the chance. You're stupid to feel any love for her.

We got through the meeting and everything went well. There were no surprises. I was shocked. After we walked outside, everyone disappeared and we were left alone once again.

"I'm sorry, Jordan."

I damn near fell off the steps. "What?"

"I said that I'm sorry." Her eyes were glossy. The same eyes that never felt remorse. The same eyes that only saw things from their owner's point of view.

"For what?"

"For dragging you through all this," she whined, while dabbing the corners of her eyes. "You have been so good throughout these months. I would've been a different person than you were."

"It's not about who did what," I said trying to be the voice of reason. "Sometimes, things happen that we have no control over."

"I know, Jordan, but if there is anything that I can do to rectify the situation, I will."

"Anything like what?" I said as I started tapping my feet. I knew she was trying to work on me.

"I'm saying, do you really want this divorce? Do you really want to leave your son and me? Can you really just walk out on us?"

She was working on my sense of pity and the love I had for my child.

"Serene, don't do this. Why do we have to bring Kendal into this? He isn't to blame for any of this."

"I know, Jordan, but don't you love me?"

"Huh?"

"You heard what I said. Don't you love me?"

"Yes, but it's not the same as-"

"See, you just said that you love me. Doesn't that mean anything to you?"

"Right now it doesn't mean much because of the situation we're in."

"Why? Are you seeing someone?"

"Not really."

"Not really? Then you *are* seeing someone."

"Kind of."

"Who is the bitch?" Serene screamed. Her eyes had that look

of unfamiliarity. When she got mad, I couldn't recognize her. Someone else seemed to take control of her body and mind.

"See, there you go. You're out of control."

"No, I'm not. Are you saying that you have total control?"

"No," I said, walking to my car. "I have to have some control. I gotta leave."

"Jordan, wait," she pleaded, attempting to grab my arm.

I shook my arm free. "I said I gotta go. Call me later."

"Will you come over and talk?"

"Maybe." *Dumb thing to say. Never open up the window of opportunity.* I rushed to my car making sure I didn't turn around. I felt like Lot.

I got home, sat down and relaxed. I was tired as hell. Court has a way of draining a person but I had to get this job application in.

I made it to Renee's job and as soon as I walked in, I smelled medication and shit. *Relax, Styles. Pretend you're in a nursery. Hell, no! This is grown people's shit.*

I got to the front counter and a skinny black man with thick glasses turned around with a weird look on his face.

"Hi. May I help you?" He was definitely swinging from a different tree than I was.

"Yes. I'm looking for the personnel office, ma'am. I mean, sir."

He flashed me a little smile.

"That's okay. You so funny. You look familiar," he said, rubbing his chin for knowledge. "Say, aren't you that man who sings the song, "Love in a Limo?"

"That's not me."

He bit on his forefinger. "So, you ain't no kind of superstar?"

"No!"

"You look so familiar. Maybe I've seen you at the Fat Cat."

"You definitely haven't seen me there." I said. Just then, a revelation came over me. *Why in the hell am I answering these questions?* "All I want to know is where is the damn Personnel Office?" I shouted.

"Gosh. Why are you getting so testes? I mean testy," he smiled, giving me a wink. He pointed to the elevator. "It's on the fourth floor."

"Thank you!" I barked.

"Wait a minute. You have to sign in," he said pointing to a pink pad. *How fitting.*

I signed the pad and as I walked away, he yelled, "Bye, Mr. Smiles."

I went upstairs to the Personnel Office. I gave the lady at the counter the application and asked her to get Renee.

She went to the back and came out a minute later.

"I'm sorry sir, she's not in. They said she'd be off for a few weeks. Would you like to leave a message?"

"Nah. That's okay," I said, walking back to the elevator.

Chapter 15

It was Saturday evening and I was supposed to meet the fellas at this bar called, The Matrix, near the White House. Even though the sun was out, it was rather breezy. The traffic on the highway was at a standstill so I flashed an occasional wave at some of the fine women that were at a standstill with me.

I got near the White House and quickly tried to find some parking, but to no avail, I ended up driving in circles for five minutes. If only I had it like the President: free parking, waiters, servants, personal aids, cigars and chicks in blue dresses. Must be nice. I got out, walked toward the restaurant and I knew that Dallas was gonna be mad because I never called him back.

I strolled to the table, "What's up?"

Dallas and Tony were both sitting down having drinks.

Tony belched. "What's up, Late Man?"

"Up yours buddy!" I said, raising my long finger towards him. "What's going on, Dallas? Cat got your tongue?"

"No, actually the cat got my beeper."

"Ha ha, very funny." I said to him.

"What happened? I thought you were supposed to call me back. What the hell were you doing anyway?" Dallas snarled.

"Business."

"What kind of business? It was definitely not work related."

"Fuck you, Juice!"

"There you go with that white girl shit again."

"You know I'm just joking D. Get me a brew and shut the hell up," I said, slapping him on his back.

Tony said, "I already ordered you one. So, what's been going on? I haven't heard from you in a bit."

"You know, a little bit of this and a little bit of that."

The waitress brought another round of beer and set them on the table.

I looked at her and pointed to the table. "Thanks. Keep a tab."

"You must've met some new chick or is that one from the day care still coming around?" Tony added.

Dallas chimed in, "Yeah, you know Styles starts forgetting the fellas as soon as a new piece comes into the picture."

"You can kiss my black ass! You know it ain't even like that."

"Yeah, right," Dallas said.

I downed my beer and asked a waitress who was in ear shot for another. "Yo', D, what's up anyway? You said you wanted to talk to me, right?"

"It's kinda late now."

"What was it?

"You know at my job, I hear a lot of stuff, right?"

"Yeah, and…"

"Well, a call came in from your sister's house."

I jumped out of my seat. "Is she okay?"

Dallas motioned for me to have a seat. "The question is, is Andre okay?"

"What happened?" I was nervous as hell now.

"Well, the other day, when I paged you, there was an argument at her house. Apparently she and Andre had words because she caught him with another woman."

"Where?" I was boiling with each passing second.

"I guess she went to his job to surprise him for lunch and got surprised. And when he got home, he was surprised." He was getting hype now. "She threw his shit out of the house and when he came home, she tried to hit him with a pot."

"She should've hit his ass with the stove," I belted, knowing all the shit that she went through.

"Well, that's why I told you to come by the house that night. But when you didn't show up, I went over there and spoke to her myself."

"You what?"

"I went over there and spoke to her. Somebody had to speak with her."

"So how is she doing?"

"You know," Dallas shrugged his shoulders. "She'll eventually deal with it and then let him come back."

"That is some stupid shit! And that's why I don't get involved because she always ends up back with him. I'm going over there now."

"That's a good idea," Dallas replied.

I gave them both the pound and stepped out. I called Renee's house and didn't get an answer, so I drove by. Nobody was home.

Relax, Styles. There is nothing you can do about it. Chill out. Call Traci. I dialed Traci's number and her answering machine picked up.

"Traci, this is Styles…I mean, Jordan. Give me a call when you get a-" Before I finished my word, she picked up the phone.

"Hi, Jordan. How are you doing?"

"Not so good. Are you able to hang out for a bit? You told

me that when I needed to speak to someone, I could call you." I knew I sounded pitiful.

"What's wrong?"

"Nothing really. I'm just a little depressed."

"You can come by and talk if you would like. I was just sitting on the couch reading. I'll put something comfortable on. You know where I live."

"Okay, I'll be there. And Traci?"

"Yes?"

"Thanks again."

"No problem."

"Would you like me to bring anything by?"

"No, I'm fine."

As I was walking up the porch, I wondered what the inside of her house looked like. I hate messy women

I rang the bell and waited. I heard someone walking down the stairs. She opened the door in a black, silk robe. I was definitely not ready for this.

Yes you are. If it happens, it happens.

"Come in, Jordan."

She really worked my name. It rolled off her tongue so sweetly.

"Thank you very much, Traci," I replied, taking off my jacket and handing it to her.

The apartment was beautiful. It definitely had an Afro-centric appeal to it. She had a beautiful black leather couch with a matching love seat and there was some beautiful African art on the wall.

"You can have a seat, Jordan," she said, pointing toward the couch. "Do you want something to drink?"

"Do you have any beer?"

"I don't have beer, but I do have wine."

"That's fine."

She went into the kitchen and came out with two glasses of red wine.

"Here," she said, handing me a glass. Relax, Jordan." Traci sat down and nestled next to me. "What's wrong?"

"My sister. She and her husband go through a lot of bullshit and I don't know what to do about it."

"Well, there isn't anything you can do. Sometimes it's best to let nature take its course. Nothing you say will make her think any differently than she already does, right?"

"You're right."

I hated feeling this way. When I get upset, the only thing that makes me feel better are playing ball or having sex. Everyone has their own way of releasing frustration. And as I looked around, I didn't see any hoop courts in her house.

"So, what's up Traci? Are you feeling me or what?" *Where the hell did that come from?*

"What?" Traci said, turning and looking at me with surprise.

"Are you feeling me or what?"

"Well, Jordan, we really haven't spent that much time together for me to be having any feelings like that."

"I'm saying though, can a brother get some love in this piece?"

"Some love?" She sprung off of the couch. "I think maybe you should go home and relax."

"I'm sorry," I said, patting the couch, inviting her to sit back down. "I'm just going through a lot and I don't know exactly what to do. You're the only one that I feel like I can talk to right now."

"What about your boys?"

"They don't understand shit like this."

"Well, I'm here for you to talk to whenever you need to talk," she explained, sitting back down. "But that other stuff is…"

"I know. I'm sorry. I don't know where my head was."

Apparently I was wearing out my welcome. *Too much drama, Styles. No woman wants to have a brother with more drama than E.R. Fuck it, Styles, make your exit.*

"Well, it looks like you were going to bed and I don't want to keep you late." *Please say, 'It's no problem, Jordan. We can talk all night if you want to.'*

She walked to the door. "Well, I do have to get up pretty early. If you need to talk tomorrow, leave me a message and I'll get back to you."

I wasn't used to getting turned down, even though I wasn't asking for anything.

"Actually, I have to get up early myself." *You fucking liar! But what the hell, she's not feeling you anyway.* I got to the door and before she opened it I turned around and faced her.

"Thanks for everything." *Work it, Styles, work it.* I reached down and gave her a hug that a long lost girlfriend would've been envious of. I felt her body for the first time and she was incredibly soft.

Do something before the Sambuca wakes up. He was yawning and started escaping the confines of my boxers.

I moved my head from the side of hers and found her lips, giving her the gentlest kiss I could. Suddenly, her lips parted and like Moses, I entered the sea. She moaned with approval as I backed her up against the door.

I kissed her lips while pressing against her. I traced her lips with my tongue. I kissed her softly and then kissed her cheek. There was no resistance, so I moved to her neck. She squirmed when I put my mouth on her neck, gently flicking my tongue up and down, until she moaned, "This isn't good."

"No?" I asked, in between licks.

Traci pushed me away. "Okay, Jordan, maybe that's enough."

It was not enough, but what was I going do, beg?

Beg, brother, beg.

"Alright," I said, walking out of the door, trying to adjust myself. "Thanks for everything. Hopefully, I'll speak to you soon."

"You will," she said, wiping the corners of her mouth.

Needless to say, I was on my way home to put on one of my porno tapes and finish the job myself. I thought about calling someone, but sometimes you want the end results without putting up with all the bullshit to get it.

Chapter 16

Kendal was leaving for the weekend and I had to see him off. He was going on a camping trip that his church group sponsors every year.

"Dad, hurry up. We're getting ready to leave in a few."

I was just walking through the door.

"Do you need anything?" *Boy, why did I ask him that question?*

"Yeah. I need about fifteen dollars to cover me just in case we go into town."

"I don't have fifteen," I answered, reaching into my pocket and pulling out a bill. "All I have is a twenty. Go ask your mother if she has change."

"She just gave me ten. Thanks," he said, snatching the twenty and disappearing into the crowded van.

Now I was stuck in the house with Serene and I knew what was coming. *Run, Styles, run.*

Serene came into the living room with two glasses of wine.

"Serene, I got to get going."

"Why are you leaving so fast, Jordan?" Serene scooted in front of me as I tried to walk to the door.

"My sister has something going on over her house and I need to check on her."

"So, you're saying that you don't have time to talk about things?"

I didn't have a good feeling. *Fuck it, Styles. Just keep your guard up.* "I have a few minutes. What's up?" I asked, sitting down on the couch.

"Nothing really. I just wanted to talk," she smiled, flashing that little smirk of hers.

"About what?" I said, tapping my foot.

"Jordan?"

"What?"

"Can I be truthful about something?" Serene asked, positioning herself next to me.

"Go ahead." I turned my head to avoid eye contact.

"Are you saying that you don't want things to work out between us?"

"What us?" I rose suddenly. I was fed up already.

"You know. You, Kendal and me. Kendal needs you. I need you." She turned her head the other way, probably because of embarrassment. "Fine. It's out. Is that what you've been waiting to hear?"

I placed my arm around her to comfort her. Even though she got on my nerves, I didn't like to see her upset. "It's not even like that."

"You want me to get down on my knees and beg you? You want me to kiss the ground you fucking walk on?"

"No, I don't want anything like that."

"Well, what do you want?" she pleaded.

"I want…I want some normalcy. Ever since I've been with you, it's been one thing after another. What do we have to do, kill each other?"

"You act like I never gave you any happiness," she cried. Tears streamed down her cheeks.

She should win the Academy Award for the tears of bullshit. You want me to come back to you so I can be back in your web. Misery loves...

"I can't do it, Serene." I said, moving away from her.

"Why?"

"Serene, how would you feel if you came home and saw me fucking Tony? Would you still want me?" The thought nauseated me.

"Things happen."

"Rain falls on your house and you happen to get a leak. Snow comes and you may happen to get caught in a blizzard. You may happen to lose your job to a merger. But you do not, and I repeat, do not, happen to fall and slip into your friend's pussy. There is no excuse!"

She threw her face inside of her hands and cried. The passion and love I had for her went out the window, and I was pouring it on.

"I mean, did you think I wouldn't find out?"

Serene lifted her head up and shouted, "Okay, Jordan. You got your point across."

"I'm not trying to get a point across. I am dealing with cold, hard facts. How do I know if that was your first time? As a matter of fact, was it?"

Serene was bawling now. For a woman that had the strength of a hundred men, she sure was crying like a little baby. She sawed her nose with her arm, leaving remnants of mucous across her sleeve. *Go wipe your damn nose. How pathetic.*

Her voice was quivering. "Y-y-yes, and I am so sorry. I know that I hurt you and..."

"You didn't hurt me, you hurt our son and you hurt the

marriage."

"You can't say that you never did anything to hurt me!"

"You're right, but cheating, and with a woman no less. Have you always been like that?"

"Like what?" Serene cried, grabbing a tissue from the end table.

"You know. Gay. A lesbian. A dyke. A carpet muncher. A muff diver. A..."

"Fuck you, Jordan!"

"How does something like that just happen? I mean, do you just wake up one day and crave it? As a matter of fact, why did you cheat on me anyway? Wasn't I pleasing you, or is that you needed more, like a nympho?"

"I swear on our child that it was only once and I don't crave it. It was just that you weren't giving me the attention I needed."

"And she did. She gave you more than attention, huh?"

"You were always at your job and..."

"And making us some damn money! I can see if I was out all night partying or out there sleeping with somebody!"

"I am so sorry."

"You sure have a fucked up way of proving it. You try to mess me up with anyone that I get with. You constantly call my friends bitches, you get mad and leave fucked up messages on my answering machine. Is that how you prove to someone that you love them?"

"Sometimes, I just don't know how to act."

"You damn right you don't."

Get the hell out of Dodge, Styles.

"I gotta go."

Serene got up and followed me to the door.

"Jordan, I'm sorry. Will you forgive me?"

"Not right now. Not right now," I said, shaking my head.

As I closed the door, Serene pushed the door back open and shouted, "I love you, Jordan."

I tried my best not to throw up.

Chapter 17

Traci and I had been out on a couple more dates and we got to know each other pretty well. I found out a lot about her and likewise. She understood about Serene and was willing to still see me; what a relief. The only problem I had with her was that she dated other guys, openly. Even though we never talked about our relationship, I just naturally assumed that we would try to date until we went either forwards or backwards.

Ever since the job came through, Traci and I hadn't really been able to hang out. I was doing a lot of crappy work at the new job. Basically I was the guy that gave the showers and fed the disabled people. When I started, I knew that it wasn't for me, but for some reason, I was starting to get attached to some of the people there.

The phone rang, jolting me out of my daydream.

"Hello."

"Hello, Jordan." The voice on the other line was Traci's. She could sure brighten up the day.

"What's up?"

"Nothing. I was just in the area and was wondering if I could stop by and see you."

"Of course you can." I looked around at all the junk. "My place is a mess, but you can still come. How far away are you?"

"About ten minutes. Are you sure it's okay?"

"No problem. I'll see you in ten minutes." I got up and put on a tee shirt and shorts. I threw the cordless on the bed and started trying to organize the confused mess. Traci had never been to my place, so I didn't want her to come and see a bunch of shit lying around.

Sure enough, ten minutes later, my doorbell rang. I buzzed her in. I threw some extra oil on my body to make it glisten and then opened the door.

"Hello," I said, giving her a peck on the lips.

"Hi." She walked in and I led her to the couch.

"This is quite the bachelor's pad, Mr. Styles," Traci said, surveying the place.

"Thank you," I replied, showing off the dimples. Chicks dig the dimples.

"What's been going on?" Traci asked, making herself comfortable on the couch. "I haven't had the chance to talk to you in awhile. Did I scare you off last time?"

"Nah. I don't scare that easily," I said as I plopped on the couch next to her. The reason I hadn't called her was because I was in the mood to get my freak on and if she wasn't going to give it to me, I figured I'd wine and dine her, but eat out at another diner.

"So, what was the hold up? I was thinking that I had some bad breath or something," she laughed, blowing her breath into her hands and smelling it.

"It wasn't the breath, it was the feet."

"Yeah, right. But you just seemed to fall off the face of the earth. Is your job holding you down like that? How's it going anyway?"

"It's fine. I'm just now getting used to the medication and

shit. You know at first, I didn't want to be there. Now it's kinda different. I'm getting attached to some of the clients."

"That's nice, Jordan. Besides your job, have you been on a bunch of hot dates? Are they keeping you busy, too?"

"A bunch of women?"

"No, I said hot dates, not a bunch of women. You could be going out with men." She was obviously amusing herself.

"Not really," I said, not wanting to lie.

"You mean to tell me that you haven't gone out with other women?"

"No. I don't *go out* with any of them." *Styles, get out of this conversation quick.* "Would you like…"

"Hold up," she interrupted. "We're not done talking about this. What exactly do you mean that you don't *go out* with them? What do you do then?"

"I got friends that call me."

She ain't buying it, Styles.

"Friends?"

"Yeah, friends."

"Friends, like Dallas and Tony, friends? Or friends like, you and I friends?"

"Friends, like being cool friends. What's wrong? A guy can't have friends?"

"You were the one that got upset when I had dinner with a friend."

"Hold up. I never said that there was anything wrong with having a friend. It was just embarrassing to see you with one while I was with my friends."

"What was so embarrassing?"

"You know."

"No, I don't know, Jordan."

"You know. The fellas thought that we were making that move."

"Hold up a second. What move?" She stood up with her hands on her hips and her neck on a swivel. *You can take the girl out of the ghetto but you can't take the ghetto out of the girl.*

"I told them that we were starting to really feel each other."

She started laughing. "You said *we*, or you said that *you* were starting to feel me?"

"I said that we were starting to feel each other."

"So, how do you know that you want to go any further? Where the hell is my ring?" She thrust her empty ring finger at me. "I'm just joking," she smiled.

"So, what you're saying is that you're not feeling me?"

"I never said that. You said that." She sat back down on the couch next to me. "How do you know that I'm not crazy? I could have a nervous tic or something. Aren't you afraid of running into a crazy one?"

That made shit hit home.

"You're right. Are you crazy?" I said, giving her the eye.

"Not really. I just don't like to take crap from anybody."

"See, maybe that's your problem. You don't trust anyone."

"Do I have a reason not to trust you? Have you been honest with me?"

"Yes." I had to think about that one for a second. "Hell, yeah! Why would I have to lie to you? We're not sleeping together."

"Oh, so, you're saying that if we were sleeping together, you would lie to me?"

"Boy, you are a piece of work," I replied. I slid to the edge of the couch. "Do you want something to eat or drink?"

"No, I'm okay. Sit back with me and get comfortable. I had

a long day."

"If you had a long day, I can help you out," I insisted.

"How can you help *me* out?" Traci said, arching her eyebrow.

"Calm down. I'm talking about giving you a massage. I work wonders with my hands."

I got up and walked behind the couch and stood over her. "Sit back, relax and let me bang out all that tension." I rubbed my hands together. *Don't rub her with these crusty hands.*

I forgot the lotion *and* the music. "Stay right here. I'll be right back."

I walked over to the stereo system and put on a smooth jazz CD by Stephon Harris and broke out the love lotion.

I dimmed the lights and strolled back to the couch. I looked at her from behind and was stunned by her attractiveness. The dim light bounced off her brown shoulders, somehow lighting the room. "Put your head down," I commanded, gently pressing her head down. I began rubbing her shoulders, but her blouse was getting in the way, so I slid the blouse down past her shoulder blade. *Damn, she has some smooth skin.*

She moaned with an approval that made us jump.

"Do you like poetry?" I whispered in her ear.

"Yeah, but I don't write. Why?" Her head swayed back and forth with each deep-pressured rub.

"'Cuz, I write a little bit."

"Yeah, right."

"I'll hit you off with a little."

"Okay, but whatever you do, don't stop rubbing," she moaned.

I started running my hands vertically along her spine until her body shuddered.

In a deep voice, I began:
 "Right now, your spine
 is all mine.

 this sweet chocolate skin
 makes me not want to finish but to begin
 to molest each one of your shoulder blades
 as the pain you had before you came, fades
 like pictures in a broken glass
 hell, I'll lick from your toes 'til you're ass-king me to
 continue this pleasureful ride
 do I have to stop here, can I go inside
 of you…"

BANG…BANG…BANG…BANG. BANG.
I froze like I got caught with my hands in the cookie jar.
Who the fuck is that, Styles? Keep calm. Don't get rattled, hopefully its Tony.
BANG…BANG…BANG…BANG. BANG.
"Are you going to get that Jordan?" Traci huffed as she started pulling her blouse up.
"Nah. It's probably Tony and I don't feel like being both-ered." I was sweating. My palms were filled with tiny drops of perspiration. I wiped my hands on a pillow and went to turn the music down.
BANG…BANG…BANG…BANG.BANG.
Someone yelled, "Jordan." *Panic, Styles.*
I put my finger to my mouth to quiet her.
Fuck that. This is your house. Get some balls. It wasn't as easy as that.
"Jordan, I know you're in there!"
What the hell is Serene doing over here? She's pulled this shit

before, but since I laid down the law, she hasn't been back, unannounced.

I gingerly walked Traci down the short hallway and into the kitchen, so we could talk. By the look on her face, I could tell that she wasn't pleased.

"Jordan, what's going on?"

I shook my head.

"I don't know, Traci. I don't know, but I'm about to find out," I yelled, leaving her in the kitchen while I left to handle Serene.

Traci yelled, "What the…"

I turned around and shot her an icy glare. "Shhhhhh. Keep it down, please."

Her cold stare hit me in the abdomen.

"Shhhh for what? Why is she buggin' like that?"

"I don't know." I didn't know what to tell Traci. I felt bad that she had to be in this position, especially after I was getting somewhere with her, mentally as well as physically.

"Well, something has to give. I am not going to be hiding out like some kid in high school. I'm not used to this," she murmured, folding her arms and pouting.

"You act like I wanted her to pop up. Do you think I said, 'Serene, come on over. Traci wants to meet you?' Hell, no." I tried to put my arms over her shoulder but she pulled away.

"Well, you better do something about this," she said walking back in the living room. "Or do you want me to go out and answer the door?

Ohhhh Hell, no! You must be out of your motherfu…

"No, that's alright. I can handle it," I said, walking toward the door.

I worked myself up and yelled, "Who is it?" There was no

answer. I felt a little better. "I said, who is it?"

Traci grabbed her jacket off of the couch. "Looks like she must have left," she said sarcastically.

I was relieved. "I was about to get in her ass."

Traci gave me the 'yeah, right' look.

"Well, Jordan, this is more excitement than I could ever ask for," she sneered as she threw her purse underneath her armpit. "I have to get going."

I walked her to the door, opened it and looked out. I was waiting for a pipe to go across someone's head. It didn't.

"Alright, Traci. I guess I'll give you a call."

"Make sure the coast is clear next time," she said with an attitude.

I gave her a kiss on the cheek and when she left, I counted my blessings. It was not time for them to meet.

Chapter 18

Renee called and said she and Andre had decided to go their separate ways, for a while. It was something that she didn't want to discuss at length. She also said she and Dallas had planned on hanging out sometime the following week because he was nice to be around.

I rolled over and looked at the clock and realized that it was already noon. I called Kendal and told him that I would be there in about forty minutes to pick him up. We were supposed to grab something to eat and then hit a movie. I hadn't seen him since he went on the trip with his church, so I know he would have a lot to tell me.

I beeped the horn and waited for him to come out. I saw Serene's car outside and hoped she would let him come out without being nosy. Kendal came flying out of the house. He had an Afro now. It seemed like every time I grew my hair out, so did he. When I got my hair cut short, he did too. He swears that it's all his idea.

Kendal got into the car and put his seat belt on. "What's up, Dad?"

"Nothing much."

He reached into his pocket. "Can I put this in?" he asked,

sliding the tape in.

"Yeah."

"Did you hear the new Wu-Tang album? It's bangin', ain't it?"

"I didn't hear that yet." I yelled over the loud music. "Turn that music down some."

"Alright," he replied with a sigh. "How come you don't mind loud music when you're playing all that old stuff?"

"Because that's the good stuff."

"What's so good about that old stuff? I bet none of them could sing better than Destiny's Child," he boasted. He started singing. "*I'm a survivor, I'm not gon' give up.*"

"That ain't music. You need to hear the old stuff like Marvin Gaye."

"What about Method Man? He'll be rapping for years and years. And what's so good about Marvin Gaye? How many platinum albums does he have?"

"I don't know, but it wasn't about that back then. It was about putting out good quality. How long do you think Method Scam will be rapping?"

"It's Method Man, and he'll be rapping forever."

"Nothing happens forever. Do you think that all that stuff that you listen to is original?"

"What do you mean?" he asked, trying not to let me see him look at a young lady that passed by.

"I mean, do you think that those guys make up all those beats? I'll answer that for you. No, they don't."

"Dad, not to get off of the subject, but I need some money for some new sneakers." He hated when I told him about our days.

"You just got new sneakers. Did you ask your mom yet?"

"Yes, and she told me to ask you."

"Ask me?" I said, pulling into Old Country Buffet. When you have a growing boy, the best place to eat is a place where he can eat all he wants without emptying your pockets.

"Yeah. She said that if you could wine and dine all those women, then you should be able to get me some new sneakers."

I abruptly stopped the car. "If I could do *what?*"

"Wine and dine women," he mumbled.

"What else did she say about me?"

"Aw, c'mon, Dad." He was obviously upset that he gave up too much information.

"I'm not going to say anything," I coaxed.

Kendal admitted, "She said that you can't get yourself together with all those women and…"

"I can't get myself together with all those *women?*"

Kendal shrugged. "I guess."

"Well, let me tell you about all of these *women*. I date just like your mother does. There's nothing wrong with dating women. It's a natural thing to do." I paused. "Do you like females?"

"No," he said quickly.

"I see the way you look at the young females. You ain't gotta lie to me. I know what it was like to be your age."

Kendal put his head down.

"Look Kendal, there's nothing wrong with me dating a female. Your mother and I aren't together, so I don't know why she continues to talk about me. At some point in time, she has to let go. Did she tell you why we aren't together anymore?"

He lowered his voice and looked at me sullenly. "Yes."

"What did she say?"

"She said that you didn't want to be there anymore."

"Do you think that that's true?"

"I don't know."

"I'll tell you the truth. We are not together because..." I paused, not knowing if I should go there. "I didn't think that we could work out our differences."

"I understand." He paused. "I guess."

"It's not something that you'll be able to get right away, but maybe one day we'll sit and talk about everything."

"That's cool. Not to change the subject again, but I'm starving."

With that, we went to eat and then we headed to the movies.

I was supposed to meet the fellas at this new club called Fender's at eleven-thirty. I asked them what kind of club this was and all Tony said was that Dallas had gone there a couple of times. So, when I put my clothes on, I decided I would wear some jeans and a tight-fitting black shirt. Hey, I wanted to fit in. It never failed. Whenever, I went to one of those white bars with Dallas, it was always the same, a bunch of white women and black guys who all looked alike. The men all had bald-heads, tight black shirts, blue jeans and one of those tight-ass gold chains on.

I got there and just as I expected, a plethora of brothers with that white aura. Right away, I knew I was in trouble.

I didn't see Tony or Dallas, so I stood in line. As soon as I got inside, an unattractive slender white chick walked up to me.

"Hi."

Boy, if I had a slab of ribs, I would have hit her across the damn head. "Hello," I responded dryly.

"Did you just get here?"

"No. I was just waiting for some friends of mine."

"Can you save me a dance?"

"I don't dance, Miss. I'm sorry. The lord blessed me with two left feet." *And I don't want you to step on either one.*

Why was I in this place? I must really like hanging out with these guys to be in this place. If I had a dollar for every tight shirt and gold chain I saw, I'd be able to quit that shitty job I was at.

After ten minutes in this joint I was ready to be out. I was tired of waiting, so I went to the coat check, got my jacket and stepped towards the door.

"What's up, Styles?"

I couldn't mistake that voice.

"Tone." I said turning around. "Where the hell have you been?"

"Me and D had to stop by Renee's house to bring her some ice cream."

I looked at him like he was crazy. "You went and gave her *what?*"

"Ice cream." He hesitated and began thrusting his pelvis. "No, better yet, we went over and laid pipe to her."

"If you ever think about…" I shook my head. "Wait a minute, she wouldn't give any to your tired ass no way."

"Don't be too sure," Tony replied, slapping me on the back. "I might be your brother-in-law one day."

"And I might be your stepfather," I replied, shoving his hand away.

"Whatever. D should be here in a minute."

Dallas came running out of nowhere. "What's up, Styles?"

He had a stupid grin on his face. He was like a kid in a candy store.

"Nothing D. What's up with you and Tone going over to

Renee's house?"

"Nothing." Dallas put his arm around my shoulder. "She paged me and asked me to bring her some butter pecan."

"Oh," I said, looking at him out of the corner of my eye.

"Styles, is this shit the bomb or what?"

"It's definitely 'or what.'"

"You gotta relax and let the vibe hit you. You ain't gotta walk around like Malcolm X all the time. Enjoy some good old-fashioned white women." Dallas invited me to survey the room with him. "Hell, if you play your cards right, you may not have to work."

"I would take a homely chick that looked like Celie before I dated a white woman. These chicks just don't appeal to me."

"You got to give it some time." Dallas wasn't even looking at me; he was scanning for potentials. As the flat butts walked by, he would smile and say 'hi.'

"Styles, I think that one is checking you out," he said, pointing to a white chick with some 44DD's.

"Yeah, right. You know how I feel about them." I turned around to see what she looked like though. I could look as long as I didn't touch. White women to me were like garnish. Sometimes they were attractive, but terrible to devour.

"She doesn't look good to you?"

I looked at her again. "Well, she does have the butter face."

Dallas wrinkled his eyebrows. "What's a butter face?"

"When everything looks good on her, *but her* face."

Dallas laughed halfheartedly. "You heard what they say about white women. Once you go pale, black women look stale."

"What I say is, once you go pale, if shit goes wrong, your black ass goes to jail."

Tony had made his way to the dance floor and was getting

his groove on with these Spanish mommies. I went over to help him out. When I got there he gave me the 'get the hell out of here' look.

"You alright, Tone?"

The Spanish females turned around and looked at me. The one with the bouffant looked at Tone with a confused look.

"What did he call you, Chad?"

Tony turned to her and shrugged his shoulders. "He's been calling me Tone for a while. He used to say that I looked like Tone Loc."

"Oh," she said, apparently satisfied with his answer.

I sometimes forgot that Tony didn't give out his real name when he went out, so half the time I didn't know what to call him.

"Styles, I guess you gotta go, huh?" When the ladies looked at me, he nodded his head for me to get out of there.

Just get going, Styles. His scary ass is always afraid you'll take the chicks from him.

After I left Tony, I walked past Dallas and he was working on this tiny red head. I found a corner where I could sit down and have a cold one. I settled in the back where there were televisions showing old Lakers' games.

"Give me a Molson," I barked at the waitress. She had a booty that would make a pancake proud to be a relative. *Ilk.*

She walked back with a Molson in hand. "Why is a fine man like you sitting in the back? Scared to mingle?" She laughed and walked away. I didn't want to be messed with tonight. All of a sudden, I wished Traci were here with me. I walked over to Tone and the Spanish chicks.

"Tone, I'm ready to leave."

"Where you going? We just got here."

"Out of here."

Tony whispered something to the females and turned his attention toward me. "You got to relax, Styles. You got to be versatile. Your aura should be able to switch like a faggot."

"Don't go there, bodybuilding man with the big pecs," I said, snapping my fingers, imitating some of the homosexuals I had seen chasing Tony.

"If you want to go, I'll see you later."

He gave me the pound. "I'll tell D that you gotta run. Ring me later."

I left Tone in a hurry. The chick I met on my way in was making her way over to me.

"Leaving so soon?" she shouted. I didn't bother to answer.

I got in the car and called Traci. Even though it was late, she had caller ID and I figured I would let it ring one time and register my number. If she saw the number and called me back, she obviously wanted to talk.

Sixty seconds later the phone rang.

"Hello, Traci. What are you doing?"

"Just laying in bed, relaxing."

"Relaxing?"

"Yes. I worked very hard this week and I need a break."

"You do? Is there anything I can do to aid and abet?"

"Yeah. You can come over here and do my dishes."

"Okay. I usually don't get a chance to-"

"I'm joking. But would you have really come over here and done my dishes? That is so sweet of you, Jordan. Are you trying to get brownie points?"

"No, I'm just keeping it real."

"Okay. You can come over for awhile."

"And Jordan?"

"Huh?"

"Hurry up. I gotta get up early."

Yes, Styles, work it out. Work it, J. Styles.

I arrived at her house and she was waiting by the door. She waved her hand. "Hurry up, Jordan. I have nosy neighbors."

I ran up the stairs and my foot got caught on the top step. The next thing you know, I was sprawled out on the porch.

"Are you okay, Jordan?" she whispered with a straight face.

"Yeah. I guess I'm okay," I laughed, dusting off my pants. "You gotta get them steps fixed because you know a brother without a good job will sue you in a minute."

"I hope you're okay," she said, biting back a smile.

What happened to 'do you want me to kiss your boo-boo?' I went into the house, found the couch and made myself comfortable.

"Traci, do you have-"

"Jordan, I know already. I have a Molson Ice just for you."

Damn, she knew what I wanted and provided it. I hope it works out like this with everything I want.

"Thanks."

She sat down next to me.

"So, Jordan, how's everything going?"

"Fine, I guess," I replied, taking baby sips from the beer.

"I have a personal question for you," she asked, looking at me inquisitively.

"Go ahead. Shoot."

"Are you sure about that?"

"No. I don't mind. There's no question I wouldn't answer."

"Are you sure about that?" she repeated.

"As sure as I am that most men have two testicles."

Traci turned up her nose. "You're so nasty."

"Nasty ain't always that bad is it?"

"Well, I want to know some personal things. Now, they may sound stupid, but they are things that I want to know."

"Go ahead. I told you I don't mind."

"Well, have you dated anyone in between the time of Serene and me?"

I put my beer down. "What?"

"You heard what I said."

"No. Not really."

"What is not really?"

She's digging, Styles. Watch what you say, this could be a setup. You know women are deadly.

"Well, like I was saying before I was so rudely interrupted," I laughed. "I was seeing someone, but it wasn't really anything."

"What do you mean it wasn't really anything? Either it was or it wasn't." She was working my answers like Judge Judy.

"I *kinda* dealt with someone a little while ago."

"Damn, you and Serene were only apart for about nine months and you're saying that you slept with someone since then?"

"Hold up. I never said I slept with anyone, you're assuming I did."

"Well, that's not important anyway, as long as you and Serene weren't still married, that's all that matters."

Whew! Thank God. She let you off the hook, Styles.

"You're right. Well, do you have any other questions to ask me?" I inquired, pointing at myself.

Traci scratched her head as if she was thinking. "As a matter of fact, I would like to know more about you and what makes you tick."

"What do you mean what makes me tick?"

"You know, what makes Jordan fall in love with a woman? What makes Jordan commit?"

"Wow!" I started laughing. "What makes me want to do what?"

"You know, commit. And why are you laughing?" she frowned.

"It's just funny, that's all."

Traci got serious. "What's so funny about commitment?"

"Nothing at all. You act like I'm scared of it."

"I never said that you were scared of commitment but now that you've had some time, what do you think?"

I was shifting on the couch because the conversation was getting deeper than I had anticipated.

"I think that commitment should be taken seriously. One should'nt make that move unless they're willing to be monogamous."

"Ohhhhh! You used the word monogamy," she chuckled, nearly falling over in her seat.

"I have no problems using that word. As a matter of fact, I was monogamous once."

Her eyes widened. "Once?"

"Yeah. Once."

"What happened the rest of the times?"

"Well, I haven't been in a relationship since then."

"You mean that you were faithful to Serene?"

"Yes."

"So, what about now? Would you ever be faithful to a woman again?"

Trick question, Styles. Don't fall for the bait.

I shrugged. "Probably."

"What does probably mean? It's either you would or you

wouldn't."

"I'm thirsty. Do you have another Molson?"

"Yes." She got up and went into the kitchen to get another beer. I looked around and wondered what it looked like upstairs. The whole house was well kept. Mom always said to check the kitchen and the bathroom.

"Here, Jordan," she said, handing me the bottle. "I hope you appreciate what I did for you because I never stock my refrigerator with anything that I don't use."

I got up and kissed her on the cheek. "You're right. That was very special and I do appreciate it. How can I repay you?" I replied, looking at those luscious lips.

She smiled, winking at me. "I'll keep it in mind that you owe me." She looked very sexy when she smiled.

I got up and looked around the room and down the hallway. "Can a brother have a tour of the mansion?"

"Sure you can." Traci grabbed my hand, leading me to the stairs. "Follow me. I'll show you the rooms upstairs."

I would follow her fine ass into a burning building with my nuts dipped in gasoline. We walked upstairs and she showed me her bathroom and two guest rooms. The guestrooms seemed untouched. The bathroom was well coordinated. She had matching everything.

We got to her bedroom. "This is probably the only time you'll ever get to see this room." From the back I could tell she was smiling.

She opened the door, stepped to the side and let me in.

"This is my bedroom. Do you like?"

"It's very nice," I said, nodding my head. "I must admit it's very nice." I walked in and looked around, taking in the uniqueness. She had a big brown sleigh bed. There was a matching dresser set with a huge vanity mirror. I noticed that she had Ansel Adam pictures on the wall. "So, you like nature, huh?" I commented, rubbing the wood, feeling the many ridges.

"Yes. I look at the pictures and I can smell the fresh air."

The hell with the fresh air. I look around here and all I can see is that big ass bed.

"Yeah, it's peaceful," I nodded.

"So, you're into nature too?"

"No," I laughed.

"Well, you've seen enough for one day. Let's go back downstairs."

As we got near the door, I stopped and grabbed her arm. "Traci?"

"Yes, Jordan?"

"Come here for a second." I pulled her close to me. "What's up? I come here to visit and what do I get? No hug, no high five, no peck on the lips?"

"Hold up. You're the one that ran up the stairs, fell, then ran to the couch embarrassed," she said, pulling away while laughing.

"Well, I'm here now. So can you show me some love?" I said, pulling her back toward me.

She reached up, grabbed my face and gave me one of the sweetest kisses that I had gotten in a long time.

"Now are you ready to follow a sister downstairs?"

With a smile as big as Texas, I grabbed her hand and in my best western imitation, I shouted, "Yes, ma'am."

We sat on the couch and decided to watch a movie. I took my sneakers off and lay sideways on the couch with Traci lying in front of me. I put my arm around her waist, and the last thing I remembered, was the beginning of the movie.

Chapter 19

My brother, Darnell, was coming in from out of town. He's ten years younger than I am and we never really got along. Between the selling of the drugs and the prison time, I couldn't keep up with him. The only time I hear from him is when he needs me to send him some sneakers. Who was he trying to impress in jail anyway? I hope it wasn't a man.

I was supposed to pick him up at B.W. I. It was one-thirty and his plane was already thirty minutes late. I grabbed a bag of chips and sat down in the lobby. There was a female reading a paper next to me. We made small talk and exchanged numbers. I probably wouldn't call her, it was just habit. I had a weakness for two things: Kendal and women. The only thing about that was, I had more control over Kendal. I don't think I'm the finest thing walking around but for some reason women just come. Maybe it had something to do with the ratio of women to men. The last time I heard, the ratio was nine women to every man and I was happy to be on the good end.

"Old man, I'm over here."

I turned around and looked.

"What's going on Method Man?" All of his teeth were covered in gold. He looked like he just ate someone's Movado watch.

"Nothing man. It's been a long time."

"Yeah," I said, giving him the pound and a half hug.

"Let's see. It had to be about four years, right? I think you and Serene were together for about ten years then. What is Kendal now? Fourteen or fifteen?"

"He's thirteen."

If your ass would stay out of jail long enough, you would know a little about the family.

"Walk with me to pick up my luggage." Darnell led the way to the luggage department. "How's Renee doing? Is she still with that asshole what's-his-name?"

"You mean Andre?"

"Yeah. Andrew, Andre, whatever. Is he treating her any better?"

"Well, actually, they just broke up for the umpteenth time. Hopefully, this time it will be for good. So, what's up with you? Where are you living?"

"I'm in between apartments right now. I had an argument with my girlfriend and I decided it was time for me to leave. I need to start all over and get away from all the drugs and that night life I'm accustomed to." Now that would've impressed the regular Joe, but I've heard this often.

"So, you think coming here will help you out?"

"Hey, you never know."

"Well, where did you plan on staying?" I was hoping he would stay with a friend because I had enough bullshit on my plate.

"Well, I didn't really know. I was going to wing it. If you said that Renee broke up with Andre, I could keep her company."

I didn't want to offer but I had to.

"Well, if Renee says that you can't stay with her, you can stay with me for a while. It might be a little cramped but what the hell, you're my brother regardless of all the bad shit you do."

He smiled. "Thanks, Styles. I knew I could always count on you." We grabbed his things and left the airport.

We decided to grab something to eat at McDonald's. He ordered two Big Macs, fries, a diet soda and then got a sundae to go.

After eating and listening to him talk about jail, we got up and left.

"Take me over to Renee's. Maybe she can still get me a job where she works."

Oh, shit. Here it goes.

"Her job is still hiring."

"How do you know? You act like you work there too."

While I manuevered out of the parking lot, I decided to tell him before someone else did. "I do."

"What happened to your job? Weren't you working at some computer firm?"

"Yeah, but there was a merger and the next thing you know it was the last one hired, first one fired."

"So, they gave you the ax?" Darnell asked, munching on an ice cream sundae.

"Yep. It was me," I said, watching him spill nuts all over the place. "And stop spilling those nuts in my car." He was beginning to work my nerves.

We made it to Renee's house. I beeped the horn to see if her nosy ass would look out the window. Just as I thought, I saw a huge head peer out of the living room window.

I peeked my hand out of the window and shouted, "There's someone here to see you."

She came outside and walked to the car, screaming, "Oh my goodness! Is that really you Darnell?"

He leaped out of the car.

"Hell, yeah! It is Darnell in the flesh. Now come over here so I can give Ms. Renee a hug."

Renee hugged him and took a step back.

"Let me take a look at you."

He brushed his pants with his hands. "I look good, don't I?" he asked, self assuredly.

"I must say, you do look good," she smiled admiringly.

Well, he should look good with all the time he had to lift weights.

"Why, thanks." He pulled her away from the car and whispered, "So, what's this I hear about you and Andre?"

She turned, looked at me and shook her head. "Oh, nothing. It's nothing that can't be dealt with."

Renee hated telling Darnell anything because she knew how he could get. He would beat the hell out of Andre. She turned back around as they headed up the stairs and shouted at me. "What are you, the valet parking? Get your tired ass in the house!"

I went in the house and they were sitting in the kitchen talking about everything. I didn't want to go in there and listen to old war stories about how they used to sell weed. I went to the couch and fell out. Fifteen minutes later Darnell hit me on my foot.

"Styles, get up!"

"What!" I screamed, wiping green eye boogers.

"Renee said I could stay because she told Andre not to come back."

"But what happens when he does come back?"

"She said that regardless of anything, she could use some family in the house."

I sat up, trying to focus on Darnell. "Are you going to stay here tonight?"

"I might as well."

I quickly woke up, gave him the pound and told him I would see him tomorrow.

Phew! That was definitely some good news. I don't think that would've been a healthy situation. On my way back home, I decided to stop at the Zanzibar for happy hour. A lot of the city workers went there to release tension from a hectic week. It was usually an older crowd. No bandanas, shorts, Timberlands or weed filling the air. It's nice to listen to Hip Hop every now and then, but damn, did it have to come with all of that?

I sat down, looked around and realized that I didn't know any one in the bar except for the waitresses. The one with the fat ass wouldn't give me any play for shit, but the skinny one with acne always gave me free drinks.

I ordered my usual and quickly surveyed the room and there was not a fine woman in the building. I was happy that no one was bothering me because it gave me some time to reflect on what was going on with my life. My mind began to drift to my work.

"Excuse me sir," someone politely said. I turned around and saw one of the finest chicks that I've seen in a minute. "Is this seat taken?"

Hell, no! Is your fine ass taken? "Actually, this seat is not taken," I said, trying to remain calm and cool.

"Thank you. I am so sorry to bother you."

"That's okay. My name is Jordan," I said, standing up and extending my hand.

"My name is Darlene," she said, accepting my hand. "My

friends were supposed to meet me, but I guess they haven't made it yet." She took seat and swiveled her chair so she was facing me. "You know, I've been here for an hour and I've had almost every drunk, married man over forty hit on me. I was just looking for someone that didn't look desperate," she smiled.

"Well it's nice to know that I'm a safe haven for distraught out of town women," I said, laughing at my own joke. Honey was definitely sexy. She was about six-foot and gorgeous. The red business suit that she sported accented her size and shape.

Darlene smiled. *Jackpot, Styles. Fifteen minutes of informal phrases and where are we gonna be... back at the crib.*

"Would you like a drink?" I asked.

"Yes, I would."

"Let me guess. A little lady like yourself would like a glass of red wine."

"Well, a big man like yourself is wrong," she laughed, hitting the table. "I would like a Hennessy and Coke."

"Damn!" I moved closer and pretended like I was looking down her shirt. "You must want to get rid of unwanted chest hairs."

"Now that you mentioned it," she said, reaching into her shirt and acting as if she was pulling out chest hairs, "I do want to get rid of some these."

Don't run. Remember the chick with the hairy nipples?

"Where are you from?" I asked.

She swerved her stool around, exposing smooth, creamy thighs. "Queens."

"Ah shit. I got me a city slicker. Isn't that a coincidence, two New Yorkers down in D.C.?" I was trying my best not to look at her legs, but I couldn't help myself.

"What part of New York are you from? The Bronx, right?"

she said assuredly.

"No."

"Manhattan?"

"No."

"Brooklyn?"

"Nope. I'm from Albany."

She started laughing hysterically. "I thought you said that we had *two* New Yorkers here. That ain't the city. You're from the country."

"Now you're trying to play a brother, right?"

"I'm just joking," she said, patting me on the knee. "What made you come down here?"

"A woman."

She moved her chair away from me and looked around. "Is it okay to sit with you? I don't want anyone coming and shooting up the place."

"No need for the concern. I got everything under control."

She looked me up and down. "I'm sure you do."

Our drinks arrived and she swallowed half her drink in one shot. I took human sips. "Damn! People in the city get their guzzle on, don't they? I guess it's true what they say about you guys."

"And what is that?" she questioned, finishing her drink off.

"That you guys like your men and liquor, hard and fast," I replied with a chuckle.

"Very funny, country boy."

"It ain't that country and quiet as kept, you'll be hearing a lot about the Albany area in a while."

"Why? Is somebody gonna go postal?"

"My cousin is writing a book that's going to be off the hook," I enthused.

"I hope it's not the *Best Man* all over again."

"Mark my word. It's going to be good."

She looked at me as if I was lying. "What's his name, just in case I'm at Border's?"

"Muddy Bosom."

Darlene started cracking up. She stood up and walked away, holding her stomach. "Hold up. You said that Albany will be put on the map because of a cat by the name of Muddy Nipple?"

"Very funny Darspleen."

"It's Darlene," she said, calming down. "Well, cousin of the famous Muddy Nipple, can a sister with normal nipples get a ride home? I took a cab here and you know sisters from the city aren't shy. We ask for what we want."

I took a long look at her and thought how lucky I was to run into her. As we got up to go outside, she stumbled over her chair, apparently tipsy from all the drinks. We made it outside and as we got to my car, someone shouted, "Hello, Jordan!"

I didn't have to turn around to know who it was. I opened the car door and covertly pushed Darlene inside like I was Secret Service. I turned around and saw Traci coming across the street with two other people.

"What's up, Traci?" I greeted her awkwardly with a hug. "How are you doing?"

"Fine," she responded, looking past me and into the car. "How is *your* evening going?" she asked sarcastically.

"Everything is okay." I was nervous as hell. I looked back toward the car, making sure Darlene stayed put.

She sucked her teeth. "Do you have to go, or do you have time to meet some of my friends?"

She saw everything, Styles. Take your lumps like a man. You weren't doing anything anyway.

"No, I can chat," I replied, massaging my face. "I was just giving a friend a ride home because she got a little drunk."

Traci rolled her eyes, apparently not buying the story I gave her. "Let me introduce you to some of my friends."

"Alright," I answered glumly.

"Sharlana and Yana, this is Jordan," she said, pointing to me. "Jordan, these are two of my good friends, Sharlana and Yana."

We exchanged handshakes. "It's nice to meet you," I said.

Yana, the taller of the two, replied, "It's nice to finally meet you. We've heard so much about you."

Sharlana, the prettier of the two, chimed in, "Yeah. We've heard some interesting things about you, Jordan."

"Well I've heard a little about the both of you," I lied. "Maybe one day we can all sit down and have dinner." *Just not tonight.*

Traci turned to her girls and said, "Get some seats and I should be right in. And order me a glass-"

Sharlana butted in, "Wine."

"Alright, I'll see you in a bit," Traci said.

"Nice to meet you," Sharlana and Yana said in unison.

Traci turned around and faced me. "Are you going to be at home this evening or are you going to be *tied up* tonight?" She didn't take her eye off of my car.

I started tapping my foot on the ground. "I should be at home in about a half an hour."

"Are you sure?"

"Yes."

"I'll call you later, okay?"

"That's fine," I said. Just as I reached her cheek, to give her a kiss, I heard someone yell, "Who is that bitch?"

Darlene had gotten out of the car and was staggering toward us. My palms were crying.

"Hold up, Traci!" I screamed as I left to grab Darlene. I had to get to her before she got near Traci. I ran to Darlene and screamed through my teeth, "What the hell are you doing?"

"Hi, Jordan," Darlene slurred, grabbing my arm.

"What's going on Jordan?" Traci yelled.

"Get back in the car!" I yelled, pushing Darlene back toward the car. I left her draped across the car and ran toward Traci to diffuse the situation.

"Are you sure you didn't have something else planned? Why is she bugging like that?" Traci snapped.

"I don't know." I turned around and saw Darlene trying to make her way back to me. "Let me handle this, Traci."

I quickly scooped up Darlene and hailed a cab. The cab driver asked me where she was going and I told him, "Anywhere, as long as it's away from here!"

As I walked back, I wondered what I would tell Traci. I knew that I had some explaining to do because Traci stood waiting for me with a look of disgust and her hands on her hips.

"Traci, let me apologize for my behavior. I know what it must look like."

"I want you to tell me what you *think* it looks like."

"It must've looked crazy. I just feel bad that your friends had to see that. The first time they meet me, I'm escorting a drunk woman to my car."

"I don't care about them seeing. They don't have to deal with that. I have to deal with a crazy woman jumping out of the car, calling me a bitch!"

"I said I was sorry. She asked me for a ride and I didn't see anything wrong with it."

"So what are you, a freedom rider?" Traci challenged.

"No. I'm just a nice guy, I guess."

"What if a homosexual came and requested a ride home? Would you give him a ride?"

"Hell, no!" I snapped back.

"If you have to pick and choose who you give rides to, maybe you shouldn't be giving rides."

"Is that so?" I said, getting quite agitated at the tone of her voice.

"Yeah, but maybe it was a blessing in disguise."

"What?"

"I was starting to develop feelings and I really don't know you well enough to be feeling this way."

"What do you mean, you really don't know me?" People were starting to stare at us. I reached for her hand. "Come over here, please."

She took a step closer to me. "I'm saying, Jordan, I don't know if you want a commitment. You haven't told me if you were looking for love or someone to sleep with."

It started to drizzle and neither one of us seemed to care.

"Why does a man have to be looking for anything? What happened to just meeting someone and letting the chips fall where they may?"

"That's bullshit," she yelled.

"Why? Do I have to be looking for anything?"

The rain began coming down and my shirt was starting to feel like paper. Traci moved closer to the building. She raised her hand and yelled, "It would be nice!"

I massaged my wet hair, trying to find words to express my feelings. "I don't think I mind commitment. It's not like I'm scared to commit, I just haven't found the right person. All the women that I've met lately have done nothing but give a brother grief."

"Just admit it, Jordan, you are afraid of commitment."

It seemed as the rain came down heavier, so did the conversation. It was pouring, but for some reason, I didn't back off.

Traci pulled on my shirt. "Jordan, please get out of the rain."

"Hell, no! Just ask me what you want to know. You say we don't know each other. Ask me a question that you should know the answer to and you don't."

"Okay. Where were you born?"

"Philadelphia. I'm not talking about questions like that either. Ask me something that, if you're my woman, you should know."

"Okay, Mr. Mouth. What is your favorite color?"

"My favorite color? Where did you get that question from?"

"Nowhere in particular. Say I want to buy you something, don't you think that color is important?"

"I guess so."

"So, what is it?"

I thought about it for a few seconds. "Honestly, I don't know."

Traci came into the rain and pointed her finger at me. "That's a damn shame. You can't even commit to a color, fearing there's another color out there that may be better!"

"You're crazy! Colors have nothing to do with relationships."

"Yes they do. When people talk about relationships, their true colors always come out. I'm glad I got a chance to see you tonight."

I went to kiss her goodbye, but she was already inside of the door. Before she closed the door, she shouted, "Goodbye, Jordan!"

Damn, Styles. You fucked that one up. Trying to get something for nothing sure backfired.

Chapter 20

I just received an invitation to go to Darnell's coming out party. The dumb ass got caught selling to an undercover cop and was just now getting out after doing two months. Renee was excited, but I knew that his ass would end up back in the joint.

Since our little argument at Zanzibar, I hadn't spoken much to Traci. We played phone tag because I guess neither one of us wanted to take the extra step and make a day happen. Deep down inside, she must've still thought I was a nice guy because she still called.

I dated about two or three chicks since our little tiff, but it never evolved into anything other than conversation or meaningless sex. I even went to the local poetry spot, Soul Kitchen, and read a poem called *Meaningless Sex.* I sat down the previous evening and put on Joshua Redman's new jazz CD and wrote:

Meaningless sex
I guess
Is not knowing who's coming next.
I think of sex as a meaningless fling,
  it's like a noun, all I need is a person, place, minus the thing.
It's not even unique
how we meet.

Meaningless conversation
is all I need for initiation.
This is a serious time, so no need to laugh
as I pull out my tool, my rod or call it my staff.
What used to be love
is now only termed sex while using a glove.
Do I want meaningless sex
or do I want what comes next?

Tony went with me when I did the poem. He went for the women, while I went to hear the words, as well as the women. When I came off the stage, he said that I was getting soft since I quit talking to Traci. I couldn't talk to Dallas because he was always at Renee's house, talking about her 'problems.'

I missed Traci. I hoped she had time to talk me today.

"Hello, Traci."

"Hi, Jordan. What do I owe you for making the call?"

"I-I-I was just calling to ask you if you wanted to come to a party that we're giving for my brother."

"Is it his birthday?"

"No, it's his coming out party."

"Is he gay?" she giggled.

"No. He was in-"

"I'm just joking," she butted in. "What day?"

"This Friday."

"Wow! You sure don't give a girl a chance to make plans, it's already Tuesday."

"I'm sorry, but you know I've been trying to reach you. You've been kind of busy lately. I made my request."

"What request?

"I left flowers and a note at your job asking you to meet me for dinner last Friday. The lady at the front desk said that she would make sure you got them."

"I never got them."

"You had to. I left them with Don King's sister; Donna," I laughed.

"Oh! That's the problem right there. The lady that sits in the front is Sharlana's mother and I think Sharlana told her what happened that night."

"So, I guess your friends don't particularly care for me, huh?"

"Well, to be honest, they didn't like what happened. They suggested I cut my losses while I was ahead."

"What did you tell them?"

"Honestly, I told them not to worry about it. I also told them that they didn't see everything I did."

"That's right, they don't know me," I boasted.

Traci hesitated. "I didn't say all that."

"I know, but-" My other line rang. "Hold up for a second, Traci."

"Why don't you call me when you get done."

"Okay."

"Bye, Jordan."

"Traci, hold up. Are you coming?"

"I'll think about it."

Something was better than nothing.

The next day I decided to kiss a little ass, so I went back to Tasha's Florist. This time, I picked up a dozen red roses. I didn't care if it sent a strong message. At this point, I was ready for something.

I went to Traci's job to leave her the flowers and the same lady was sitting in the front.

She smiled at me as if I didn't know what she did the previous time. "Would you like for me to deliver these to Miss Johnson?"

"No, thank you, Donna," I said with a smile of my own.

"What did you say?"

"I said, no thank you, Mom. Aren't you Sharlana's mom?"

"Yes I am," she said, sticking out her chest.

"Well, if you don't mind, I'll bring these upstairs myself."

"Okay," she said begrudgingly.

I walked upstairs hoping that Traci wasn't in her office. I slowly approached her office door and knocked. There was no answer but the door was slightly ajar. I tiptoed into her office and placed the roses on her desk. She had a fairly large office with a lovely view of downtown D.C. Next to her phone was a piece of paper with "Jordan" written all over it. She had lovely handwriting.

"Are you a peeping tom as well as a stalker?"

Her angelic voice startled me.

"I-I-I was just stopping by to bring these roses," I stammered, pointing to the flowers.

"Do you have a delivery job now?" she chuckled.

"Funny." I searched my pockets and fiddled nervously with my keys. "Well, I gotta go," I said, brushing by her as she stood in the doorway. "Bye."

I felt like a kid in elementary school.

As I drove home to make plans for the party, I received a message on my pager. When I got in the house, I checked my messages. "Thanks for the flowers; they were very nice. And to answer your question, yes I will go to the party with you. Just call me before Friday and let me know what time it is." *Jackpot,*

Styles. You are still the man.

Truth be told, I had a bunch of shit to do to get this party going. Who in the hell was going to cook all the food? It wasn't gonna be me. I hit the phone book to look for a caterer.

Three Star, on L Street, delivered soul food for ya mama. Their ad read, "We make potato salad that will make you slap your grandma." One down and liquor to go. We needed some beer, Hennessy, Vodka and Alize. My cousin Little Man always said that vodka always brings out the "nigga" in people. I saw a lot of spades games go wrong when the vodka came. All you would heard was, "pass the vodka" and "you reneged."

I still had to invite everybody. Renee wanted me to stick with about twenty heads. I'd speak with Tony and Dallas tonight and let them know what time the party was. I still had to call Serene and make sure she brought Kendal.

"Serene, what's up?"

"Who is this?" she asked, knowing good and damn well she knew my voice.

"This is Styles."

"Oh. Hi, Jordan. What do you want?"

"Darnell is coming home this Friday."

"And."

"And I want Kendal to come to the party."

"For a coming out party?" she snapped. "Jordan, please. You called me to bring *my* son to a grown man's, 'I'm getting out of jail' party."

"Look, I wouldn't be giving him a party either, but Renee wants to do it."

"When?"

"Friday."

"What time?"

"Seven-thirty."

"What if I had something to do?"

"I'll pick him up."

"It's not that easy."

I was ready to cut this call short. "Just bring him to see his uncle, alright?"

"Yeah, but-"

I slammed the phone down, not waiting for an answer. The phone rang ten seconds later and I didn't bother to answer it.

Chapter 21

I pulled up in front of Dallas' house, turned the car off and beeped the horn. Dallas lived in a pretty decent neighborhood in Silver Springs. I didn't like the hustle and bustle of the area. Too much shit going on. I loved Mitchellsville because it was near the stadium and I was too far out for people to just stop by and visit. I turned the car back on and put in the new Eric Benet single. He was on some Maxwell shit nowadays. I threw my head back and tried to figure out what I was going to do with this job. I was getting tired of doing mundane stuff. I wanted to be challenged. Hell, I didn't go to college for five years for nothing. I wish I would've known what I wanted to do when I was there. A degree in African American Studies, wow! I couldn't use that anywhere if I tried. Half the time when white people found out I was an Afro Studies major, they definitely didn't want to hire me. I waited for another five minutes and called his cell phone. There was no answer, so I left.

At the End Zone I took up my usual table and drink, but was surprised when the waitress came over with two bottles.

"Thanks, but what's with the two bottles?" I said, gladly accepting both.

"One's on me."

"Why thank you."

She smiled, wiping off a table next to mine.

"Hold up for a second," I yelled.

She turned back around to face me. "Huh?" .

"Why all of a sudden are you starting to be nice to a brother?" I checked her nametag. "Mia." She wasn't the friendly type.

She admitted, "This is the first time you've come in and not made a comment about my butt."

I slapped the back of my hand. "Shame on me. I don't really mean it. I just like to talk shit."

"I'm sure you do. Actually, I like to joke too," she laughed, covering her mouth. "The beer was not on me, it was a gift from Brenda."

I raised my eyebrow inquisitively, leaning to the left to get a better look at who this Brenda was.

She pointed over to a waitress that wasn't too attractive. "That's Brenda over there." Brenda just happened to be looking over and waved. *You sure couldn't bring her home to mom.*

"Well, tell her I said thank you," I murmured.

Mia smiled.

I shook my finger at her. "And nothing else."

"Actually, she wanted to know if you were married."

"Tell her that I just got a divorce about three weeks ago." *That's an invite.* "As a matter of fact, tell her that I'm not mentally prepared to date yet."

"I'm sorry to hear that," she frowned.

"Nah, don't be sorry. I haven't had a chance to celebrate yet."

"Was it that bad?"

"No."

Mia lowered her voice, leaned in close. "Was it your fault?" She was leaning over the table exposing cleavage.

"Why does it always have to be the man's fault?" I barked,

looking down her shirt. "Can't a woman do some bad shit some-times?"

She pulled her shirt up, backing away. "Whoa, Killer. I was just asking a question."

I put my hand on top of hers. "I'm sorry. It's just that it was a rough time in my life. And by the way, it was her fault."

"Alright, I understand. So, I should tell my friend that you aren't taken, right?"

"Hell, no! Tell her that I'm seeing someone."

She straightened up. "Well, are you or aren't you?"

"Well, not really. I just met somebody and we've been kinda hanging out for awhile."

Her jaw dropped. As she walked away, I yelled, "What's the problem?"

"Nothing."

"Then why the long face?"

"It's just that after all this flirting, I thought…" she paused. "You know, maybe you and I could hang out sometime."

Damn, Styles, you played yourself. Think, think… Traci. What the hell are you thinking about her for? You better stop bullshittin' and go for the kill. You've been after that fat ass for a minute. Do your thing Bro-heem!

"I'm sorry. I wish I would've known. I mean, it always happens like that. When it rains, it pours."

"Excuse me?"

"Nothing. I was just saying that hopefully, we can still hang out."

"I don't like to interfere with others," she said.

"It's not like that." I paused. "At least not yet."

"Well, I wish you all the luck." She walked away, not allow-ing me any comeback.

Damn, Styles. You waited for this chick for the longest, she finally pushes up and you front. Faggot.

I looked at my watch and was gonna give them a few more minutes when I looked up and saw Tony and Dallas making their way to the table.

They settled into their seats. Dallas had the same withdrawn look that he'd had for the past few weeks.

Dallas looked around, searching for a waitress. "What's going on, Styles?" He gave no eye contact.

"Nothing. What's up your ass, D?"

"I'm just having a bad day."

"I can understand that. What do you guys want, the usual? The first round is on me."

Tony piped up quickly. "Get me a Molson and a shot of Cuervo."

I looked at Dallas and he was in another world. "What do you want?"

He shook his head, snapping back into reality. "I'll take a triple shot of Hennessy. Straight."

I went to feel his head. "Are you sure you're okay? I've never seen a triple shot from you."

"Well, you know, sometimes shit happens!"

The waitress brought us our drinks and shook her ass at Tony and Dallas.

"Did you see your favorite ass, Styles?" Tony said, pointing to Mia.

"Yeah. I already spoke to her."

"What happened? Did you get the digits?"

"I didn't try. I'm really trying to get this job thing straight and I'm trying to make myself a one-woman man," I said with a straight face.

"Yeah, right. *You* a one-woman man?"

"You watch. I think I finally met someone I want to be with."

Tony moved closer. "You know what the problem is?"

"What?" I huffed.

"Traci is the first woman that won't give you any pussy and that makes you want her."

"Yeah, right."

"I'm serious. Women think just like men nowadays. They want to fuck just for the hell of it. Hell, I've met more than one chick that came up and said out of the blue that she just wanted to fuck me."

"Did she have any teeth?" I cracked.

"Nah, man, I'm serious. Women like to get theirs. Shit, they're just like us. They love the chase."

I downed a shot of Hennessey and wiped the corners of my mouth with my hand. "Who likes the chase?" I coughed.

"Come on, Styles. When we go out, would you rather go for the woman that's kicking it to all the men or do you go for the one that's in the corner minding her own business?"

I thought about it for a second. "I see what you're saying."

"I know what I'm talking about. Women have walked up to me in the club to get away from all the bullshit. They don't like the hound. Unlike us, *they* watch what *we're* doing. They probably know every woman in the bar that we tried to kick it to. Perception is a mutha."

"I know," I agreed.

"And if you really think about it, most of us like when a female doesn't give it to us right away. I know I do."

"You're trying to say if I slept with her, I really wouldn't want her as bad?"

"You mean to tell me that you never thought you wanted to be with someone and after you had sex with them, you thought that you were crazy to want them so bad."

"Yeah, once or twice," I agreed reflectively.

"See, it's the chase. Wait until you sleep with her and if you still feel the same way, then take it to the next level."

"That's why you don't have a woman now." I took a sip of beer. "Your theory is all fucked up."

"Whatever, but when you find out that the woman of your dreams has some stinkin' ass pussy or something, then don't come complaining to me."

"If it smells like hot garbage then I got to let her go." I gave him the pound. "I just couldn't tell a woman something like that."

"Why wouldn't you tell her?"

I looked at him in disbelief. "Now, c'mon, Tone. Have you ever told a woman that her pussy stinks?"

"No, but I would."

"How?"

"I would tell her that maybe she needs to get a checkup."

"Please. I can't go through that."

"What do you mean, you can't"

"Just what I said. My man told me his girl had an odor problem and it kept him from going down. He would only hit it in the shower."

"If it's that bad, then why put up with it?"

Dallas was quiet as hell. Even he would've jumped in this conversation.

Tony nudged Dallas. "Damn, D, what's up? Usually you're in our conversation trying to get some dirt to bring back to Becky."

"Her name is not Becky and if the news flash didn't hit you

by now, I'm not with her," he said downing another shot. He was starting to sweat.

"Get the fuck out of here!" I said in disbelief. "So, that's been your problem? Well, are you at least dating a sister now?" I joked, knowing he would never go there.

"Kinda."

My eyes widened. "What?"

Tony jumped in. "Did I just hear D say he was dating a sista?"

"Hell, yeah. Ain't that some shit?" I answered.

"Enough of this bullshit," Dallas said, cutting me short. "What's going on with the party on Friday?"

I had forgotten all about it. "I need you guys to help me bring the stuff over to the house."

"Whatever you need, just let me know," Tony said.

"I'll be around too," Dallas said.

"Thanks. I just gotta find a way to have Serene bring Kendal over without stopping in."

Tony finished his beer. "Just tell her to drop him off and get to steppin'. Man, you're hard with all the other chicks you deal with, but with her, you turn straight bitch!" Tony looked at me awaiting my response.

"Bitch?"

"Yeah, bitch!" Tony repeated. "She can do anything she wants and all you say is that you don't want to cause conflict with the divorce proceedings. Well, *hello*, you two *are* divorced and you don't have to kiss any ass, but you do."

"You need to watch your mouth. That ain't none of your business," I warned.

"You offer your opinion all the time to me, so why do I got to watch *my* mouth?" Tony eyed me, knowing I wouldn't take it there. First of all, we were cool and secondly, even if I did want to beat his ass, I would need the army *and* the navy.

"I'm out," I said, getting up to leave. *Styles, relax. Take this shit in stride. They should think you kiss her ass 'cuz you do!* The revelation came over me.

I sat back down. "You're right, Tone," I agreed. "When people get into your marriage, it hits home."

Tony gave me a slap on the back. "Styles, you got to realize that everyone is not out to get you. You're not the only one going through things. People go through shit every day. People get divorced every day and you have to understand that Serene is going to use Kendal against you every chance she gets. You got to get through the bullshit."

"You're right."

"You damn right, I'm right. How long have women been using kids as pawns?"

"For as long as I can remember," I admitted, reflecting on what I had seen as a child. My aunt used to make me and my cousin start shit with my uncle's new wife. "The sad thing is, the kids don't know where it's coming from."

"There's nothing you can do about it."

"I know, but what do I do when Serene tells Kendal all this shit about me?"

"He'll know the truth later in life."

I thought about it. "You're right." Tony was dumb in many areas, but when we spoke about the drama he was usually on time.

Dallas was soaking everything up. He was still uncharacteristically quiet. He would have at least said something about Tony getting on my case.

I grabbed his drink and he still didn't move. "D, what's the deal?" He didn't answer. I poked him in his side. "Cat got your tongue?"

"What?" Dallas said, shaking the cobwebs out of his head. He had his head in his hands trying to wipe the worry away.

"Where have you been the last fifteen minutes?" Tony said to Dallas. He didn't look right.

"I've been here," Dallas answered glumly.

"Well, you could've fooled us," Tony replied.

"Yeah, you had us wondering who was occupying that little ass body of yours," I jumped in.

"I've been going through a lot this past month."

I was getting annoyed by his silence. "Like what? Every time we try to talk to you, you act like it's some top of the line security shit. Well, you know what? Fuck it! I have enough problems at home. I just hope you ain't on crack or some shit."

Dallas scooted to the edge of his seat and stared at me. "On crack?"

"Yeah! On crack!" I stabbed him with a stare of my own.

"Who told you that?"

I looked at Tony and then at Dallas. "No one told me. You've been acting strange lately, that's all."

"People *do* go through things," he shot back.

Tony got up to use the bathroom. "Yo, Tone," I said. "I won't be here long so hurry up back." I turned to Dallas. I felt his hurt for the first time. He did look like he was aging faster than the average crackhead.

"I'm sorry, D. I have to be a little more sensitive to your problems. You always seemed to be the stable one. Me and Tone are just walking around looking for something that seems to evade us. Even though we make jokes, sometimes I wish I could have someone to actually love me and I mean it."

"You do have someone that loves you."

"Who?"

"Serene." He hesitated. "She loves you and you should think about getting some counseling."

I pulled to the edge of my seat, turning my head to the side. "Some what?"

"You heard me. You need some counseling. What's wrong with working things out? If she had caught you cheating, what would you want her to do?"

I didn't move. I had thought about it.

He pulled his seat near mine. "Just like I thought, you never even considered it."

"Actually, I have, but I can't see myself doing it. Every time I think about being with her I would think about that other woman. It just wouldn't work."

"Have you ever really given it your all?"

"No. She fucked up and I will never forgive or forget. I'm just gonna continue to do what I'm doing."

"Which is what? Playing all these women?"

"What do you mean, playing all these women?"

"You know, Styles. You act like it's a game with these women. How many can you sleep with without committing?" His voice had risen a few octaves.

"Keep it down, D. Damn, you make one good point and you think you're the Head Shrink!"

"Well, how many?" he continued.

"Dallas, it doesn't matter how many women I sleep with. I could stop at any time, if I found the right one to commit to. And what are you talking about playing games?"

"I'm talking about the games you play. After the games are played, why should any of them take you seriously? Women know when men aren't serious about them."

"I don't have any problems with these women. I know what I'm doing." I settled back into my seat. Who was Dallas to be asking me any questions about commitment? "Hey, listen, there are no games being played if I let them know exactly what's going on. They know the deal and if they want to deal with what I'm bringing to the table, more power to them."

"And that's why you're by yourself. You have the potential to be the best at anything you do but you're just...here. You don't have any motivation. You've been working at that job that you can't stand for a while. The Styles I knew would've been out of there and back at a job he felt comfortable with. You don't even like cleaning up your own shit, let alone somebody else's."

He's definitely right, Styles. What the hell is happening to you? To us?

I was surprised by Dallas' aggressiveness. He was never the one to bring out valid points. "You're right, Dallas. Shit has gotten real raggedy and I'm not feeling anything at this time. I am definitely glad we got to sit down and have this conversation. I needed it from a friend."

"Anytime."

"So, what's going on with you? You still haven't confessed your problems to the world. Spill the beans."

Dallas shook his head. "You wouldn't understand if I told you."

"Try me," I invited.

"Well, it's been a tough situation for awhile. I told you about my girl, right?"

"I know you are not crying after she got you put in the squad car because she said you hit her?"

He put his head down in embarrassment. "It's kinda hard to

explain."

"Well, whenever you need to talk, I'll be here for you." He looked at me like I was crazy. "Honestly, Dallas, I mean that."

"No matter what?"

"No matter what. Look, I gotta run. I just came to tell you guys to come to the party on Friday."

Tony came back just as I was leaving.

"Damn, I didn't even tell you guys what time the party is jumping off."

Dallas cut me off, "Seven-thirty."

Chapter 22

I told Traci that I would pick her up at seven o'clock. I still had to pick up Darnell at the jail. I knew he would be happy to finally come home. This was his tenth time in the joint. I don't see how he could sit in jail for months and months without freedom or women. Those cats in jail lived for the new guys. We all knew what went down, but we figured Darnell could handle himself. This time, I hoped he had enough sense to stay out.

I was supposed to arrive at the jail at noon, but the Beltway traffic was at a standstill. When I arrived, I waited for a few minutes and no one came out. I sat at the gate for a little while longer and decided to go the Security Office.

"Did Darnell Hankins get out today?"

"I guess so. There were about five people who were let out earlier and each one left. No other prisoners will be let out to-day, so if he was supposed to be getting out, he's gone."

"Alright." Where the hell could he have gone? I know he's pissed off, but he knows that I always run a little late.

I figured he could have only gone to one of two places; my house or Renee's. I drove back to my place and there was no sign of him. I called Renee's house and there was no answer. I de-cided to go over there to see if he was waiting on her porch.

As soon as I got to Renee's, a cab pulled up. I couldn't mistake that head for anyone else.

"Darnell, what's going on? Why'd you leave, you know I'm always a little late," I said, giving him a hug.

"After being in the joint for so long, when it's time to go, it's time to go," he smiled. Darnell looked just like his father, while Renee and I, looked like our father. I guess mom couldn't get anyone to come out looking like her. He definitely had mom's temperament. He didn't take any crap from anyone. If a fight was going down, I wanted to make sure he was on my side.

"I'm glad you're out. Maybe this time you'll stay out," I playfully scolded.

"I'll put some loot on that," he said, sticking his pinky out to make the bet.

We interlocked pinkies. "Bet!"

I noticed that Renee's car was in the driveway, but for some reason, she hadn't answered her phone.

Darnell grabbed the crotch of his pants and grimaced. "Styles, I gotta go use the bathroom before we get out of here. We need to hit up Chocolate City or something. I ain't seen no chicks in a minute and a brotha is thirsty."

"You look like you gotta get your shit on. I just called Renee and no one answered the phone," I said, trying to peek into the window.

"Well something gotta give 'cuz I have to take a mean shit."

I walked to the front door and knocked; nobody answered. I walked around to the back and yelled to Darnell. "No one is answering the back door either. You may be out of luck." I said, walking back to the front. By now, Darnell was holding his stomach like he was ready to explode all over the grass. It would've been good for the plants, but not for me.

"Styles, I'm getting ready to break into the joint. At least this time I won't get arrested," he said with a sly grin.

I chuckled. "Don't count on it because you know your luck."

"Which window does she usually leave open?"

"The kitchen, but it might be too small for you."

"The hell with that. When a brother got to take a shit, he'll travel through broken glass."

We went to the back and I pointed to the window. "It's right there."

Darnell walked to the window and lightly banged on the pane. The window opened. "It's open. And what are you talking about," he whispered, "I can fit right through here?"

"Good, but before you jump on the toilet, make sure you open the front door."

"I knew you wanted to smell it like old times," he joked, putting his head inside of the house.

"You're right. But instead of smelling it, I wanted to see Big Bubba's come drip out your ass."

"Kiss my ass!"

"Not until it's thoroughly sprayed with pesticide."

"Go to the front," he ordered, climbing inside. "I'll be there in a minute."

After Darnell shut the window, I walked to the front.

Five minutes had gone by and nothing. What was taking him so long? I sat down on the stoop, figuring that he couldn't wait to use the bathroom.

Bam!

I jumped up. *What the hell was that?*

Bam!

I heard another thump, followed by Renee's screaming, "Leave him alone! Leave him alone!"

My adrenaline started flowing. I started banging on the door, but no one came. A minute had gone by before Renee finally made it to the door.

She was sobbing hysterically. "Jordan, tell him to stop!"

In the backround, I heard Darnell scream, "I'm gonna kick his ass; fuck that!"

I grabbed Renee and shook her. "What the fuck is going on Renee?"

She started crying even harder. "D-D-Darnell is going crazy!"

"What do you mean, crazy?"

"Just like I said, crazy!"

I was getting agitated by her lack of answers. Something was going on and apparently I had to find out for myself. "Darnell?" I yelled toward the back.

All I heard was Darnell screaming, "Get the fuck up!"

I turned to Renee. "What happened?" She didn't respond. Her nerves were beyond shot. Then it dawned on me that it was Andre getting his ass whipped. Darnell hated the sight of him.

I grabbed Renee's shoulders. "Was Andre hitting you again?"

She jerked her body away from me. "Close the door, Jordan," she wailed. "We don't need the cops and everyone else in our business."

Oh shit! Darnell just got out of jail and the last thing he needed was for the cops to come and lock his black ass up again.

I ran toward the back and yelled for Darnell to come out. Usually when he was angry, I would stay out of his way because he was like a pit bull. Before I went to the back, I prepared myself for the worse.

"Darnell," I whispered, tiptoeing into the bedroom.

I walked into the room and I could barely see a thing because it was so dark. Renee didn't have a window in the back room. I saw Darnell's shadow crouched over Andre's body with his fist in the air yelling, "Get up, punk ass!"

Darnell was in rare form. He must've hit Andre and the faggot was scared to get up. Punk-ass. How can you put your hands on a chick, but won't fight another man?

I grabbed Darnell, whispering, "Let's get out of here. He ain't worth you going back to jail."

Something must've clicked inside Darnell's head because he snapped out of his daze. "You're right. It sure ain't worth going back to jail. I was just trying to save *you* the trouble."

"Trying to save *me* the trouble? You know that I don't even get involved in their shit."

"Apparently you should," he replied, pointing to the limp piece of man.

I wanted to make sure the bastard was still breathing, so I walked over and nudged him with my foot. With the aid of the light shining from the hallway, I could see the shadow of a lifeless piece of meat. He didn't have on any clothes and he was rolled up in a ball, apparently trying to soften the blows to his dome piece.

"Get up!" I yelled. "I don't have total control over Darnell and if I was you, I would bounce now!" I pushed Darnell out of the room.

Andre lifted his head and when I got closer, I damn near fell to the ground. I shook my head twice to make sure I was seeing what I was seeing. I bent down.

"Dallas?"

He tried to stand up, but fell back down. I was stunned. "Dallas, is that you?"

What the hell was going on? First of all, why was he in my sister's house butt naked? What the fuck was going on? I walked away and tried to answer the question myself, but couldn't. *Relax, Styles, think. Think. Think. Think.*

I walked into the hallway and the only thing that occupied my mind was Dallas being naked in Renee's house. It looked like Darnell had beaten the life out of him. When did all of this start? Was this why Dallas was acting so weird lately?

The yelling in the front room brought me back to reality. I ran into the kitchen and Darnell was on the stool, sitting with a blank stare as Renee stood, yelling. She continued screaming as he got up and went to the refrigerator.

"What the hell is wrong with you?"

Darnell didn't say a word. He got the pitcher of water out of the refrigerator and opened the cabinets to get a cup.

Renee screamed again, "What the hell is wrong with you? You just can't climb through someone's window and start beating people up!"

With a stoic look, Darnell poured himself a cup of water.

Renee went over and slapped the cup of water out of his hand. "And don't touch none of my shit," she yelled. Darnell stood there with a drenched shirt and his fist balled up tight. "And you better unball your fist too because the next person you punch, will be the last!" Renee was soaked with perspiration.

I jumped in. "Darnell, let's go."

He looked at me with an unfamiliar look that he gets when he reaches his breaking point. I had often seen that face when he was in trouble. He sorta blanks out. I remember when he was about eight and I had taken him to the park to play ball. While I played on one side, he was on the other side dribbling. I guess some older kid decided to try and take his ball, that's when Darnell went berserk. Next thing you know, I was looking down on the kid as he grabbed the side of his head. Darnell stood over him with two things: a blank stare and his basketball.

"Let's go."

He gave no resistance as I whisked him away. When we got outside, we sat in silence, watching the heat waves dancing up and down the streets. As kids in Georgia, we used to watch the waves move against all the different cars that rode by, making them look like wavy colors.

"My fault, Styles," Darnell apologized.

"What the hell were you thinking?"

Darnell walked down the stairs and put his foot on the first step and gazed at the waves. "I don't know. I guess I just snapped." He was close to tears. The only time I had seen him cry was when he first went to jail.

"What the hell happened?" I asked, not wanting to let up.

Darnell shrugged his shoulders, shaking his head. "I went through the window and as soon as I went in..." Darnell fell silent.

"As soon as you went in, what?"

He continued, "As soon as I got inside, I heard Renee yelling."

"Yelling?" I asked, putting my hands over my eyes, shielding the light.

"Yeah. She was yelling."

"Yelling what?"

"I don't know what kind of yelling. All I know was that she was yelling."

The sun was doing a number on my eyes. I got up and sat under the awning. "What happened after that?"

"I ran into the room and that's when I saw that Renee was bent over, screaming."

"Bent over?" I shook my head in disbelief. "Are you sure she was bent over?"

"Believe me, I know my positions, even in the dark."

"Damn!" Just the thought of Renee being naked made me sick to my stomach. There's just something nasty when you think about your sister or your mother getting busy.

Darnell continued, "She was screaming and I didn't know what the hell was going on, so I ran in and grabbed him. You would've done the same thing if you saw what I saw."

Apparently the sun was getting to Darnell too because he came and sat down next to me under the awning. "I just snapped. I didn't know what to think. I just went in and grabbed him. The fucked up thing was, when I snatched him up, he turned around and I saw that it was Dallas. That freaked me out more than anything."

"You damn near killed him. I mean you can't just start punching people. What would've happened if you killed him?"

"I don't know what would've happened. And how am I supposed to know that we have a kinky ass sister that's bangin' your boy?" His mood went from sorrowful to anger.

I didn't want to touch that statement. *Take his ass back to your crib, Styles.* "Let's get out of here before someone decides to call the cops."

"That's cool, but I want you to know that it's fucked up what your boy did!"

"I'm not worrying about that right now."

"Well you should be. If that was my boy, I would've definitely-"

"There you go again," I interrupted. I had to get him out of there before Dallas came out. Sometimes I didn't know where Darnell came from. He seemed to be the only wild one. Renee and I didn't fight that much. Darnell was the one that always ran with the wild group. Maybe he needed an activity to do when he was younger.

I stood up, reached in my pocket to get the car keys and realized that with all the commotion going on, I had left them inside the house. *So much for the smooth departure.* "Darnell, I'll be right back."

I really didn't want to go back in there, but at this point, I had no choice. I rang the doorbell and Renee yelled, "Come in."

I went into the house and Renee was sitting on the couch, crying.

"Renee, where are my keys?"

She pointed without glancing my way. "In the kitchen."

"Alright." I didn't know what to say. I just hoped Dallas would stay his black ass in the bedroom. I reached for my keys and noticed the lighter fluid. *Oh shit! What about the cookout?* The lighter fluid reminded me about the party. *Does he even deserve a fucking party? Fuck it! Let's try to get him off on the right foot.*

I walked over and sat down next to her. "Are you alright, Renee?"

"Yeah," she said, wiping her face with her hands.

"I'm sorry about all of this," I said, putting my arms around her.

"It's not your fault. You didn't have anything to do with *his* stupidity," she snarled, pointing to the front door.

"I know, but if I was thinking anyway, I wouldn't have brought him here with the party going on." I looked at her, awaiting a response on the party.

"I forgot all about the party. Well, I guess that's all fucked up."

I didn't know where to bring it after that statement. "What

do you think we should do?" I was hoping she would kind of forget about the bullshit, at least for the day. Call it selfish.

"Jordan, do you expect me to forget about what he just did? Do you expect me to act like nothing ever happened? I mean he did just walk into my house, wait," she paused. "he actually just *broke* into my house and caused chaos."

I stood up and walked over to the mirror that hung above the fireplace, trying to regain focus. *Be gentle. Naw, fuck that! This is bullshit!* I turned around and walked towards her. "Forget about the party, I wanna know what the hell is going on with you and Dallas. I mean, when did all of this start?"

"It isn't even like that," Renee scoffed.

"What do you mean, it isn't even like that? How is it?"

Renee patted an empty space on the couch. "Sit down for a second, please." I hesitantly sat down next to her and laid back, rubbing my fingers through my hair, trying to make sense of all this.

"Go ahead."

She took a long, deep breath. "Well, where do I start? It's all so weird." She nervously scooted to the edge of the couch. "As you know, Dallas and I have been hanging out for a while and I just feel like he's been a good friend."

"Friends don't spank each other with spatulas."

"Spatulas?"

"I was just trying to make light of the situation. I'm not going to go nuts like Darnell did."

"I hear you," she said, feeling relief. "Like I was saying, it's been kind of weird the way it all happened. We were just hanging out. He was having problems with his girlfriend, I was having trouble with Andre and we just started talking. Next thing you know, I was looking forward to our talks."

"So what you're saying is that it didn't start out with you liking him."

"Right."

"But did it ever occur to either of you that he is a friend of mine? A very good friend at that."

"Jordan, sometimes things happen."

"No, things like that don't just happen."

"I don't need this shit," she screamed, getting up to leave. "If you want to argue, you can argue by your damn self!"

"Okay, Renee," I pleaded, grabbing her hand and pulling her back down. "What do you want to do about Darnell? We need to look at the bigger picture."

Renee moved deeper into the couch, looking at me through tear stained eyes. "What is the bigger picture?"

"The bigger picture is that we need to help Darnell through this rough period in his life. He needs to come out knowing that he has a purpose in life."

"I really don't know what to do."

"Well let's do it Renee. Even if it's a small gathering, let's do it. I have a couple of surprises for him."

"A couple of surprises?"

"Yeah, so hold tight and let me handle things."

"I'm only going along with this because you came in begging," she smiled. Right then, I knew that I had my sister back on track.

I had a lot to do before the party. I had to get the food and invitations out. Being a brotha, I always waited until the last minute to do everything. Oh well!

Chapter 23

The party was starting in about an hour and I still had a lot to do. I had to call Traci and let her know when and where the party was. I hated doing things last minute, but I couldn't help myself.

Traci was on my mind a lot lately. I wanted to make that move for some reason. I didn't know if I wanted an exclusive relationship, but I know if I ever did, it would be with her. She had me buggin'.

Darnell was knocked out on the couch. I closed my bedroom door and stretched out on my bed to speak privately. "What's going on, Traci?"

She sounded like she was just waking up. "Nothing much, Jordan. I was just lying down on the couch reading. What's up?"

Damn it felt good to hear her voice. It was a while since we really hung out. I was definitely missing her. "Are you coming to the party?"

"You know I am. I haven't seen my baby in a long time."

"You're right," I said, smiling to myself.

"And after I see him, I'll stop by and see you," she laughed.

Maybe that's why I fell for her so hard. She had a sense of humor that always kept me on my toes.

"Okay, Traci. I'll pick you up at seven-thirty, and this time I'll try to be there a little earlier than usual. I'm bringing Darnell with me too."

"That sounds good. And Jordan…"

"What's up?"

"I really miss you." She hung up before I could respond.

I decided to call Serene and let her know the exact time to get Kendal there.

"Hello, who is this?" Kendal asked.

I don't know how many times I told him that it wasn't proper to answer the phone like he was on *Good Times*. "Didn't I tell you that you're not supposed to answer the phone like that?"

"Sorry. Sometimes it just comes out."

"Where's your mother?"

"She went to the store. Do you want me to tell her to call you when she gets in?"

"No. Just let her know that the party starts at seven-thirty."

"I'll let her know."

"I'll see you later, okay?"

"Okay."

"Love you."

"Okay, me too."

It was hard for him to express himself the older he got. I didn't take it in a bad way because I'm sure I went through that stage too.

I walked back into the living room and Darnell was still asleep on the couch. He was in a deep sleep too because he was slobbing all over the sheets I gave him.

"Darnell, wake up!" I shouted. There was no response. "Darnell, wake up," I shouted again, poking him with my finger. A bomb could go off and he would probably wake up and tell them to keep the noise down.

He turned his head toward me. "Can't a brotha get some sleep around here? I just left a place where we had to wake up when they wanted us to."

"Shut the hell up and get your ass out of the bed. As a matter of fact, get your ass off the couch." I snatched the covers off him.

"Asshole!"

We got dressed and left. He still had no idea what was going on, especially after the incident this afternoon.

"Where are we going?"

"I gotta pick up Traci; we 're gonna go over to her nieces' party for a second. You're welcome to come with us," I said. "Tone and some of the others are stopping by. They're bringing their nephews."

"Alright. I don't have anything to do anyway." I was happy that he didn't want to be dropped off anywhere. Everything was going as planned. Now, hopefully Renee had gotten over that bullshit that happened earlier and took care of business.

I almost forgot to call Tony. I grabbed the cell phone out of the glove compartment. "Tone, what's up?"

"Nothing much. What's going on?"

"Did you remember the party?"

"Yeah. You know I don't forget about no party. I know there's gonna be some chicks there, right?"

"I guess so. Renee is supposed to be inviting some of her girls and before you ask, no, I don't know what they look like."

"You know me like a book, huh?"

"Yeah. Unfortunately I do."

"Did you get in contact with D?"

I didn't want to bring it up with Darnell in the car. "Yeah, I did, and some crazy shit happened."

"What?"

"I can't get into right now, but when you get there, I'll let you know all about it."

"Alright. I'll see you at seven-thirty."

"Yo', Tone, do me a favor and get there a little early."

"I know you're not telling someone to be early. If that ain't the pot calling the kettle black."

"No, if that ain't midnight calling you black." I hung up before he could respond.

Darnell was slouched over in the passenger side, looking out the window. This was the most peaceful I had seen him in awhile. After he finished rapping along with a song on the radio, he looked at me and asked, "So, what about Traci?"

"What do you mean, what about Traci?"

"Have you two made that move yet?"

I arched my eyebrow inquisitively. "Huh?"

"I know you must want her because if not, you would've treated her like all the others."

"What are you talking about? I treat all the women the same. As for Traci and myself, we haven't really been together for a while. We kind of wanted to get our lives together before jumping into anything."

"What happened? She dumped you?" Darnell snickered, trying to read between the lines.

"No, she didn't dump me. I don't get dumped." My ego kicked in and took over my mouth. "Why would you think she dumped me anyway?"

"I was just saying that you wouldn't have wanted to do that on your own, so I figured it was her idea."

"Well, you're wrong. It was a decision made by the both of

us." He was definitely trying to work on my last nerve but I wasn't going to let his mouth affect me or my plans to straighten his ass up.

We neared Traci's house and I hoped she wouldn't slip up and mention anything about the party. I pulled up and she wasn't outside, so I guessed this would be a good time to get out and remind her not to say a thing. Just as I stepped out of the car, she opened the door and walked out of her house. She looked simply amazing. The baby blue blouse she wore really brought out her skin tone. She was so fine that I would take her on a platter right now.

"Hey, Baby. How are you doing?" Traci beamed, giving me a nice hug.

"I'm cool." I stepped back and gave her a once over. "You sure are looking good."

"Why, thank you, Jordan. You always know how to make a girl feel like a woman," she winked.

"Uh hum." Darnell cleared his throat. I guess he was feeling left out.

"How are you doing, Darnell?"

"I'm alright." He jumped in the back seat. He was an asshole sometimes but he still had some manners. I guess everything wasn't lost in the fire.

Traci looked back at Darnell. "You are looking like a hundred bucks, Darnell."

"Thank you," he replied, patting her on the shoulder. "You are looking rather good yourself. My brother sure is a lucky man."

"Do you know something that I don't know?"

They both laughed.

"Alright, it's gang up on Styles day, huh?"

Darnell reached over and put his hand on my shoulder. "If the shoe fits."

"Yeah, yeah, yeah," I said, pushing his hand away and pulling off.

Darnell settled back into his seat and Traci was in the front giving me the goo-goo eyes. I winked at her so she could get the message to play along.

"How is your niece doing? Does she know about the party?" She winked back. "No, she doesn't know anything yet. I'm sure she will enjoy herself though. Darnell, are you sure you don't mind coming by for a second?"

"No, I didn't have anything to do today anyway."

"Okay, I really do appreciate you stopping by."

I grabbed Traci's hand. "Did you pick up the gift from Renee's house?"

"No. Not yet anyway." She didn't seem to know where I was going with this.

"You must've forgotten that Renee brought a present for your niece. She used to baby-sit for her way back in the day and I told her that she was graduating so she decided to get her something."

It must have hit her because she got really enthused and shouted, "I almost forgot, Jordan. Where was my mind?"

Apparently, not where it should have been. We drove near Renee's house and I started getting a little nervous. *What are you getting nervous for, Styles? Its just people you've seen all your life.* I didn't know why I was getting nervous. Maybe it was because it was like a coming out party for myself as well. It was an important day because no one had seen me with anyone in particular before. If they had, it was always when I was going to dinner or something, but today was different. I would be amongst family and friends and Traci would be on my arm. Not like an arm piece but like my woman. Kendal would get to meet her for the first time. Renee already knew her, but everyone else will be formally introduced to her. Shit, it was scary.

We pulled into Renee's driveway and there were a lot of cars around. It looked like there was a concert going on. I gave Traci a look over and realized that she looked simply splendid. She had her hair pulled back, with some form fitting jeans on. Simple buy sexy. I loved the way she could fit in anywhere we went. I didn't have to sit under her when we went places because she could hold her own. I loved that about her. Serene would always want to follow me around. She had no sense of self.

"I'm going to run in and get the present." I opened the door and left them to talk. I walked a few steps, turned around and shouted, "As a matter of fact, why don't you guys come in because I know Renee would tell you guys to stop being rude."

Darnell gave me a crazy look. "You too, Darnell. She'll let bygones be bygones. Relax and take the stick out your ass."

Traci looked at me with bewilderment. I hadn't told her about what happened earlier that day. She wouldn't have wanted to be around drama. That's one thing I learned from her; she hated drama.

We walked up the stairs and I snapped my fingers like I had just remembered something. "Go inside. I gotta lock my doors. Somebody apparently tried to break into Renee's car the other day."

"Alright," they responded in unison.

I walked to the car as Darnell walked inside. I heard a loud, "Surprise!"

Darnell ran back outside, stunned. He sat by the door with his hands over his head. He kept shaking his head over and over again until Renee came and hugged him. I was overcome with emotion because of where they were, after all that happened earlier.

"Welcome home, Darnell. Welcome home," Renee said.

"I can't believe…" Darnell stopped his sentence short and began crying. Literally crying.

My mother came and gave him the biggest hug of all. She held him for what seemed like an hour. I sat on the car and enjoyed the moment. Traci walked over to me and put her arm around me and said, "That was a nice thing for you guys to do. Even though he's been in and out of jail, it's nice to know that you guys still care. That is special and it tells a lot about a family." She gave me a kiss on my cheek.

"So, what you're saying is that I'm a helluva guy, right?" I boasted.

"I guess I am. You seem to be able to impress me when I lose faith in men."

"Lose faith in men?"

"Yeah. Men do things to make you realize that sometimes they don't think."

"Oh, so now we don't think things through?"

"Don't take it personal."

"I'm not," I frowned.

"Am I the problem?"

"It's not just you, other guys do the same things too. It just seems like they are out to conquer and control."

"Is that why you wanted to take a break from me? You think that all I want to do is conquer as many women as I can? Well, I am here to tell you that I used to do that, but now that I'm older and wiser. I know that it isn't about getting into a woman's panties."

She leaned her head back and looked at me out of the corner

of her eye. "It's not, huh?"

"That's right," I said, grabbing her hand and leading her toward the house.

Traci stopped before we got to the steps. "So, you're saying that if we never have sex, you'd be able to refrain from sleeping with another woman?"

"I didn't say that," I said, amusing myself. "I ain't gonna lie, though. Sex is important to me. It's not the most important thing, but it's important. Without sex, you don't have that love part. You know, the intimacy that making love brings." *Work it, Styles. Work it.*

"So, you're saying that you can go without sex?"

I paused. "Yes."

"I have a question for you."

"Go ahead, shoot."

"Have you had sex with anyone since we've met?"

Traci stared at me, waiting for me to crack. *You really didn't have sex. The president said that oral sex is not considered sex.*

"No!"

"It sure took you a long time to answer," she smiled. "Were you nervous?"

"No. I was just digging deep, trying to remember if I slept walk and fell inside some helpless woman." She laughed. "What about you?"

She began, "I'm black and I grew up-"

"Cut the bullshit," I interrupted. "You know what I mean."

"No, I don't. I don't read between lines."

"Okay. Have you had sex since you met me? As a matter of fact, have you had sex since the first day I ran into you?"

She hesitated and her voice went soft. "Actually, I did."

"Y-y-you did?"

"Yes."

"What the hell! With who? Are you still-"

"Slow down, Jordan. We never had any commitment. What am I supposed to do, wait for a knight in shining armor to come and take me away? I believe in reality. Men have been doing it for years. When you guys want some, you simply go out and get some." She took a breath and looked at me. "Do you think I was wrong?"

"I'm saying."

"What are you saying?"

"Are you still seeing this guy, guys or whomever?"

"As a matter of fact, I'm not."

"So when was the last time you guys had sex?"

"It's been awhile now."

"What's awhile? A day, week, month, or a couple of hours?" I was getting worked up. My armpits were weeping and my shirt was soaking up all the tears. Why was I acting like this? *Get a grip. You've been doing it for years. So what if someone has finally done what you've done. Deal with it!*

"When I met you the first day, I had a date that night."

"What's going on with you guys now? Do you guys still sleep together?" I was boiling inside. She was driving me crazy.

"We were an item for quite sometime and I knew that it wasn't going anywhere so I decided to end it. I have needs just like you do, so why not?"

"So you guys were just fucking partners?"

"No!" she said adamantly. "We were not just *fucking* partners. We were in a relationship and things soured. Rather than go to another man for sex, I decided to call him when I need some."

"What happened to getting yourself a dildo?"

She let out a hearty laugh. "A dildo?"

"Yes!" I said seriously. "A dildo."

"Would you go out and buy a plastic doll or a plastic mouth?" I had no response. "No you wouldn't, so why would I?"

"Because."

"Because what?"

"I mean, I'm not used to women coming out in the open and saying they have people they can just call."

"To tell you the truth, Jordan, a lot of women have ED."

"What the hell is ED?"

"Emergency dick!"

I threw my hands in the air. "I've heard it all. What the hell are you talking about?"

"We have a person that we want to be with just for sexual reasons and there is no commitment. It has to be someone that we trust. Someone that comes when we break the glass. They will come without any questions. And do you know what the good thing about that is?"

"What?"

"They know their role."

"Are you and your *Emergency Dick* having sex nowadays?"

"No."

"Why not?"

"I just felt that it was doing me no good. Meaningless sex is not high on my list of priorities. What about you? What do you do when the feeling comes?"

I was embarrassed at the thought. "I handle my business," I mumbled.

"What does handling your business mean?"

I dropped my head, not wanting to answer the question.

She put her finger under my chin and lifted my head and in

a baby voice, she asked, "Does that mean that Mr. Jordan Styles masturbates?"

I yanked my head away. "What's wrong with that?" I snapped. "Everyone's done it once or twice. Haven't you done it?"

"Yeah. Do you feel like I'm a skank or something for having sex with someone that I'm not with?"

"No. Right now, I don't know what to think. It's been a lot to swallow." Renee looked outside and yelled for me to get my narrow ass in house. I took Traci by the hand and led her into the lion's den.

We walked in and people were everywhere. The first person to come up to me was Tony. I told Traci to give me a minute. Tony pulled me to the side. "Styles, what's going on? I went to Dallas' house to get him and he was all broke up." I motioned for him to follow me into the kitchen. "Yeah, Styles, he looked like he had just run through Arizona with a 'Kill Whitey' tee-shirt on."

We got into the kitchen and I sat on the counter, shaking my head. "Tone, you wouldn't believe it if I told you."

"What?"

"I had to piece together the story from what Darnell *and* Renee told me."

"Huh?" Tony was still puzzled.

"Darnell went into the house to use the bathroom and he heard Renee screaming. Next thing you know, he was in there whipping Dallas' ass."

"What?"

"Yeah. Splitting his skull."

"Dallas was with Renee?"

"He had Renee bent over while he whipped her."

"What the hell was she doing?"

"Your guess is as good as mine. I guess she's into that type of shit."

"Get-the-fuck-out-of-here!" he drawled.

"You're right. Our main man Dallas was banging my kinky ass sister. Do you believe that? How would he feel if I was banging his mom?"

"That's wrong, Styles, but then again, so is banging your sister and not telling you."

"That's right. So, I figured the little nigga got what he deserved."

"You think he deserved the beat down that he got?"

"Listen, Tone, shit happens. If he wasn't stepping somewhere where he shouldn't have been, his feet wouldn't be all messy."

"I see it from your point, but damn, did he try to fight back?"

"By the look of things, he didn't. He did beat up Darnell's fist with his face," I laughed.

"Did you speak to him since you left your sister's house? Did you even try to call him?"

"Nope," I admitted. "I just left it alone. I didn't know whether Renee was inviting him, so I didn't bother."

The doorbell rang and I heard Renee shout, "Hey, Kendal."

I ran toward the front to see him and as I got there, I heard the rest of Renee's sentence, "Hello, Serene. How are you doing? Come in."

That damn Renee! What the hell was she thinking? She should've remembered that Traci was here. *Relax, Styles. Just grin and bear it. Where's Traci at anyway?* I looked around and spotted Traci talking to Uncle James. He was looking her over like she was a fried pork chop, except he didn't eat pork. Right about now he would've thrown away his Koran if he owned one. It was like a family reunion all over again. Even though I only invited twenty people, more came. Everyone had to bring a friend.

I walked over to Kendal and gave him a big hug. "What's up?"

"Nothing." And with that, the relatives came and scooped him up.

"Hello, Jordan."

I turned around and there was Serene. I forced my lips into a smile. "Hello, Serene. How are you doing?"

"I'm doing fine, Jordan, thanks for asking. How are things with you today?" Serene was looking through me.

I knew she was up to something, but what, I didn't know. "I'm fine, but it's been kind of a long day so I'm ready to get out of here."

She nodded toward Uncle James and Traci. "Is that her?"

"What?" *You knew it was coming, Styles.*

"I said, is that her?"

"Who?"

"The one that's talking to Uncle James?" She nodded in their direction again.

"Yeah."

She had that smirk on her face. "So, you can't talk to me because she's here? She got you on lockdown like that?"

"It's not even like that, Serene. As a matter of fact, she's very understanding. Unlike-"

"Unlike who?"

"Nobody," I said, not wanting to argue right here.

She pointed to herself. "I wasn't understanding?"

"Well, to be honest, you weren't. You were just too..." *Why in the hell are you even going there with her, Styles? Cut your losses.* "I'm not even going to go there with you. What's done is done." I looked around to distract myself from her bullshit.

"Just like that. You can turn your back on me after all these years?"

"I'm not turning my back. I consider myself to be moving forward." I walked away, knowing that I was going to piss her off, but I wasn't in the mood to kiss any ass today.

I walked to where Traci and Uncle James were standing. "Can I steal her away for a second, Uncle James?"

"If you promise to bring her right back. If I'm not mistaken, I think Traci likes her some Uncle James. Hell, if I was thirty years younger-"

"Yeah, yeah, yeah," I interrupted. I winked at Traci and led her away.

Traci shook her head laughing. "Thanks, Jordan."

I pulled her close, whispering in her ear, "Let's get out of here. I've had enough of this party." Then I remembered that she still didn't meet everyone, so I walked her around to meet everyone.

I heard Kendal yelling outside. We went to the back yard. "Kendal!"

He was eating everything in sight. "Yeah, Dad?"

"I want you to meet my friend, Traci."

"Okay," he said, putting down his burger and fries.

"Traci, this is Kendal. Kendal, this is Traci."

Kendal extended his hand. "It's nice to meet you."

Ketchup was all over her sleeve now. "Pleased to finally meet you," she said, wiping her hand and sleeve off.

In the middle of Traci asking Kendal a question, Serene came outside. "What the hell is going on, Jordan?"

Aw shit! "Serene, relax," I yelled, walking toward her.

"Relax, hell! Why should I relax while you're out here trying to make a happy family?"

Traci looked with disgust as Serene continued her tirade. I jumped in front of Traci and Serene.

"Serene, you need to calm down. You're going to have everyone in here watching a scene. Is that what you want?"

"Who's causing drama? Just a minute ago you were in there asking me when you could stop by and visit!" she lied.

"What?" *What the hell was she talking about?*

I was fuming now. "What the hell are you talking about?"

Serene continued her lies. "Like I said, you were just asking me about coming over tonight!"

"You got to be out of your mind! If I wanted to…" I remembered that Traci and Kendal were still standing there. I wanted to end the conversation now. "You know what Serene, I gotta go. You can argue by your damn self." I told Kendal that I would speak to him later and I grabbed Traci's hand and left.

Chapter 24

The previous evening was still in fragments as I tried to get up and head for the bathroom. I couldn't decipher between my dream and the reality of last night. Tony called as I entered the bathroom to shave. He was talking his head off about what happened at the party. I really didn't want to relive the episode, so as he talked, I put the phone on speaker and began to shave. I was looking like shit. I needed to do something about everything. I sounded like Yogi Berra. I finally told him that I would just meet him at Ben's Chili Bowl, on 13th and U Street, in an hour. I looked out the window to see what I should wear. It was drizzling, so I threw on some jeans, sweatshirt and my Minnesota Vikings hat. People always asked me why I wore that hat when I lived in D.C. I always responded, "Because I hate the sorry ass Redskins."

I arrived at four o'clock as the sun was starting to peek around the dark gray clouds.

"Table for one?" the hostess asked.

"Two," I responded, holding up two fingers. I remembered Tony said that Dallas might be showing up. "Actually, three."

"Follow me." She led me to a table that was right in the middle of everything. It was good because I like to sit where I can the see entire place.

"Thank you."

When the waitress came to my table, I realized that she's the same waitress that waited on me the last two times I was here. I was beginning to see her everywhere. The last time I hit *DC Live* I saw her. We danced a few songs but when the Reggae came on, I broke out. She liked doing all that winding and if I wasn't getting none, Sambuca wouldn't have appreciated the teasing.

"Hi, Jordan."

"What's up…" I pounded the table, trying to remember her name. "Sophia."

"Very good." She sarcastically patted me on my back.

I got up and gave her a hug. "How can I forget the Dance Hall Queen?"

"So, what have you been up to?"

"Nothing much. Just a little beat from last night. I had a rough night."

She looked around to make sure it was alright and then took a seat next to me.

Surprised at her gesture, I scooted my seat back a little and smiled.

She smiled broadly. "I'm not going to rape you."

You can't rape the willing. "I really had a rough night last night, that's all."

"I understand. We all have nights like that. Would you like something to drink?"

"I'll take a Long Island Iced Tea."

"The regular bartender isn't here and Pat over there," she nodded toward the bar, "doesn't make the best drinks. They're kind of weak," she quietly advised.

"Well, give me a Molson. He can't fuck that up."

I really wasn't feeling too social today. Sophia was nice though. She didn't ever want anything from me, and likewise. It was hard to find a female to hang out with. I wasn't losing my sex drive or anything, but I wasn't in that hunting mode either. Traci was getting me to change some of my views. She seemed to make me care about life again.

Sophia came back with a beer and sat down.

"Thank you." I looked toward the bar and saw Little Ben checking her out. "You better get up and start working before Baby Ben tells you to take your black ass home," I joked.

"Ben can *kiss* my black ass if he thinks I'm gonna bust my ass and not take any breaks. And besides, who calls themselves Baby Ben? Is he giving us a little insight into his underwear?"

I was cracking up because she was right. I would never call myself baby anything. The name isn't very manly if you ask me.

She leaned over and rested her arm on mine. "Let me ask you a question."

"Alright."

"I need a man's point of view and you seem to be the only one in here with any sense," she said, looking at all the other patrons in playful disgust.

"Is that a compliment or did I win by default?"

"It doesn't matter how you won," she grinned. "Anyway, my girlfriend and I were having a discussion about why men would rather lie than tell the truth."

Run, Styles. I knew that no matter what answer I gave, I would be representing all men. What a load to carry. I sat there dumbfounded.

"I mean, when you meet a woman, why would you rather lie and try to get somewhere with her rather than telling the truth and letting her decide?"

In my best Jack Nicholson impersonation, I yelled, "Because you can't handle the truth!"

She damn near fell off her seat. "You are crazy."

"I know," I laughed, acknowledging the looks by the other patrons. "But seriously, not all men do that. Actually, I just started telling women exactly what I felt."

"What do you mean?"

"I just started telling them the truth. If you think about it, the hardest part for a man, after lying, is trying to tell the truth after he starts caring about a female. After that, he's scared of the repercussions."

"Damn right! You should be scared. As a matter of fact, why are you saying he? Don't you mean you?'

She's slick, Styles. Real slick. No, we should come out in the open right away. Let the woman make the decision whether or not she wants to deal with whatever the guy has going on in his life."

"We had another question, too." She looked over to make sure none of her customers were in need of anything. She continued, "Why do men cheat? I mean, if everything at home is going well, why do they go outside of the home?"

Damn, Styles, she's getting talk show on you.

"Wow, you sure got the important questions down, huh?"

"Something like that," she grinned. "I don't want to get too personal though."

"No, I'm fine," I replied, shifting in my seat. "I can handle myself."

She looked me up and down. "I bet you can."

"Huh?"

"I said, you're the man."

"Oh," I replied, knowing exactly what she said. "Well, men

cheat because they're human." Obviously, by her facial expression, that wasn't the answer she was looking for.

With a look of exasperation, Sophia pushed her seat away. "If you don't want to answer the question, you don't have to."

I had to think about it. *Do I give her the secrets that men have promised never to tell women, or do I keep it real?* "Well, to keep things real, I'll tell you. Men cheat because a lot of them love sex. It's not that we can't be faithful, a lot of times it's because we don't want to be."

"Really?"

"It's hard for a man to turn down sex. There's no other way to explain it. For example," I hesitated. "If a man is in the club and a fine woman walks over to him and starts talking, his ego kicks in. He has to respond. It's human nature."

"Human nature?"

"Yeah, human nature. And to make it worse, the numbers are in our favor."

"What numbers?" She seemed a bit puzzled.

"We are outnumbered almost anywhere we go. And the sad thing is, a lot of women nowadays just don't care. I've spoken to women about it and they've said that if they met two men, one single and the other married, that creates dilemmas."

"What kind of dilemmas?"

"Well, for example," I paused, taking a sip of beer. "If a woman has a choice between two men; a single man she didn't really want or a married man that she does want, it would make for a difficult choice."

"Why?"

"Because, she could be with the single one, that she doesn't really like, everyday, or the married one for two nights a week. Nine times out of ten, she's going for the married one. So that means that we have women out there willing to deal with that and we are going to act on it."

"Did *you* act on it?"

"When?"

"When you were married."

"No. I tried to stay faithful to my wife at the time."

"Tried?"

"Yes."

"You tried, sounds like it doesn't come as second nature to you. Was she faithful to you?"

"No, and that's the fucked up thing about it. The first woman that I respected and didn't cheat on, cheated on me. Karma's a bitch."

"You're right."

I looked at her and she wasn't all that pretty. But body wise, she was bangin'. The more I saw her, the sexier she became.

She looked toward the bar and saw Ben waving at her. "Well, Jordan, it was definitely nice talking to you and I hope we can get together one day when I'm not working."

"That doesn't seem to be a problem as long as your man doesn't mind."

She turned around. "Actually, I don't have a man." I smiled. She finished, "But, I'm sure my woman would let me go." My smile quickly faded. I didn't like lesbian jokes anymore.

"Alright, sweetheart, I'll be speaking to you."

"Bye," she said softly, escaping into the smoke filled lounge.

Now that I had Traci back in the picture, everyone and their momma was on my nuts. How come it is that whenever you're single, women stay away but when you're not, they come running? Chicks must smell desperation. Tony always said when you go to the club with a condom in your pocket, you always come home with a condom in your pocket. Anticipation is a bitch.

"What's up, Styles?" Tony said, sneaking up on me.

"What's up, Tone? You solo?"

"Nah, man," he murmured, nodding toward the door. "Dallas is parking the car."

I shook my head in disgust. "Damn, Tone! Who you supposed to be, Mandela?"

"You know I gotta keep the peace," he bragged, throwing up the peace sign.

"Truthfully, I ain't ready to see him right now," I said, getting out of my seat to leave.

Tony pushed me back down. "Just relax. I think he's coming now. I gotta run to the bathroom."

Punk ass!

Dallas looked like he was lucky to have made it through the night after the ass whipping he had received. One of his eyes was swollen shut.

"What's up, Styles?" Dallas greeted me a bit awkwardly.

Put your best hand and foot forward. I offered my hand. "What's up, Dallas?"

There was an uncomfortable silence that followed. Unintentional silences between friends are deadly. Luckily, Sophia came and broke through the thick air.

"Hello. May I get you something, sir?" She gave her full attention to Dallas.

"Yes. I would like a triple shot of Hennessy," Dallas blurted, wiping his forehead.

"On the rocks?"

Dallas looked in her eyes almost disdainfully, "No, thank you. I'll have it straight up with no chaser."

He sounded like he was in a Dirty Harry movie. This was a very awkward time for the both of us. It was very weird. Most of the time we talked at each other, we never really had anything to discuss of this magnitude. I didn't know where to start the conversation. *Fuck him, Styles. You weren't the one that fucked up! So start talking like a snitch, Dallas!*

"My fault, Styles."

"Huh?"

"I said, my fault."

His casualness pissed me off even more. "My fault, hell! How do you even think of some shit like that?" I pointed at him.

Dallas threw his hands in the air. "What are you talking about?"

I beat my fist on the table. "You know damn well what I'm talking about!"

"Haven't you ever fell for someone without knowing?"

"No!"

"Come on, Styles. You mean to tell me that you never liked someone because they were unique? You act like I wanted to sleep with Renee," he paused, "from the start."

"I didn't say you wanted to sleep with her from the beginning. As a matter of fact, that's not the point. The point of the matter is you crossed the line." *Swell his other eye.*

He hemmed and hawed. "What line, Styles? What line?"

Did he not get it? Did he not understand the code? "What if I was runnin' up in your mother, would you be happy with that?"

Disgust filled his face. "No, I wouldn't be happy with it. But I wouldn't be able to do anything about it. And if you were treating her right, then why should I worry?"

I fumed, "You are so full of shit, Dallas! If I was fuckin' your mom, you wouldn't be saying this shit!" I knew he was full of shit. He would not be sitting all calm, cool and collected if I was laying pipe to his old lady.

"Do you think I'm treating your sister wrong? Do you think that I'm trying to get over on her? Huh?" He was standing up, pointing to himself.

"You want the world to know?" I complained, looking at the people watching us.

"Alright, Styles." He sat back down. "I'm getting a little loud, but I'm just a little pissed at the whole situation. Look at my fucking eye," he screamed, pointing to his eye.

"You're pissed?" I yelled back at him. "If you're pissed then what do you think I am? Do you think I'm bubbling over with joy thinking about you and Renee doin' your thing?"

He dropped his head. I guess maybe he didn't understand. Maybe he was out of touch with the Negroes. *Fuck that! If you can't stand the heat then maybe you shouldn't be in the kitchen.*

I looked toward the door and couldn't believe what I was seeing. *Here comes the pain.* It was Darnell and some chick. I really didn't need this right now, but at the moment I didn't care if Darnell came over and bashed his head in again.

I got up and walked over to Darnell. "What's up, Darnell?"

"Nothing much." He looked over my shoulder and saw Dallas. "My fault, I didn't know you were chillin' with your brother-in-law," he giggled.

"Funny."

"Damn, Styles, you can't take a joke." I wasn't ready for this shit. Not today. *It seems like everyone is working your nerves today, Styles.*

"What's the deal, Darnell? Did you come over to work my last nerve too?"

"Nah. This is my friend, Pam." Darnell stepped aside and Pam shook my hand.

Damn, Pam was packing a trunk full of...Spam.

"Hello, Pam. How are you doing?"

"Fine, thank you. I've heard a lot about you."

Well, I haven't heard a damn thing about you! "Likewise," I lied. Damn, she had some soft hands. Where the hell did Darnell find this one? This was not his usual chickenhead. Maybe he was serious about leaving all the bullshit behind him.

Obviously, Darnell knew I was pissed because he grabbed Pam and left for their table. "Alright, Styles, I'll check you later."

I nodded.

We dapped and they left our section. I know Dallas was over at the table shittin' on himself. Oh, well, I wasn't gonna help him clean it. *Diaper spill on table 7.*

As I walked back to the table, Tony was returning. "How's everything going?" He was looking around like there was going to be blood all over the place.

"Okay. Nothing to brag about though." I had to be honest.

"What about you, Dallas?"

"Okay."

There was silence that would've killed the lambs. *Let's get the hell out of here, Styles. This shit is wack.* I got up. "Tone, Dallas, I'm out of here. I gotta go pick up Traci." I was lying. Hell, I hadn't even spoken to Traci. Since the party, I didn't know what to say to her. Serene sure enough fucked that all up.

"Styles, what the hell happened at the party last night?"

I turned back around, shaking my head halfheartedly. "It was crazy, Tone. Serene just went off."

"How?" I knew Tony was laughing inside because he always told me about messing with Serene. And like a dummy, I never listened.

"You were inside with everyone else and I had just got done talking to Serene. Next thing you know, she came running outside when she saw Traci talking to Kendal. Man, I felt like shit. All I could think of was how Traci must've felt."

"What did Traci do?"

"Thank God, she's calm." I had to take a breath to calm myself down. "I mean I don't know what I would've done in her position."

"You wouldn't have done shit," Tony laughed.

"You don't know what I could do when I am pushed. People get angry and get all kinds of strength. Look at how strong your retarded mom gets when you drink the last of the Kool-Aid. You know that's her strength juice." I turned around to leave again.

"Kiss my black ass," Tony shouted.

I came closer to the table. "What?"

"My ass. My buttocks. My orifice. My puffy pillows."

"Damn, anytime someone refers to their ass as a puffy pillow, it's an ass that doesn't need to go to jail," I cracked.

"Anyway, how does Traci feel about the situation?"

"I don't know. I can't really call it."

"What do you mean you can't call it?"

"I don't know what's going on. I should just say the hell with it."

"When you do, give her my number."

"You wouldn't know what to do with that."

"Try me. The blacker the berry, the sweeter the juice."

"If your juice gets any sweeter, you'll be a walking cavity."

"You know the deal," he responded, brushing aside my comment. "What about Serene?"

"Serene is crazy. What would you have done? Would you have confronted her or would you have just left?"

He thought about it for a while. "That's a good question. Now that I think about it, I wouldn't have even given her the chance to say any of that shit."

"What would you have done?" I asked while throwing fake punches in the air. "Punched her in her lip."

"You know I don't hit women. It's against my nature. I'm nonviolent."

"Nature my ass."

"It's a tough call. Sometimes women back us into a corner and make us defend ourselves. But do you know what the difference is?" Tony asked.

"What?"

"How you defend yourself. You can defend yourself the way you did, which is to get out of there. Or the other way, which is with your hands."

"I know what you mean. Sometimes I feel like just knocking her fucking head off, but I don't. I'm better off laying low."

"Yeah, before you got laid low."

I was getting tired of his snide comments. "Well, fellas, I gotta get going. I'll ring you guys later," I said, not waiting for an answer.

I got in the car and badly wanted to call Traci. But then again, I didn't want to pester her. She won again.

"Hello, Traci. How are you doing?"

"I'm fine." I listened to her voice, trying to read her mood, but couldn't.

"Well, I have something to apologize about."

Before I could go on, she jumped in. "Don't worry about it,

Jordan. Things like that happen and we have no control over what others do."

"Believe me, I know."

"I do have a question, though." I hated that statement. When women had questions, it was always something personal.

"When was the last time you two slept together?"

Coughs interrupted my breathing.

"W-w-what did you ask me?"

"I said, when was the-"

"I know what you asked me. What I meant to say was why would you ask me that?"

"Because women don't usually act like that for no reason."

You didn't really sleep with her, Styles. It's time to get technical.

"I haven't slept with her in awhile."

"What's a while, Jordan?"

"I don't know. A while."

"How come men never know when they last slept with someone but they know exactly how much money they paid for dinner on the first date?"

"What are you talking about?"

"I'm talking about a man's selective memory. Was it like a week, two weeks, a month, a couple of months?"

She was confusing the shit out of me. "Traci...Traci?" I shouted.

"Huh?"

"Traci, I can't hear you. My phone is dying. I'll call you when I get home, okay?" Click.

I didn't want to bullshit her. But I didn't want her thinking I was waffling either. Hell, when was it anyway? Three or four months since Serene got high off Sambuca.

I got home and decided to tell the truth…well, kinda.

"Hello, Traci."

"How is your phone?"

"Huh?"

"Your phone."

"Oh, it's okay, I didn't know what you were talking about."
C'mon Styles, keep up with the Jones'.

"You're acting strange. Did you take your medication to-day?" she joked.

I started laughing, happy because she was in a lighter mood.
"No, but I'll try to remember the next time."

"Anyway, I was asking you how long was it since you last slept with Serene?"

Damn, she didn't miss a beat, did she? "About a year."

"A whole *year* since you two last slept together?"

Yeah, you're right, Styles. It's been about a year since you two slept together. Technically, you can have sex without sleeping to-gether. You never did go to sleep. Farfetched, but what the hell. I wasn't lying. And anyway, what she didn't know wouldn't hurt her.

"Yeah, I guess it's been a while. And why do you ask?"

"Because," she paused. "when a woman is bugging out like that, it's because she and the guy have feelings and usually, they are still intimate with one another."

"Well, with *this* other, she isn't."

"I just had to ask because sometimes what you don't know might hurt you."

Damn, she had this woman's intuition thing down.

"Would you tell me if you met someone that you really en-joyed spending time with?" I asked, trying to pick her brain.

"Probably not," Traci responded.

"Why not?"

"Because you would blow it all out of proportion. You would probably make something out of nothing."

"Are you saying I don't think that men and women can be friends?"

"No, but do you think that men and women can be friends without it going anywhere?"

"Yeah. And speaking of friends, what about you coming to see me tomorrow?"

"Where did that come from, Jordan?"

"My heart." Damn, I had the right answers when I needed them.

"Do you miss me or something?"

"Something, like that. I've been thinking about you a lot lately."

"You have?" She sounded surprise. Hell, I was surprised.

"Yeah, so why don't you come over about eight o'clock tomorrow and I'll make you something to eat and then you can go home. Scouts honor."

"You weren't no damn scout," she mused.

"I know, but it sounded good."

Chapter 25

When I got up to work out this morning, I had a funny feeling. I didn't know why, but for some reason I knew that something was going to happen. I felt like Cleo. Hopefully it wouldn't be Serene and her crazy ass. Thank God she started dating. I never understood why women wouldn't leave you alone until they found a replacement. I guess it didn't matter what sex the replacement was either. I wouldn't be surprised if it was another woman. It wasn't my cup of tea, but whatever floated her boat.

I decided to go to the YMCA to get a workout. When I came out of the locker room, I headed straight for the exercise bikes. I had to warm up before hitting the weights.

I was riding for about ten minutes when a lady came and sat next to me.

"Mind if we race?"

I turned around. *Damn, she looks familiar.* "Sure, no problem," I smiled, accepting her invitation.

"So, have you been working out for a long time, Jordan?"

"Huh?" I gasped. I damn near shit on myself.

She gave me a huge smile. "Mr. Jordan, how are you doing?"

"Fine," I nervously responded, trying to figure out who she

was. I placed my full attention on the bike while I mentally ran her through my Rolodex.

"Cut the shit, Jordan. You don't even know who I am, do you?"

Think, Styles, think. Turn around and let me look at your... "No, I don't. I'm sorry; you'll have to forgive me. I don't usually have this bad of a memory."

"No, problem. I'll forgive you this time. But, I'm not going to tell you who I am right away. I'll let it bother you while I kick your ass in a little race," she smirked.

I gave her a devilish grin of my own as I set the timer for fifteen minutes. I thought hard as hell but I still couldn't figure her out.

After about five minutes of sweating profusely and sneaking peeks at her beautiful chocolate legs pumping away, I couldn't take it anymore. "Where did we meet?" I huffed.

She quickened her pace. "Are you sure you don't remember me?"

"No," I said in between deep breaths.

"Well, I'll quit being mean to you." She stopped her furious pace and turned around in her seat to face me. "Do you remember being on a cruise six months ago?"

I almost fell off the bike.

She was the barmaid. How could I forget her? Those drinks? Those lips? That... "Oh, shit! I do remember. I'm sorry it took me so long. I've got a lot of things on my mind." I felt better now. "So, how have you been doing?"

"Fine. You know, the same ol' shit, different day."

"Tell me about it," I said, turning off the machine. "Umm..."

"Shannelle. My name is Shannelle."

"I knew that."

"Just like you knew how much alcohol you could consume," she teased.

"Ha ha."

"I never did get a chance to see you before you left the boat."

"I know." It all started coming back to me. She was the barmaid on the boat about six months ago when I went on a cruise with my job. Or shall I say, the job I used to have. She was giving me date rape drinks. The Long Island Iced Teas tasted like she mixed a lot of alcohol with a sprinkle of soda. At that moment, I didn't care as long as the drinks kept coming. Later, she asked me to come to her cabin and I happily obliged. Next thing I knew, we were butt ass naked, tearing her cabin up. In the morning I awoke in my own cabin. I left when we docked.

"Hello?" she screamed, poking me in the arm.

"Yeah, I'm here," I replied, trying to regain my focus.

"So, what's going on with you now? Are you married or did you get that divorce?"

"No. I'm happily divorced."

"How does one become happily divorced?"

"It happens after one becomes unhappily married for too long," I laughed.

"I understand. But how does a fine brother like yourself stay single?" She looked at my legs as I started pounding away on the bike again.

"Who says I'm single?" I replied, visually caressing her smooth dark skin while taking sips from my water bottle.

"Oh, I'm sorry. I didn't see a ring on your finger, so I naturally assumed you were single. That was so inconsiderate of me. Are you single?"

I thought about it for a moment. *Actually, you aren't an item, Styles. What do they say about putting all your eggs in one basket?*

"Well, kinda," I said, sounding unsure of myself.

"What kind of answer is kinda?" she scowled. "Either you are or you aren't."

Boy, she was trying to back me into a corner. I really didn't want to answer her. "Well, I just met this female a couple of months ago and we've been hanging out a lot."

"Have you spoken about it?"

"Spoken about what?"

She gave me this look like I knew exactly what she was talking about. "You know."

"Not really. I want to take things slow. Just coming out of a relationship, I don't want to rush into anything."

"You're right. Take things slow." She seemed to have a million things running through her head. "So, what are you doing tonight?"

"Relaxing." My hormones were racing. *What about Traci?* I snapped my finger as if I just remembered something. "Oh, I'm sorry Shannelle, I almost forgot. I have to help my mother out today around eight." For some reason, I didn't want to close all the doors.

"That is so nice of you to take time out of your schedule to help your mom."

"It's not a big deal. I just do what anybody else would do for their mother." The brownie points were building up.

"Well?"

Go for it, Styles. You got her where you want her. Right about now I didn't know what I wanted. My brains and balls were set to square off in the tenth round and it seemed as though I wasn't invited to this fight either.

"Well…umm," *Has Traci done anything to you for you to go*

do your thing? Nope, I didn't think so. I looked at her and even though she was so damn fine, it seemed as though my brains had won this one. "I'm going to go home and prepare to cook."

Depression seemed to cover her face instantly. "That's okay, Jordan. I can take a no," she said softly.

"It's not like that. I would love to try and woo you again," I smiled, playfully patting her leg.

She sucked her teeth and poked me in the leg. "*You* are very mistaken."

"Why am *I* mistaken?"

"You couldn't woo me."

"I'm pretty sure I could."

She motioned for me to come closer. "Can I let you in on a little secret, Jordan?"

I turned around and kicked my leg up on the pedal. "Please do."

"Do you know what women do when they see men?"

"No."

"We know within minutes if we have any intentions of sleeping with you."

"Get the hell out of here," I laughed.

"Remember on the boat? Do you think you talked me into having sex with you?"

"I had a good part in it," I boasted.

"I don't mean to burst your bubble, but when I saw you, I knew I wanted you."

I grinned. "Yeah?"

"Yeah. The trick is, you don't talk your way into the booty. Most of the time, we wait long enough for you to talk your way out of it."

"That's some funny shit."

"It's true. I went over to a guy's house, knowing that I would give him what he wanted, but he opened his mouth and ten minutes later I left."

"Damn!"

"That's just the way it is sometimes. Next time a woman shows up at your house, don't lead her away by talking. Just shut the hell up and let nature take its course."

"Thank you for the advice."

"You're welcome."

"Maybe we can get together another time?"

"Okay. At least I know where to find you."

I got off the bike, gave her a hug and a kiss on the cheek.

I walked toward my car and saw Tony approaching the Y.

"What's up, Styles?" He looked at his watch, then at me with surprise. "What the hell are you doing here so early?"

I shrugged. "Just trying to get a little workout on. You know, beating the muscles a bit. What are you doing here so early? Don't you work out in the evening?"

"I'm supposed to meet these two females so I can help them with their workout." Tony raised his arm and made a muscle. "I can't help it that the women find me extremely attractive."

"My ass. If they think that you're attractive then maybe there's hope for the homeless."

Just as he was about to respond, Shannelle walked out.

"Damn, Styles! Baby girl is fine!"

"Yeah," I responded short, not wanting to let on that I knew her. He would ask me questions that I didn't want to answer right now.

His eyes followed Shannelle across the street. "You don't think *she's* fine?"

I turned around to see Shannelle walk away. "She's alright."

"You couldn't get that even if you tried," Tony challenged. "That's your problem. When you can't get a female, you say she's alright."

"You wouldn't believe me if I told you."

"Told me what?"

"Nothing." I didn't want to get into it right there. At least not while she was still near. Tony had a bad habit of staring and letting people know exactly what we were talking about.

"You know her?"

"Something like that," I mentioned, pulling my keys out of my pocket.

"What happened?"

I hesitated, waiting for her to get a little further so she wouldn't overhear me talking. "Remember that time I went on the cruise and told you I met a barmaid?"

"Yeah."

"Well, that's her."

"Stop playin'."

"Why do I gotta lie?"

"Seriously?"

"Yeah."

"Didn't you say you got drunk and tore that ass up?"

"Something like that."

"Well, did she speak? As a matter of fact, did she even remember you?" he quipped.

"Actually, I didn't remember who she was. I was trying to remember where I knew her from and then she kindly reminded me of where we met."

"And that was it?"

"What are you talking about, was that it?"

"You know. Did you try to get the number, the address, the bra size, anything?"

"No. She tried to get me to hang out tonight."

I was starting to get frustrated with his twenty questions.

"Did you set it up?"

I shook my head.

"Why not? Are you sick or something? She's fine as hell."

"To tell you the truth, I thought about Traci."

"Traci? What would make you think about her? Are you turning gay or something? Only a scary ass would worry about what their female friend thinks. I mean, you two ain't even together."

"Do we have to be? Look at us. We're both over thirty and have never really been in more than two committed relationships. I know it sounds stupid, but I'm tired of all the running around. Don't you get tired of it?" I paused. "Tired of all the lying, cheating and manipulating?"

He thought about it for a while and rubbed his chin. "Now that you put it that way, hell, no!" We both burst out laughing. "Styles, who gets tired of women? Who gets tired of countless women at your beck and call?" He went to feel my muscle. "Are you going soft on me?"

I snatched my arm away. "Nah. Not really. But this time, I want to do things right. Now, don't get me wrong, there are times when I want to go out and get my freak on, but something's holding me back and until I find out what it is, I'm gonna try and chill."

He shook his head as he looked toward the ground. "Damn, that's a bitter pill to swallow."

"I know but try swallowing it from my end."

He was stunned. Hell, I was stunned. "Well, I guess I can

respect that." He gave me the pound. "As a matter of fact, it could be good," he said, grinning from ear to ear.

"Good for what?"

"That means there'll be more for me."

I mockingly took off my hat. "I take my hat off to you. As a matter of fact, do you know the song the Temptations were singing about poppa being a rollin' stone?"

We both sang, *"Wherever he laid his hat was his home."*

"I will leave you my hat that I laid all over Maryland and DC."

"Those are some big shoes to fill."

I looked at my own feet. "You're right and if you didn't know, it ain't a myth. Look at these size fourteens." I pushed my foot towards him.

Tony looked down at my feet. "Whatever, small fry."

"Go ask your momma."

He walked in the building whispering to himself, "Styles done went and gave up the game."

I hollered, "And like the other Jordan, I can come out of retirement and reclaim my title anytime I want!"

I walked towards the car thinking about everything that we had talked about. It has been a long time since a female made me feel the need to be with one person. It was a scary and good feeling all at once. I just didn't want to fuck this one up but for some reason I always did something stupid.

I was near the house when my cell phone rang.

"What's up, Serene?"

"Hello, Jordan. I was just calling because I wanted to ask you to watch Kendal this weekend. I'm going out of the country."

She wanted me to ask questions but I didn't want to know. At this point I wouldn't have cared if she said she was getting married. "I had something to do but I'll cancel it."

"Really?" She sounded surprised but she shouldn't have. She knew that I did everything I could for my son.

"Yeah, I can swing it." Dead silence followed. "What's going on?" I knew she wasn't going to get off the phone until she said her piece.

"Nothing. I just wanted to let you know that I met someone, so we gotta stay away from all that stuff."

"Whatever, Serene. I don't know what you're talking about. We don't have anything going on. It's all in your head."

"You can say what you want, Jordan. I know that I'm not just your baby's momma."

I couldn't take the drama today. I wanted out of the conversation so I abruptly ended it.

I was concerned about what I was going to do about dinner. I was confused about what to cook. Did I want to break out my Italian cuisine, my French platters or my Ghetto Surprise? Italian won over because who wants to make love after a plate of soul food. If I made the ghetto surprise we both get the "itis" and find the nearest bed... for sleep.

I went into the house and checked my messages. Mr. Simmons had left a message telling me to call the office immediately. My heart stopped for a few seconds. Was this why I had that feeling today?

"Mr. Simmons, how are you doing today?"

"Fine, Jordan." He hesitated. "I know that I'm the last person you want to hear from today, but I had to give you a call."

"Okay."

"I have a friend that is looking for support staff in another company." He paused to clear his throat. "They're an upstart company that has a lot of room for advancement. Now I'm not saying that it's anything definite, but it's something to start with."

"Thank you. I really do appreciate it."

"I'll tell you the truth. I liked the way you handled yourself when the merger took place. You were very professional about the matter. There were other people that cursed and screamed at me like it was my fault. I was just the one delivering the news."

I was glad that I kept my cool.

He gave me the number and we briefly discussed the direction that the firm was taking.

I was so happy at the thought of being back in the field that I was speechless. "Thank you, Mr. Simmons."

It was about seven o'clock, so I decided to start on dinner. She would be here at exactly eight. I made dinner and awaited her arrival. For some reason I had a knot in my stomach.

At eight o'clock sharp, my doorbell rang. I opened the door and damn, she was looking tough. I wanted her so bad I could taste her. She wore jeans that fit nice and snug around her hips. I loved the way she looked. Her brown skin danced off of the lights and a light breeze spread her fragrance throughout the room.

"Jordan, the place looks nice," Traci said, looking around.

I smiled. I loved when she was pleased. "Thank you."

"You're welcome." She exhaled, taking in the atmosphere. There were a dozen long-stemmed red roses on the table.

"Wow, you definitely went all out," she smiled, pointing to the roses.

Even though I wanted her to go on forever, I had to stop her. "It wasn't too much to do for someone you really like." Without waiting for her comment, I grabbed her hand and led her to the table. I pulled her chair out for her before sitting across from her. She looked beautiful in the candlelight. "Everything looks gorgeous, Jordan. I just can't get over you."

"Are you ready to eat?"

"Yes I am, but first, can I please give you a kiss?"

I pointed to my cheek. "On the cheek, right?"

"No, on the lips."

"Yes, but Traci?"

"Huh?"

"No tongue."

She smiled. "Just meet me halfway so I can taste those nice full lips."

"How can I deny someone when they ask like that?" I reached across the table and gave her a kiss on the lips. Her lips tasted of sweet berries. I drew back and tasted my own lips and quickly went back to hers before she sat back down.

"Damn, you got some sweet lips, woman."

"Well, yours aren't too shabby either." We both laughed and sat down.

Traci gazed at the flowers while I stared at her beauty. She wore no make-up, except for the gloss that covered her lips. The natural beauty thing was working in her favorite.

"Waiter?" I shouted. There was no response. I shouted again, "Waiter?"

Traci turned her head and looked around. "Jordan, who are you talking to?"

"Relax. I got this under control."

"I hope there's nothing you forgot to tell me."

"Like what?"

"Like telling me that you talk to yourself," she said, looking at me curiously.

Just as she finished her sentence, Tony walked out of the kitchen, wearing an apron over a black suit.

"Hello, Tony," she said softly, slightly embarrassed. "I didn't know you were here. I thought Jordan was talking to himself."

"That's okay, Traci." He walked over to her and shook her hand. "You are looking extremely beautiful this evening."

"Why, thank you. You look nice tonight also. Are you going on a hot date or something?"

He looked at me, laughed and turned his attention back to her. "No, I was just in the neighborhood and thought I would start waiting tables." He gave her a little wink and disappeared into the kitchen.

"Jordan?"

"Huh?"

"What are you up to?"

"What do you mean, what am I up to?"

"Just what I said." She was starting to try and pick me for information. *Hold onto your guns, Styles.*

"Oh, waiter," I screamed, motioning towards the kitchen. In my best French imitation, I turned to Traci and said, "You know, good help is hard to find."

"I heard that!" Tony yelled. We all laughed.

I reached over and took Traci's hand. "You know, Traci…" I was at a loss for words.

Don't let the cat get your tongue, Styles. Speak your mind. "You know, Traci, I've been thinking about you and me."

Before I could finish, she started laughing.

"What's so funny, Traci?"

"You." She was obviously feeling me right now. "When you get nervous, you are so cute."

"Cute? Who wants to be cute?"

"Cute is good, Jordan. Who wants an ugly brother?"

"I hope not you," I smiled.

"Anyway, what were you saying before I so rudely interrupted you?"

"What?" The confidence I had, quickly faded.

"You heard what I asked, Jordan."

I knew good and damn well what she had just said, but my confidence was gone.

I fumbled with my napkin, trying to muster up the nerve. "Well, if you must know, I'll tell you." As soon as I was about to finish my statement, Tony came out of the kitchen with dinner in hand.

"Are you guys ready to eat a little dinner?"

I was starving. I didn't mind the interruption because it gave me a chance to avoid the question that I didn't want to answer. Traci turned to Tony. "Did you cook all this food by yourself, Tony?"

He looked at me and then back at her. "I can't lie. Jordan made all of it. I'm just here to serve it."

Traci looked at him appreciatively. "Well, I think it was very nice of you to come over and help your friend out."

"It's the least I could do for my man, Styles. And anyway, I am a romantic too." Tony sure was laying the shit on thick. I couldn't take it. He was no doubt making a bid for one of her friends. I knew him like the back of my hand.

"Jordan, wasn't that a nice thing for Tony to do?"

I put my head inside of my hands, trying to block out all the adulation. "Yeah, that was a nice thing for him to do. I owe him one."

He was enjoying all the praise.

Tony smirked my way. "And you'd better believe that I will

be collecting on it."

"Kiss my ass and get steppin'."

"Jordan," Traci chastised, playfully slapping my hand. "Is that a nice thing to say to your friend who just served us dinner?"

"Yeah, Jordan, is that a nice thing to say about me? I canceled a date to help you seduce your woman," he lied.

"He knows I'm just joking with him." Tony had to get the hell out of here before I threw up from all the compliments he was receiving.

"Alright guys. I'll speak to you later." Tony took off the apron and threw it on the chair and headed for the door. "And Traci?"

"Yes?"

"If you have any friends let them know that an eligible bachelor is available."

"Only if you let your friends know that I'm an eligible female."

They both laughed. As soon as he left, she picked up right where she left off. "So, Jordan, what was it that you wanted to talk about?" Traci started nervously picking at her spaghetti.

I was nervous and the sad thing was that I didn't know why. *Don't get scared now, Styles.* "Well, Traci, I was wondering if you've thought about us?"

She had a puzzled look on her face. "What about us?" She took another bite and laid her fork down.

"You know what I'm talking about."

"Actually, Jordan, I don't know what you're talking about. So, if you can, please, explain it to my agent. As a matter of fact, have your secretary call mine," she joked.

The comedy was flying everywhere. *Relax, Styles.*

"Well, I was wondering about us." Before she interrupted, I

continued. "I wanted to see if you wanted to take it to the next level."

Silence followed the words that dripped out of my mouth slowly, like lava from a volcano. I wish I could have taken them back, but it was too late. I felt like a little boy asking for something I knew I wasn't going to get. I waited for words to form out of those beautiful lips that I had kissed only minutes ago.

She picked her fork up and fiddled with it before placing it back down. "Wow, Jordan. I don't know what to say."

Say something. Anything. I picked my pride off the floor. "You don't have to say anything." My mood was changing for the worse.

"I don't know what to say. I just never expected this right now."

You didn't expect this right now? See, it never fails. The minute you start developing feelings for someone and you want to do the right thing, look at what happens. I had to think. I was confused. "Forget I said anything."

"What do you mean, forget you just said that?"

We both shifted in our chairs, obviously uneasy about the direction the conversation had taken.

I got up to turn on some music to break the silence. The music moved our attentions to other things. We talked about our favorite singers and jazz artists. As I spoke about Miles Davis and John Coltrane, my mind was saturated with Traci. I wanted to tell her, "Fuck this music shit. Let's be together for the evening and talk about sunsets and moonlights. Kiss me. Taste me. Learn about what I want in life. Tell me about what you've always wanted to do. Tell me one thing that you've never told another and I'll spill to you my secret fantasy of moving to Paris and running around the Eiffel Tower until I was dizzy."

All that came out was, "Would you like to sit and watch a little TV."

"Okay."

We sat and watched *Who Wants to be a Millionaire*. To her surprise, I wasn't as alienated from the world as she might have thought. I didn't know whether to put my arms around her or to just sit like we were bosom buddies. This chick definitely had my head going in a direction that I wasn't accustomed to. I needed a fucking compass!

After the show went off, I went to ask for a kiss, but all I had the nerve to ask was, "Do you want dessert?"

"No, thanks, Jordan. I'm rather stuffed and it's getting kinda late."

I looked at my watch and it was not *rather fucking* late! But fuck it; I could play the game too. If she wants to play, then from here on out, we will play. Now the question is, once I'm done, will she still be around? An ego is a terrible thing to have but I was stuck with it. I figured that I've done everything right and what do I get? Nothing.

"You're right, Traci. It is getting kinda late and I was supposed to meet someone for business," I lied.

She looked at me and then at her watch. "You do business at this time of night?"

Stand your ground, Styles. If she shows a little concern then maybe this is all a front. "Well, you know, I'm trying to get into this prepaid legal service and some guy named Nathan is supposed to meet me."

"You've got some odd business hours." She was looking for something. For what, I didn't know.

"He's busy and I'm busy, so we have to take the time that we have."

"Well, okay. I guess I'll give you a call when I get a chance."
She looked a little dejected at this point. *No more dejected than
you were looking a little while ago, Styles. My, how shit changes.
It's all about changing the tides.*

I walked Traci to her car and left for Republic Gardens. I had
to party. Something had to help me take my mind off of Traci.
The line was long and it was chilly out. I waited for about fifteen minutes before I got tired of waiting. I walked down the
block and ended up in Ben's Chili Bowl. The smell of food
tempted my stomach because we didn't really eat anything. Traci
even had my appetite confused. I was frustrated and the only
thing that would make it go away was playing ball or a good nut.
At this time, if there was a basketball court and a roomful of
naked women, I wouldn't have any shots attempts.

"May I help you?"

Someone must've been reading my mind because I turned
around and saw Sophia looking finer than ever. "What's up,
Sophia?" I replied glumly.

She took a step back. "Damn, it must not be my lucky day
because I haven't seen a frown like that all evening."

*Damn right! And if you play your cards right, you might be
able to touch my deck...of cards.*

"I just had a rough day and I need to take the edge off. What
about you?"

"Nothing changes in here but the beans," she laughed. She
was wearing black stretch pants and a tight red blouse. She looked
better and better every time I saw her. Maybe she was starting to
grow on me. Women had a habit of doing that to me. Tone and
I had a conversation about that one time. They look okay and
then the more you talk to them, the better they look. But on
the other hand, I dated this chick one time that was fine as hell

but after seeing her funky ass attitude, she went downhill. Sophia was different. She didn't seem like she belonged in a restaurant serving food and drinks to drunk-ass married men. Her face showed the wear and tear of everyday life. She seemed like she was living a life that wasn't conducive to her skin, but her body was incredible. Cam'ron said it best, "Why do chicks with fat asses always have to wear A-cups?" Lucky for me I was an ass man. There was nothing like cuddling up next to a nice ass. The hell with a pillow.

"I'll have a triple shot of Henny."

She looked at me wide-eyed," Damn, is it that bad?"

"You could say that," I answered, not wanting to go any further than I had to.

"Well, we should both be drowning our sorrows then."

"Why? Are you having a bad day too?"

She looked at me with eyes that told it all. "Yeah, it's been a rough couple of months for me, but nothing I can't handle."

For some reason I wanted to comfort her. I didn't know why. Maybe I wanted someone to comfort me. I was confused and it was not a good time for me to be out and about. My female friends never believed me when I told them about letting their man go out angry. They couldn't understand that a golden rule was to never let your man go out to the bar pissed off. Never, and I repeat, never, let your man go out with a loaded weapon. I remember I was planning on seeing another chick and my girlfriend at the time fucked all that up. Before I walked out the door, she went down on me until I came. I lost all the drive I had. Fucked up my whole evening. As a matter of fact, I never did make it out that night.

"What time are you off tonight, Sophia?"

"Well, Ben is letting me go early. He said they don't really need me all night."

I pulled my chair close to her while she leaned against the wall. "Can you hang out with me for awhile? I'll be on my best behavior." I winked at her.

"Maybe I won't go then. What if I want to see you being a bad boy?"

"You mean you would want to see me robbing a bank or something?"

"Now, you know that isn't what I meant," she whispered, getting a little closer.

The ball is in your court, Styles. "What do you say about us getting the hell out of here?" Hopefully if my calculations were correct, she would get the hell up and offer to go to her house.

She straightened up. "That sounds good to me." I counted my blessings. Sometimes it's not good to ask any questions. This was definitely one of those go-with-the-flow nights.

"Where do you want to go?"

She went into deep thought. I hope she wasn't crazy or anything. Right about now, though, I was willing to take a chance. "How about us going to your place, Jordan?"

"That sounds…" It hit me as I spoke. What about all that dinner shit on the table? Definitely don't shit where you eat.

"Actually, that does sound appetizing but my brother is here from out of town and I don't want him all in my business." It sounded like bullshit but I wasn't about to bring her over there. Not now.

"Well, I'm in a similar situation with my sister. She and her kids are staying with me until they get on their feet. So, my place is out of the question."

I thought about it for a few seconds. I couldn't bring her to a hotel because that would put pressure on her to sleep with me.

"Why don't we go for a drive?"

"Is it nice out?"

"It's chilly," I laughed. "No pun intended."

"That's cool with me. I'll be ready in about ten minutes."

We decided to drive by the Monument and talk. We found a nice little spot on Constitution Avenue, near the park.

It was a quiet spot where no one else parked. It was a nice place to...talk.

We were having small talk when out of the blue, she turned and asked, "Jordan, what do you think of me?"

It was not a question I was anticipating but what the hell.

"What do you mean?"

"You know what I mean. Do you think that you and I can be friends?"

"I thought we were already friends." *Make her work just like she makes you work.*

She smiled, apparently amused at the games being played. She started rubbing my thighs. She massaged my legs until Sambuca yawned. "By the feel of things, Jordan, you know exactly what I mean," she grinned, resting her hand on the crotch of my pants.

I half moaned, half groaned my approval. She moved towards my zipper and unleashed the beast. At this time I didn't know what to expect. All I knew was, whatever I was about to receive; I would be ready. I started rubbing the back of her neck while she continued her quest.

She lifted up my shirt and started kissing my nipples. "You taste like chocolate, Jordan."

"Do I?" I asked rhetorically. The anticipation was unreal. I wanted her to indulge.

She moved down to my stomach and as she inched closer, I

kept a slight pressure on her neck. Nothing hard just a slight nudge. I was beyond hard.

She looked up at me. "Are you sure your woman won't mind me helping you out tonight?"

Damn! Instantly my hardness was replaced with a withering piece of bologna. She looked up at me, and then back down at my penis.

She began tugging at my flaccid penis. "What happened, Jordan? He doesn't like me, does he?"

I was mad. Fuck that, not only was I mad, I was pissed off that I could allow myself to be in this position. I started zipping my pants up. She had brought me back to reality. A reality I had momentarily lost. I didn't know what to think. Hell, I didn't know what to do at this moment!

"Did I do something wrong, Jordan?"

Hell, no! You *said* something wrong!

"No, I'm okay. I guess I'm not ready to deal with another woman right now." I didn't know what the hell was going on with me. Were my brain and nuts on the same page? I hoped not because this was some scary shit. I didn't know why, and right about now I wasn't trying to question things either.

"It's nothing, Sophia. I have to get going." I started the car and pulled off. "Where would you like me to drop you off?"

Chapter 26

I called the number that Mr. Simmons had given me and spoke with Human Services. The company was looking to relocate and I wasn't feeling that right now. Not only was my son here, Traci was here also. The head of personnel was nice because she put me in touch with another company that was looking for technical support staff. After working at the home for the past few months, I realized that my old job wasn't that bad.

I was at the disabled home working when Renee barged in.

"Hello, Renee." She looked a little better since the last time I saw her. It was still awkward speaking to her because we really hadn't spoken since the day of the "beat down."

She slammed herself onto the couch. "Okay, Jordan, let's get everything out in the open." She has a funny way of getting right to the point. The one thing about my sister that I did appreciate was that she was blunt and to the point.

"Well, for starters," I began. "I don't agree with what went on with you and Dallas." I knew that I shouldn't have gone there, but if I didn't then I wouldn't be me.

"That's cool, Jordan. You have the right to feel the way you do, but also remember that I have the right to do what I want to do." Her eyebrow was cocked and ready. She did that every time she was pissed off. "What about the times when you were kicking it to my friends? Sure I told them not to talk to you, but you guys did what you wanted to do anyway."

She's got a point! The hell with that shit! That was your boy! "I got a question for you, Renee. Why him?"

"What do you mean, why him?"

"Just what the hell I said."

She stood up and warned, "First of all, you're nobody's father in this room!"

I ran to close the door because at this time the conversation could go anywhere. "You need to calm your ass down!"

She sat back down. "Well, you know the rules, Jordan. Don't start no shit and there won't be none." I couldn't believe this was the same woman that took all that shit from her husband.

"You know, we're not going to get anywhere like this. As a matter of fact, the issue involving you and Dallas is moot because I'm not dealing with it anymore."

"So, it's like that?"

"I guess so!" And with that, Renee disappeared into the roomful of white coats.

After I got off work, I called Tony and asked him if he could meet me at the mall. I had to go pick up some new shoes. Being that I never worked at a place like the disabled home, I figured that shoes were shoes, but my corns was killing me. He said that he would get there at about six o'clock, which gave me about an hour to kill. I wanted to call Traci but since our last encounter I didn't know what to do. She had me perplexed. I went over the evening we had spent and didn't know where I had gone wrong. *And with your stubborn ass, Styles, you won't even ask.* I called it being old-fashioned while others might call it stupid.

She won again.

"Hello, Traci."

"Hi, Jordan. How's your day going?"

"I'm doing okay."

"So, what's up? You seemed kind of off last week." Her relaxed attitude had me going nuts. *Forget about her ass, Styles. Go about your business. If she wants to be chased let someone else chase her.*

Confusion followed the words that I never thought would come out of my mouth. "Traci, I love you!"

Oh shit, Styles! What the hell are you saying?

"What did you say, Jordan?" Her voice was shaking more than mines.

I didn't know why I said what I said. It seemed as though there was a midget in my mouth shouting out things I knew nothing about.

"All that came out of my mouth was, "Huh?" *Fucking, huh?* I felt like an idiot.

"Did you just say that you loved me?"

My heart was beating through my shirt. I could actually see it thumping. "Huh?"

"I said, did you just say-"

"I know what you said," I interjected. "As a matter of fact, I know what I just said." In all reality, I didn't know what I said. In between thoughts the phone beeped. "Hold up for a second."

I clicked to the other line and it was Tony. "What's up, Styles? I'll be there in a minute. I'm just wrapping up a little business."

"Yo', Tone!"

"What's up?"

"Before you get off the phone, let me tell you what just happened."

"What?"

"I just told Traci I loved her," I blabbered.

Tony gasped. "You what?"

I guess he was just as surprised as I was. I shouldn't have told him. But I did. "Yeah, man. I just told her I loved her."

"And what did she say?"

"Huh?" The anticipation was killing him but I just couldn't get anything else out of my mouth.

"What happened after that?"

"Nothing. I was surprised as you are. But after I told her, you called me. As a matter of fact she's on the other line."

"Well, what are you gonna do?"

I thought about it for a second. I didn't know what I was going to do. "I don't know what I'm going to do. Your guess is as good as mine."

"Well, you better get your black ass off the phone. Relax, man. Ain't you the one that's always telling me you've got shit covered?"

"Yeah, but this is different." I wanted to let out all those butterflies that danced inside my stomach.

"I'll be there in a few minutes."

I clicked back to the other line. "Hello, Traci. I'm sorry I took so long."

She hesitated. "That's okay, Jordan." There was silence on the phone. I didn't know where to bring the conversation. *The hell with that, Styles. Bring it to the forefront. Let her know what the deal is. Where are your balls at, man?*

"Traci?"

"Yes."

"I don't know why I said it, but I did." I thought about what I was saying and it wasn't coming out the way I wanted it to.

Start over, Styles. "I'm sorry, Traci. All of this shit has my head twirling."

"I understand. It's a shock to me, too."

"Yeah. I never saw it coming."

"Huh?"

"Look, Traci, to be honest, I never thought about love when it came to you and me."

"Why would you say that to me?"

"I don't know."

"Well, if you don't know what you're saying, do you think you really mean it?"

I pondered over the question for a second. "I must mean it. I don't just go around telling women that I love them."

"Well, I'm glad to hear that," she chuckled.

"What about your feelings?"

"My feelings about what?"

She was making this out to be more difficult than it had to be. "Your feelings about us."

"I haven't really thought that far ahead, to be honest."

My chest pounded. My heart was beating my skin to no end. "Traci, I gotta go."

"Why? You don't want to talk now?"

Hell, no, I don't want to talk right now! "It's not that. It's just that right now I'd rather be alone."

"Are you sure? I hope you're not mad. I just don't know what to say."

"You don't have to say anything. I'll talk to you later, okay?" I didn't wait for her to answer before I hung up.

The phone rang seconds later. I didn't answer.

I wanted to salvage something at this point. I was mad,

upset and hurt.

See, that's why you don't give your whole heart to a woman, Styles. Did you notice that when you open yourself up, women shit on you? I wish I would've known that she didn't think of me in that capacity before I opened up to her, but fuck it, what's done is done.

Frustration set in and I wanted some sex. I wanted to find out if I still had it. I wanted someone to please me like Traci wouldn't. I wondered if she was gay. I didn't understand why she didn't want to sleep with me, let alone be with me. Maybe I was being too paranoid.

Fuck it, Styles. Handle your business. I called Tony and told him to meet me at the bar instead of the mall. The last thing I wanted to do was look for some damn Hush Puppies.

I went to Republic Gardens and luckily there was no line to get in. I went in and headed right for the bar. I looked around and no one was appealing. I started on my beer and scanned the room again. When I finished half of my beer, I looked up and saw Sophia coming through the door. Was this a signal from up above? I shouted from across the room, "Sophia!"

We hadn't really spoken since our "car ride." At this time, I wasn't trying to remember what happened, but trying to envision how we were going to finish what she started.

She turned towards me and waved. That's funny. Usually when she sees me, she runs over. Only this time she didn't seem so anxious to come. I didn't care though, because tonight I wouldn't be denied. I would give her what she wanted. Hell, I would give her what I wanted.

"Sophia!" I shouted again.

She put up her forefinger. "I'll be over in a second," she mouthed.

"Okay." I don't mind waiting. Shit, I waited this long, what's another five minutes?

"Hello, Jordan," she smiled, finally making her way to me. "How are you?"

"I'm doing good now that you're here."

She pulled away and put her hands on her hips. "Well."

"Well, what?" I didn't know what she wanted me to say.

I pulled her close to me, squeezing her tightly. "I'm kind of here with someone." She nodded toward the bathroom.

I looked over by the bathroom to see who was worthy of taking my place. To my dismay there was no one. "With who?" I asked, continuing to survey the place.

"He went *into* the bathroom."

"Oh." My voice must've been filled with disappointment because she quickly followed my answer with a question.

"You sound disappointed. Are you?"

"Kind of," I admitted.

"You acted like you didn't want me the last time, Jordan, so what am I supposed to do, beg?"

"It's not like that," I said, reflecting on the car ride.

"As a matter of fact, what happened with your girl you were so concerned about?" she chided.

Not really wanting to answer the question I decided to make it short. "Nothing."

"What do you mean, nothing?"

All these fucking questions were pissing me off. "Just what I said. Does there always have to be something? Can't a man just want to be with a woman because he wants company?"

"I guess so."

"Well, can't you get rid of-"

The man came out of the bathroom and shouted, "Sophia!"

Sophia gently pulled me near and whispered, "Hold up for a second, Jordan. I'll be right back."

He was an ugly motherfucker. I sized him up and he couldn't hold a fucking candle to me. Why in the hell didn't she want me tonight? Was I playing myself with her too?

Fuck it, Styles. You always got backup. In all reality though, since I was dealing with Traci, I really didn't have backup. I was in a messed-up situation. At this moment, I literally didn't have anyone to call. I wanted to be in bed now. I wanted to be sucking and fucking until I passed out.

She came back. "I'm sorry, Jordan, but I've got to get going. Kevin just got a call from the office and he's upset that he has to go back to the job for a second."

"Well, tell that ugly brother he should be upset. He probably was in a good mood until he went in the bathroom and saw himself."

"That's not nice, Jordan."

"Sometimes it be like that."

She shook her head. "And sometimes it don't. I gotta go."

And with that, she split. Now, I was definitely alone. Tony hadn't gotten there yet but even when he did, there was nothing he could do to suppress my appetite.

"What's up, Styles?" I damn near shit in my pants.

I turned around and saw Dallas pulling up a stool. "What's going on?"

"Nothing much. What brings you here?"

"Nothing. I didn't have anything to do so I called Tony and told him to meet me down here."

"That's what he told me. You can't be that bored."

I looked around the bar again. "Look at my black ass. I'm here alone, ain't I."

He laughed. "Not the man of the hour, Mr. Jordan Styles."

"In the flesh. Things have been going a little crazy lately."

"You don't have to tell me."

"I know." I took a good look at him and he was starting to look a little better. "You been getting some rest, I take it."

"I guess you could say that. What about you? You look tired as hell."

"You wouldn't believe it if I told you."

"Try me."

"First of all, I think that my girl isn't feeling me."

He had a look of disbelief on his face. "What?"

"I know. That's the same shit I said."

"What happened?"

"Well, for starters. I told her I loved her."

Dallas' jaw dropped. "You told her what?"

"I told her I loved her. Check this. Before that, I cooked for her. You know, I was trying to romance her and that's when all the shit started happening."

"What shit?"

"You know. The same shit that happens when they tell us that they love…" *Oh shit! I don't believe that this is happening to you, I mean us.* I was reacting the same way that the women that I had strung out acted. I didn't know what to say. I didn't finish my sentence.

"Damn, Styles! That's some powerful shit. Did she tell you anything after you told her you loved her?"

"She told me that she hadn't thought that far. I didn't have a comeback for that shit."

All Dallas could do was shake his head. I know he felt bad for me. For the first time since I found out about him and Renee, the subject of those two didn't come up. It felt good to finally be able to talk to him, friend to friend.

"So, what are you going to do?"

"Right now, I'm about to get inside my car and make a few calls."

I stood up to leave and Dallas grabbed my arm. "Styles, wait." He stood up next to me. "I'm sorry about everything. Can I be frank with you?"

"Go ahead."

"I miss you," he confided. I mean I really miss you."

I had a funny feeling in the pit of my stomach. "What are you talking about, Dallas?"

"I miss hanging out with you guys. I miss you guys calling me the white girl lover."

I thought about what he was saying and actually, I missed him too. I put my arm around his shoulder and walked with him to the door.

"Well, I guess we can't call you the white girl lover anymore, huh?"

Dallas smiled.

Chapter 27

The next morning, I decided to give Marigold Industries a call. They told me to bring my resume down. I didn't have anything to lose. I was upset that shit wasn't going right with anything else, so I figured more rejection wouldn't hurt. If they didn't want to hire a brother, maybe I should take it as a sign that I should be doing something else.

I got to the office on L Street and handed in my resume. The black lady at the front desk sounded positive about getting me an interview. I hope she could pull some strings.

I went outside and saw someone that looked like Traci, walk across the street. My heart ceased and then reality set in. She didn't want me!

I drove around downtown D.C. and the next thing you know, I was sitting in front of Serene's house. I didn't know what brought me to her, but I was here. *Fuck it, Styles. If Traci didn't want you, you know someone that does.* So what if she's a little crazy. At this moment, I wanted someone to ride me into a coma.

"What are you doing here, Jordan?" Serene smiled, cracking the door wide enough for me to see her face.

"I need to talk."

"*You* need to talk to *me?*"

"Whatever, Serene. Can I come in or what?"

"I guess so," she said, widening the door and stepping to the side so I could enter.

I walked in and looked around. Every time I went back home, I felt bad. Not because I left, but because I wished things were different. But here I was, sitting in my old house, about to make love to a woman that I know I didn't want to be with. Rejection has a way of making you do crazy things.

"Do you have a beer?" I asked, tossing myself onto the couch.

She took my jacket off of the couch. "I think so. Are you feeling okay?"

"I'm feeling alright."

She went to the kitchen and came back with a cold beer and sat down across from me. I could see her thighs peeking out of her half opened robe. Even though she was an asshole, she had some real good...

"Jordan!"

I shook my head. I must've been in la la land. "What's up?"

"You were spacing out on me." She looked down and noticed that her robe was open. She pulled her robe shut and crossed her legs. Why in the hell was she acting like she didn't like it? I hated all the bullshit.

"I'm okay. Just a little preoccupied."

"You look like you've been through hell and back."

"Kinda."

She uncrossed her legs, invitingly. "Do you need something else besides that beer?"

I looked at her lips and then back down to her thighs and decided to do something about my pain. "Yes!"

"What?"

"I need you to shut up and make love to me!"

Anticipation filled her face. "Wow! I don't know-"

I got up and made my way to the love seat as she spoke. My tongue interrupted her words. I began to kiss her like I did when we were younger. That's the one thing I loved about her. When we kissed, it was like one big orchestra. My cello was harmonizing with her viola. The music that it made was unbelievable. As I kissed her, I put her legs over my arms and carried her back to the couch. I fell onto the couch with her straddling me. Our tongues massaged each other's as she began moving up and down, positioning my dick in between her lips. I could feel the moistness through her panties.

Serene aggresively kissed and licked my neck.

"Damn, Serene, you're a fucking animal!"

"Shut up and bite my nipples!"

She licked my neck while I was busy tearing her robe off. As she licked my chest, I fought for position. I couldn't take it anymore. I flipped her around, making her kneel over the couch so I could have full access.

"Jordan, what are you doing to me?" she panted.

She moaned as I licked up and down her back. I reached around and put her nipples in between my fingers, massaging them until they became rock hard.

"Lick my nipples, Jordan?" she begged.

I bent over, lifted her breasts toward the side so I could lick her nipples like she suggested, but something happened. I don't know why but I began to think about what Traci was doing. I wondered what she was watching on TV, and whom she was watching it with.

Serene must've noticed my mood swing because she turned around, saw my face and slumped onto the couch.

"What's wrong, Jordan?"

I buttoned my shirt up and sat across from her.

"Nothing."

"Why'd you stop? It was feeling good," she whined, massaging her clitoris. "You don't want me?"

I stood up and zipped up my pants. Serene stopped massaging herself and closed her robe. I guess she knew that I meant business this time.

"It's not that, Serene. I just don't want to go through all the bullshit."

"What bullshit, Jordan?" She walked over and sat on the edge of the love seat. "I'm not bugging. What's wrong with us making love again?" She reached over trying to undo my belt.

I pushed her hand away. I knew that if I brought up Traci, all hell would break lose, so I decided to just leave it alone and lie. "Serene, do you think this shit is healthy. We make love and the next thing you know, we're in court screaming at each other."

"Fine," she snarled. "I ain't going to beg you to sleep with me. You think I got it that bad," she spat, pointing at herself. "Well, it's not. I got men beating down my door on a daily basis."

"Good," I chided. I decided to do something that I had never done with her...be honest. "Can I tell you the truth, Serene?"

She stood up with her arms folded. "Please do." She sat back on the couch with her arms folded.

"I don't want to do anything to fuck up what I got with Traci."

Serene turned around and walked away. She threw her arms on the mantle and slammed her head inside her arms and cried. I wanted to go over and console her, but that's what she wanted.

"You think I want to hear that?" she whimpered from across

the room.

"You want me to be honest, don't you?"

"Whatever!"

Even though I didn't care for her most of the time, I still had love for her. I fought back the urge to make her feel better. I knew that I had something special and I wasn't going to fuck this up. Traci makes me see the light. She makes me care about feelings. She has me thinking about a lot of shit that I hadn't thought about in awhile. Besides that, I liked her a lot. I like the way she doesn't go for any of my shit. I like the way I can be myself and not put up a front.

"Are you going to make love to me, Jordan?"

Serene didn't quit. Usually I would've seen tears and consoled her mind and body. I would've kissed, tasted, sucked and fucked her back to normalcy. Not today!

I left Serene's house and called Traci. I knew she wasn't home, but I wanted to hear her voice. I left a message for her to call me.

I started to go to the bar, but decided against it. Before you know it, I was in my bed listening to, *In a Sentimental Mood.*

Chapter 28

"What are you doing for New Year's Eve?"

Tony was at my house early in the morning. I hadn't told him about what happened with Serene a couple of days ago, partly because he would tell me that I was stupid to go there in the first place, and partly due to embarrassment. "I don't know what I'm doing yet. What about you?"

"You know how it is, all of these women beating down my door, trying to go out with the Chocolate Man."

"So what you're saying is that you might be hanging out with me again, huh?" I laughed.

"Basically," he admitted.

"What is Dallas doing?" I said, peeling myself off of the bed.

"He said that him and Renee are having a party."

"You going?"

"I don't know. You know how his parties go. All those white people doing that Macarena shit!" I said, imitating the dance.

"I know. I'm not trying to go out and deal with all those crazies either."

"You want me to tell him to count us out?"

"I'll go, I guess. If his shit is weak then we can go find a real party."

The phone started ringing and Tony flinched. "Watch out Big Hershey. I got neighbors."

"Kiss my Hershey-coated ass."

"What's up, Dallas?"

"I'm chillin', and you?"

"I'm just trying to get an oil spill out of my living room." In the backround, I could see Tony raising his middle finger.

"Huh?" Dallas respond, apparently confused.

"Never mind. What's the deal with this party?"

"I was just calling to let you know about the party I'm throwing. The shit is going to be off the hook, so make sure you stop through."

"What are we going to do?"

"Drink and play spades."

"Play some what?" I said, surprised.

"Spades. You heard me the first time, Negro."

"When did you start playing spades?" I laughed.

"Recently."

"You gave up hearts?"

"Yeah, I had to. Now I'm ready for the big boys."

"I'm definitely down to come. Tony said to count him in."

"I'll see you guys tomorrow night about nine, okay?"

"Nine it is. Peace."

Tony must've heard everything I said because as soon as I dropped the phone, he shouted, "Did I hear you say that Dallas wanted to bust some spades?"

"Yeah. Ain't that some shit."

"It ain't no funnier then me seeing your car at Serene's house."

"Huh?"

"Huh, hell! I know your beat up looking Volvo anywhere."

"Yeah, and…"

"What's that all about?"

"What's what all about?" I repeated, turning on the TV.

Tony grabbed the remote and turned the television down. "You claim you hate the chick, but every chance you get, you're over there. Hell, you're over there more than the milkman."

I turned around instantly. "The who?"

"Damn, I was just joking," he sighed. "You're paranoid."

"Sometimes it gets like that."

It must've hit him why we had broken up in the first place because he sat down next to me, with a different tone in his voice. "I forgot. What's the deal with you guys?"

"Nothing. You know how it is," I said, quietly.

"Actually I don't know how it is. Please inform a brother on the deal."

"It's simple. I love to have sex and with her, I can be myself." I didn't feel like telling him what actually happened. He might try that "you're getting soft" shit.

"That's bullshit!" Tony lashed. "What do you mean, you can be yourself?"

"I know what she likes and where she's been." Tony gave me the eye. I continued with a more humbled tone. "Well, I pretty much know where she's been. It's just comfortable."

"And it has nothing to do with you wanting to be with her?"

"Hell, no! I can't even picture myself being back with her."

"But before it was, you couldn't picture yourself seeing her face. Then it was, you couldn't picture yourself sleeping with her."

"It does sound a little crazy, don't it?"

"Damn, right! If I didn't know you any better, I would've thought Serene had you whipped."

I stood up and pointed to myself. "I do the whipping!"

"Right now, you ain't whipping shit!"

"What?"

"I'm talking about you whipping her. I haven't heard about Traci. What's the deal with her? That's the one you should be trying to whip. You need some New Year's resolutions."

"I'll tell you the deal," I hollered. "I went over to Serene's house and guess what I did?"

Tony looked at me without answering.

"I'll tell you what I did." I paused. "Not a fucking thing. I started to sleep with her, but I didn't. I started to kiss her and then for some reason I stopped. I don't know why I stopped, but I did."

"Damn."

"Yeah, damn. So you can come over here and act like you know what you're talking about, but I know the real deal."

"I didn't know it was like that, Styles," Tony responded, shaking his head.

"As a matter of fact, you shouldn't talk about women that come in and out of people's lives. You got a woman? Hell, no! So how can you school me on what to do?"

Tony was getting fed up but I didn't give a damn.

"And to answer your question, I do have some resolutions. I'm going to tighten up my circle of women *and* my circle of friends."

"That's the Styles I know," Tony said, giving me the pound.

"Kiss my ass, Tone, because the first one going is your black ass!"

"Yeah, right. You know that I'm not going anywhere. I'm the only one that will put up with your bullshit and I'll tell you to your face what I think."

I thought about it for a second. "You're right."

"So, who's going to be the one next year?"

"What do you mean, who's it going to be?"

"Serene, Sophia, Shannelle , Traci...who?"

"Very funny," I sarcastically laughed. "Kym is definitely out of the question. Sophia is just a chick that gives me free drinks. Serene is a psycho and Traci doesn't seem to want my black ass, so I guess I'll be on my own."

"That's bullshit. Why don't you call Traci and see what's going on with her? Maybe you can bring her to the party."

"I don't know where to start with her."

"Start by calling her and getting to the meat of the problem," Tony said, grabbing his keys. "You're the one that's always saying that you never know if you don't ask."

I opened the door. "Peace, Tone. I'll talk to you later." I hated when he was right.

I contemplated on whether to call Traci. She turned me down and I didn't know why. She had my head spinning.

"Hello, Traci. How are you?"

"Fine and yourself?"

"Okay. What were you doing?"

"Just sitting here, watching a movie."

"What, a chick-flick?"

"Actually I was watching *Belly.*"

"Damn, you're a violent sista ain't you?"

"Call it what you want," she giggled.

My voice got more businesslike. "I got a question."

"You scare me with all of these questions."

"Do I?"

"Yes you do."

"Would you rather me not ask?"

"No. I want you to ask me whatever is on your mind. But Jordan…?"

"Huh?"

"From now on, if you ask me a question, you can't get off the phone when I say something that you don't agree with. I thought talking was about getting things out in the open."

"That's cool."

"So what's your question?"

"Why don't you want me?"

"What?" She sounded surprised.

"Why don't you want me? What am I doing wrong?"

"Why do you think you're doing something wrong?"

"Because you don't seem to be feeling me."

"That's not true, Jordan. We've hung out and you've come over to my house. Do you think I invite everyone over to my house?"

"I wasn't saying you did."

"Well, for your information, I don't. I'm very selective in whom I bring to my house."

"Damn, you don't have to get aggressive with me."

"Sometimes I do. Don't let my passiveness fool you. I can be a bitch sometimes."

You can be a bitch all by your damn self. "Damn! It has to be like that?"

"Like what?"

"C'mon Traci. I've been nothing but good to you. I haven't tried to run any game on you."

"That's because you can't run game on me," she warned.

"You're not as smart as you think you are," I challenged.

"Meaning?"

"Meaning just what I said."

"You think you have it all figured out, huh? The world does not revolve around Jordan Styles," she spat, sarcastically.

Hang up! Who in the hell did she think she was anyway? I wanted to hang up the phone but my pride and ego didn't allow me to.

"You think I feel I'm all that?"

"Basically."

"And why would you think that," I said defensively.

"I think you feel you can woo a woman with a little bit of this and a little bit of that."

"What do you mean, a little bit of this and that?"

"Just what I said. You think that by cooking me dinner and saying a little poetry over candlelight, I'm supposed to tear off my panties."

"It's not even like that. You're crazy!"

"If I'm crazy, then what does that make you? You were the one telling me that you loved me."

That made shit hit home. Was I playing myself? "That's why men don't tell women what they think," I snapped. "You guys get all that shit distorted and try to make us believe that you're a one-man woman, when it's the complete opposite. You think that by having a pretty face and a fat ass, we're supposed to fall down and kiss the ground that you walk on."

Her voice changed to a lighter tone. "Do you want me to be honest with you?"

"Please do. Give me the real deal."

"When we first went out, I was feeling you."

"Was?"

"Yeah, was. I think what turned it around was when you mistakenly called me Serene. You didn't think I heard it, but I did. Women catch slipups like that."

"So you thought that-"

"Hold up. I'm not done." Traci interrupted. "I let that slip by. Then I began thinking about everything else. Serene was acting up at the party and she insinuated that you asked her for sex, but I let that go, too. I even let the night I saw you ushering that drunken woman into your car, pass. I know that we weren't a couple, but I held out for you. I wanted you to get rid of all those women, but after a while, I couldn't take it anymore. How am I supposed to trust you?"

"Have you ever talked to me about it?" I yelled into the phone.

"I didn't think I had to," she quickly responded.

"Why didn't you think you had to talk to me?"

"Why should I? We weren't together!"

"How are you supposed to get together with anyone? You have to start somewhere."

"I have a question for you." Traci said, turning the tables. *Get going, Styles.* I hesitated. "Go ahead."

"Didn't you say that you loved me?"

"Yeah!"

"Was that bullshit?"

"What?"

"The reason that I asked is because I would like to know if you could love a woman while being with another?"

I didn't know where she was going with this question. "I don't know, why?"

"Do you remember the night that you *supposedly* wanted to take it to another level?"

"Yes."

"How can you want to take it to the next level with me and then turn around and do what you did?"

What the hell is she talking about, Styles? My mind was drawing a total blank. I had no clue on what she was talking about. "Never mind, Jordan. If you don't know what happened, I'm sure not going to tell you. Maybe I was seeing more into it than I should've been."

"Why don't you give me a chance to prove what I'm worth?" *You're begging like a fucking girl!* If the fellas could see me now.

"I've got a few more questions for you," she added.

"What?"

"You can have pretty much any woman you want, right? If I'm sitting here telling you that I don't want to move in that direction, then why do you bother with me? I'm pretty sure not too many women would tell you the same thing that I'm saying."

Damn right, they wouldn't! "I know," I said, confidently. "But for some reason, I think we can make it."

"Make it where?"

"We could try to make it to that next level. Maybe higher." It sounded corny but that's what I felt. Why in the hell did I want someone that really didn't want me?

"Why do you love me?"

"Huh?"

"Why do you love me?" she repeated.

I hated questions like that. All I knew is what I felt. "I don't know exactly why I love you. I just know that I do. I care deeply about you and I want you to be a constant part of my life."

There was no response. I hated the silence. "I don't know, Jordan. Things just don't compute."

I was puzzled. "Like what?"

"Do you remember my friend Sharlana?"

"Yeah."

"Well, her cousin works at a restaurant that you frequent."

"What does that have to do with me?"

"Remember the night that you cooked dinner for me?"

"Yeah." I didn't know where she was going with this one either. I really didn't want to stick around and find out either but she was worth it.

"Her cousin's name is Sophia."

"H-h-huh?"

"Are you okay Jordan?"

"Y-y-yeah. I don't know what happened. It felt like I lost my breath momentarily."

She let out a sarcastic laugh. "Stuff like that can make you suddenly stop breathing, huh?"

Hang up the phone, Styles! "I got to get going because-"

"Hold up! You said that you would finish this conversation. If it's not your cell phone battery, it's something else. You wanted to talk, Jordan, so talk!"

You ain't gotta explain shit to her! All this talk I've been doing, I sure couldn't bitch up now! "What does she have to do with me?"

"Are we going to play stupid now? Do I really have to tell you, or are you man enough to come at me like I've got some sense?"

"What do you want me to say?"

"I want you to tell me why you are wining and dining me, but freaking the other women? I mean I had my doubts, but no proof. Something just didn't compute. I didn't know what it was, but then I started doing something that I don't usually do."

I was getting heated now. "Like what?"

"Like asking my friends about you."

"They don't know me!"

"But, they know about you."

"And you believed them?"

"It's not like that. It's just that things didn't feel right."

"So you were stringing me along?"

"No. I wouldn't call it that. I have a lot of fun with you."

Fun! Fucking fun? What the hell am I, a fucking make me happy doll? "So, basically, I was just something to do to pass the time?"

Next thing you know, the phone was laying in pieces underneath the coffee table. *Call her back!* Even if I wanted to, I didn't have enough glue to piece it together.

Chapter 29

It was the morning of New Year's Eve and my head was spinning. I must've had a thousand drinks last night. I didn't remember a thing.

My cell phone interrupted my thinking.

I picked up the phone.

"Hello!" I shouted.

"Hello, Jordan," an unfamiliar voice responded.

"Who is this?"

"Sophia."

I took the phone away from my ear and looked at it. "Hold up. How'd you get my cell number?"

"Damn, you were that drunk?" she joked.

Before she could get out another word, I stopped her. "I don't feel like talking right now."

"I was just checking to make sure you made it to bed last night."

"What do you mean, made it to bed?" I tried to piece together the previous evening. When did Sophia come into the picture?

"You were pretty messed up last night," she continued.

"Yeah, right." I needed to gather my thoughts. Suddenly, fragments of the evening were starting to pop in my head. "Hold up for a second. I gotta run to the bathroom." I threw the phone on the bed and started putting together the previous evening. I was at the Republic Gardens and all I remembered was Sophia buying me drink after drink. I must've had at least five beers and a few shots of Hennessey.

Oh shit! Hennessey makes me...

I snatched the phone off the bed. "What the hell happened last night?"

Sophia laughed, which only sped up my panic. "Nothing, really," she replied casually.

"What the hell does 'nothing, really' mean?"

"Just what I said."

"Are you bullshitting me?" I desperately wanted to know what kind of ass I made of myself.

"No, I'm not." She paused for a few seconds. "I'll tell you what happened.

"Well," I shouted into the phone.

She sucked her teeth. "You're pushy for a man with no memory." She paused. "You stayed until the club closed."

"And..."

"Then you asked me to drive you home."

"I couldn't drive?"

"Apparently not. Then while I was driving you home, you said that you were hungry."

"What?"

"That's when I told you that I had something for you to eat. Now how do I put this?" She seemed to search for a better way to express her feelings. "You asked what I had to eat, so I lifted up my skirt and you started-"

"What!"

"Relax. I'm just joking. You're lucky I'm a nice lady."

I didn't know whether to jump for joy or curse her the fuck out!

"And *you* brought *me* home?"

"Like a dumb ass."

"What do you mean, like a dumb ass?"

"Because you came into the club steaming. You started talking about Traci and something about my cousin telling her something. What's with that?"

"I don't know. Maybe I was drunk and didn't know what I was talking about."

"No. I believe you knew precisely what you were talking about."

Don't burn your bridges.

Fuck them bridges! "Shit, I was pissed off."

"About what?"

"About your cousin telling Traci about me and you."

"I told her not to say anything."

"You should've kept your mouth shut," I screamed.

"You're right."

"Now look at the shit I'm in."

"It's not my fault. You shouldn't have tried to be so sneaky."

"I don't have a commitment to anybody."

"You must like her or something."

"Maybe." I thought about it for a second. "As a matter of fact, why am I talking to you about this shit anyway? Your ass got me in trouble the first time."

She hung up the phone.

Traci was on my mind. For some reason, I just couldn't shake her.

"What's going on, Traci?" I seductively asked over the phone.

"Nothing much, Jordan. You sound like you're in a much

better mood today."

"Are you going to start up?"

"I was just trying to lighten the mood."

"It's well lit," I dryly responded.

"Can we start this conversation over, please?"

I hesitated. "Yeah."

She hung up the phone.

Two minutes later I called back. "Why'd you hang up?"

"We were going to start the conversation over again, so I felt that you should call me back," she chuckled.

"Smart ass," I laughed.

"That's why you love me, right?"

"Not for your smart ass. Maybe for your fat ass."

"Funny."

I had to get to the meat of the conversation. "Are you going to the party with me or not?"

"Can I call you back and let you know?"

Can she call you back? "Can you call me back?" What the hell was this shit?

"I kinda had plans."

"Damn!" I said, dejectedly.

"My friends are coming up from Charlotte and they asked me to hang with them."

"Are you sure they're coming?"

"Pretty sure. If anything, maybe we can meet up later in the evening and spend some time together."

"That sounds cool," I replied, relieved. "Maybe we can start this next year off on the right foot."

"That sounds great to me, Jordan."

I was starting to feel better. "No more bullshitting, right?"

"No more bullshitting."

Chapter 30

It was four o'clock and there was no word from Traci. Hopefully she would find some time for me this evening. I wanted to see her soon. This next year was going to be about change. I wasn't going to wait on things to come to me. *I* was going to start dictating.

I started to get dressed, but decided against it. I turned on the TV and watched some of the college bowl games. I had a lot to think about today. What I was going to do with this job situation. What I was going to do about Traci and what I was going to do about all the extra people in my life. I needed closure.

Dallas called me about ten times to make sure I was coming. I really didn't feel like going, but fuck it! It was going to be comical, to say the least. Me, Darnell, Renee and Dallas all in the same room? I wouldn't miss this shit for nothing.

It was nine o'clock and Traci still hadn't called. I thought about calling her cell phone, but I didn't want to be a pest. Tonight, she was going to either love me or leave me.

I got dressed and left for the party.

I knocked on the door and Dallas answered. It was only nine-thirty and it was already packed and noisy.

"What's up, Dallas?" I said, hitting him in the back of the head.

"Glad you could make it, my brother."

"Me too. You know I wouldn't miss this party. Let me go holla at everyone. I'll check you out in a bit." I hung up my coat and went toward the living room. Renee was sitting down on the couch, eating chips and talking to Darnell's girl.

"What's up, Renee?" I said, bending down, kissing her on her cheek.

"What's up, Jordan? I see you made it."

As I sat down, Darnell's girlfriend got up.

"You guys want something to drink? I'm gonna go and make sure Poopee ain't getting drunk," she smiled.

"Poopee?" I asked.

"Yeah, Poopee," she confirmed.

"Well, tell Poopee to bring his brother, a Long Island Iced Tea."

"Okay," she said, switching her ass. *Freak!*

Renee patted me on my back. "You rollin' solo tonight?"

I looked around for an imaginary friend. "Looks that way, don't it."

"Styles is rollin' solo," she teased.

"I know. You gotta keep saying it to yourself so you'll believe it, huh?"

"Where's Traci?"

"With her friends."

"Is there trouble in Tinseltown?"

"Tinsel my ass."

She looked at my ass and turned up her nose. "I'd rather not."

"Fuck you!"

"That either." We both cracked up.

"Seriously though, I don't know about her."

"Why?"

"I hit her with everything."

"Everything like what?" Renee laughed.

"I cooked her dinner. I bought her roses. I-"

"That's enough," Renee interrupted.

"I know. Is she a dyke or something?"

"A what?" Renee laughed hysterically.

"I don't know *what's* going on with her."

"Apparently you ain't hit her with what you should've been hitting her with."

"What?"

"The opposite of that bullshit you give her."

"What do you mean, bullshit?"

"Traci ain't one of those chickenheads that you can hit with any old bullshit."

"Yeah, and…"

"Maybe you should adjust your style. No pun intended my brotha," she smiled, obviously amused at her play on words.

"I don't know what to do. I guess I'll just bring in the new year with you guys." I peeked into the other room and saw everyone else laughing. I shook my head. "Pitiful ain't it?"

"How do you think we feel? We're the one that has to put up with your sad looking ass. There are other girls stopping by too. And before you say anything, some of them are nice."

I stood up to go into the other room. "Not the ones I've seen."

"Beggars can't be choosers."

"I can be choosy if I want to be. I'm not interested anyway. I've got Traci on the brain. What about you? How are things going with you and Dallas?"

"Why do you have to go there?"

"Because I can, so fess up. You two still beating each other up with chains and whips?" I said, faking like I was beating her. "It ain't even like that," she said, embarrassed. "Can we move past all that?"

I moved over and frazzled her already messed up hair. "You're lucky that I'm trying to have fun tonight. I'll speak to you later," I said, leaving her for the jungle.

I walked toward the den andDarnell's girl was walking toward me.

"Excuse me, Jordan," she beckoned, nudging my arm.

"What's up?"

"Here's your drink."

"Thanks," I said, accepting the drink. "And Poopee better not have tried to lace my drink!"

I walked into the den and noticed Darnell entertaining two of Renee's girlfriends.

Darnell got up and came towards me. "What's up, Styles?" You finally made it." He nodded towards the women that he was entertaining on the couch. "I was tired of being the main attraction over there."

I smiled and waved at the ladies that were now looking in our direction.

"That's bullshit. You love the attention." I nodded back toward Renee and his girl. "Your girl goes for that shit?"

"She's cool with it. I got everything covered. And speaking of covered, what's up with you and Traci? I thought you were bringing her."

"I told her I would call her and let her know if I felt like picking her up."

Be true to the game, Styles. This is a New Year, no time for frontin'.

"Let me holla at you for a second, Darnell." I put my arm around his shoulder and led him to the kitchen.

Darnell hopped onto the counter. "What's the deal?"

"I'm thinking of making a move."

He looked puzzled. "What kind of move?"

"I don't know yet. I'm just going to go with the flow. Do you remember when I told Mommy that I would be settling down after I got the divorce finalized?"

"She told me something about that."

I went to the fridge to grab a beer. I opened it and took a sip.

"She told me that she was concerned about me and my womanizing. She said that I reminded her of Daddy."

Darnell looked at me and shook his head. "You need to keep your shit under wraps. You put your shit out there too much."

"Regardless of what I do or whom I do it with, I should be able to do what I want without everyone criticizing me."

He nodded his head. "True."

"But, I decided that I would be done with all that bullshit. The craziest shit is, when I tried to stop, look where it got me. Nowhere. To be truthful, next year, I'm about to change up everything."

"What are you going to do, turn over a new leaf?"

"I'm turning over a whole fucking tree," I joked.

"I feel you," Darnell smiled, nodding his head.

"You talk to Dallas yet?"

"Sort of. When I came in, he answered the door."

"He wasn't bleeding so I guess you didn't kick his ass again."

Darnell jumped off the counter. "I was cool with him. I'll

catch you in a bit. I gotta check on my woman."

"Peace out, Poopee," I yelled.

"Fuck you," he yelled back, disappearing into the noisy room.

I didn't know what to do. I didn't want to bring in the new year like I did the last; alone and womanless.

I decided to do something about my problem.

"Hi, Traci?"

"Hi, Jordan. It sounds noisy," she screamed.

I put one hand over my ear so I could hear. "I'm at Renee's party."

"Are there a lot of people there?"

"Yeah."

There was an uncomfortable silence.

"Are you coming or what?"

"Huh?"

"I said, are you-"

"I heard you. I told my friends about you," she explained.

"Yeah. What did you say?"

"I told them that I really enjoyed your company and that we were starting to have an understanding."

"Really," I said, sounding like a highschooler.

"Yes. I've been doing some thinking."

"About what?"

"Us."

"What about us?"

"I'd rather not talk about it on the phone." *Don't fuck this one up!*

"I'll see you in about thirty minutes?" I asked.

"Yes."

The phone call had a crazy effect on me because now I was dying for a drink. I walked into the living room and made myselff the killer drink.

Renee looked in my glass and smelled the potency of the alcohol. "And you better not throw up on my damn carpet," she screamed sternly.

"I'm here to par-tay," I sang, doing the running man.

"What woke you up?"

"I just got a call from my baby."

"Who, Tony?"

"Kiss my ass!"

"Do we got to go there again?"

"I'll tell you where we got to go."

"Where?"

"To the kitchen," I said, grabbing her by the arm.

"Why," she asked, trying to pull away.

I pulled her out of the room. "Just bring your behind in the kitchen!"

We went into the kitchen and Renee sat on the stool with her hands on her hips. "What?"

"What's the deal with you and Dallas?"

"I'm not going to be interrogated in my own house," she said, jumping off the stool.

"Hold up," I said, grabbing her hand. "I just want you to know that I don't care what you do. If you want to date him, then I guess I can live with it."

"Really?" she said, glossy eyed. "That really means a lot to me. Especially right now."

"Why right now?"

"I'll tell you later," she whimpered.

Getting up to leave, I yelled, "I hope you're not pregnant!"

She turned around quickly. "Nothing like that," she smiled, rushing back to the party.

What the fuck was going on with her? She talks about me acting weird.

Traci would be arriving in about five minutes. I needed another drink.

I fixed myself another drink and two minutes later, the doorbell rang. Dallas ran to answer the door. *Who was he, the fucking butler?*

Traci walked through the door and looked simply amazing. She took off her coat and my eyes nearly popped out of my head. She was wearing a tight ass one-piece skirt set. It had to be the most revealing thing I had seen her in. I wanted to taste her.

"What's up, Sweetheart," I said with open arms. I ran my hands down her back, tracing every inch of her spine.

"Nothing," she responded, kissing my lips.

Now this is the shit I'm talking about!

We went into the living room and I introduced her to everyone.

I pointed to the bar. "You want something to drink?"

"Who are you, the bartender?"

"Something like that."

"In that case, I'll take an Alize."

"I hope you can handle it."

"You'd be surprised."

Put a little extra liquor in there. No. I want her sober for what I got to say.

I fixed her drink and led her onto the back porch, away from all the noise.

She sat down on the bench and I pulled up a chair in front of her. I opened my legs and she placed hers in between mine. "Listen, Jordan, I have to speak to you regarding a few things before the year is up."

I looked at my watch. "You've got a little bit of time left." She took a couple of sips from her drink. "I've been thinking," she explained, pausing to take another sip. "about us and what I've been putting you through."

"What have you been putting me through?"

"You know. I guess I've been giving you a hard time about things."

"What made you come to that realization," I said, rubbing her calves.

"The New Year has a funny way of making you think about what you're doing with your life. I'm glad that it only comes once a year. I can't take all this evaluating."

She was making me smile so hard, I was cheesing. I felt like Grimace.

"So what are you going to do about it, Traci?"

"I was thinking that I would leave that up to you."

Where's the punch line?

I was stunned. I wasn't expecting that.

"Damn, I don't know what to say."

Renee came running onto the porch. "You guys have to come into the living room! I have an announcement to make!" I grabbed Traci's hand and whispered in her ear, "We'll finish this later."

We found a seat on the couch. Everyone was packed in the living room. Darnell was sitting on the floor with his girlfriend, while Renee's friend's occupied the love seat. Some guy that just walked in, was standing by the doorway while Renee and Dallas stood in front of everyone else.

"I know you guys think I'm crazy, but I have a little bit of time before the New Year kicks off. I have something to tell you," Renee stated. Dallas looked really uncomfortable.

Renee continued, "I would like to first thank all of you guys for coming. And now to the meat of the reason that you are sitting in front of me. You all know that Andre and I will be getting a divorce next month, right?"

Everyone nodded.

"Well, Dallas and I are happy to tell you that we are getting engaged."

Coughs flooded the room.

I stood up. "What the-"

Dallas quickly came toward me and gave me a hug. "What's up brother-in-law?"

This shit was getting crazy. Traci gave a look of disbelief, as did everyone else. Next thing you know, everyone started hugging and kissing Renee like she had just won a pageant.

Darnell was lying on the floor, baffled.

I walked toward Renee with a million things running through my head.

This is New Year's Eve, Styles. Give everything a chance. Traci sure gave you one!

I walked over and gave her a big hug. "Congratulations, Renee."

Renee started crying.

I pulled my head back to see my shirt. "Don't get that shit all over my shirt!" I laughed.

"Kiss my ass," she sobbed.

"Don't worry. I'm going to let you handle the situation. I want you to know that I've got your back."

"That means a lot to me, Jordan. It really does," she said, holding on for dear life.

I stepped away and kissed her cheek. "No problem. Now

go get yourself cleaned up."

She walked toward Darnell and they embraced.

There were five minutes left until the new year and I wanted to finish up my conversation before time was up.

I pulled Traci aside.

"Can we finish our conversation before the ball drops, Sweetheart?"

Traci was crying. "Yes."

As I led her to the kitchen, she said, "Wasn't that beautiful, Jordan?"

"What, Renee and Dallas?"

"Yeah."

"It was alright," I lied. In fact, I thought it was great.

"I enjoy the sight of love."

Well wait until she gets a load of me!

As soon as we hit the kitchen, I dropped to one knee.

"What are you doing?" she asked, looking around to see who was looking.

She stood above me, looking even more radiant than the day I met her. I grabbed her hands and kissed them.

"I want to talk about you and me."

I cleared my throat.

"I love you more each and every day
on bended knees I began this morning when I prayed
that you would be with me
see,
I want you to cherish the time that we spend together.
Now the question is whether
or not I can sever
all other ties
or whether or not I will continue to lie

about my feelings.

I want you.

I need you.

If being sensitive means weakness

Then my heart is unable to hold your sweetness.

What I'm saying is that I want to give you the world.

I want to take this to the next level, if you want me, girl

Take my hand and feel what I'm feeling

Marvin Gaye should've switched his words cause," I stood up
and sang as best as I could,   *"When I get that feeling, you make
a brother hit the ceiling!"*

I kissed her lips gently.

"Baby, I know I can't sing, but you make me want to
rejoice. You make me want to sing when I'm happy and cry
when I'm sad."

She was starting to cry all over again. I wiped her tears
with my hands and held her tight.

She lifted her face away from my shoulder, looked up at
me and began sobbing all over again. She turned her head,
trying to hide the tears.

I grabbed her and hugged her for what seemed like hours.

Someone shouted, "One minute until New Year's!"

While we were still locked in our bond, I whispered,
"Look, Traci, I know that I've done things the unconventional
way, but that doesn't mean that I don't care about you. Can
we at least try to make things work?"

She didn't answer. All she could muster up was a fake
smile. As we walked toward the living room, Renee came and
hugged her, asking what was wrong.

Traci shook her head.

I pulled Traci back to me.

"Are you okay, Traci?" I asked, giving her another hug. "Did I say something wrong?"

I was nervous as hell. There was less than a minute left and I didn't know what she was thinking.

Should've kept your mouth shut!

I held Traci tight, hoping she would be able to tell me something.

Renee yelled, "Does everyone have their streamers! Everyone grab the person's hand that's next to you."

The crowd cheered.

Renee grabbed Dallas' hand.

"Twenty seconds!"

Tony barged through the door.

"What's up, Styles? I made it," he huffed.

"Fifteen seconds!"

Renee cleared her throat.

Tony looked at Traci and saw her crying. "What the hell did I miss?" he whispered.

"Ten seconds!"

Traci pulled my head close to her lips.

"Yes!"

"Five seconds!"

With a tear in my eye, I whispered into Traci's ear, "Have I ever told you about the Eiffel Tower?"

The end!